Rowe is a pai

❦ ❦ ❦

Praise for No Knight Needed

"*No Knight Needed* is m-a-g-i-c-a-l! Hands down, it is one of the best romances I have read. I can't wait till it comes out and I can tell the world about it." ~*Sharon Stogner, Love Romance Passion*

"*No Knight Needed* is contemporary romance at its best....There was not a moment that I wasn't completely engrossed in the novel, the story, the characters. I very audibly cheered for them and did not shed just one tear, nope, rather bucket fulls. My heart at times broke for them. The narrative and dialogue surrounding these 'tender' moments in particular were so beautifully crafted, poetic even; it was this that had me blubbering. And of course on the flip side of the heart-wrenching events, was the amazing, witty humour....If it's not obvious by now, then just to be clear, I love this book! I would most definitely and happily reread, which is an absolute first for me in this genre." ~*Becky Johnson, Bex 'N' Books*

"*No Knight Needed* is an amazing story of love and life...I literally laughed out loud, cried and cheered.... *No Knight Needed* is a must read and must re-read." ~*Jeanne Stone-Hunter, My Book Addiction Reviews*

❦ ❦ ❦

Praise for Not Quite Dead

"[Rowe] has penned a winner with *Not Quite Dead*, the first novel in her new NightHunter vampire series...an action-packed, sensual, paranormal romance that will captivate readers from the outset... Brimming with vampires, danger, resurrection, Louisiana bayou, humor, surprising plot twists, fantasy, romance and love, this story is a must-read!" ~ *Romance Junkies:*

✿ ✿ ✿

Praise for Darkness Possessed

"A story that will keep you on the edge of your seat, and characters you won't soon forget!" - Paige Tyler, *USA Today* Bestselling Author of the X-OPS Series

"*Darkness Possessed*…is an action-packed, adrenaline pumping paranormal romance that will keep you on the edge of your seat… Suspense, danger, evil, life threatening situations, magic, hunky Calydons, humor, fantasy, mystery, scorching sensuality, romance, and love – what more could you ask for in a story? Readers – take my advice – do not miss this dark, sexy tale!" ~*Romance Junkie*s

✿ ✿ ✿

Praise for Darkness Unleashed

"Once more, award winning author Stephanie Rowe pens a winner with *Darkness Unleashed*, the seventh book in her amazing Order of the Blade series…[an] action-packed, sensual story that will keep you perched on the edge of your seat, eagerly turning pages to discover the outcome…one of the best paranormal books I have read this year." ~*Dottie, Romancejunkies.com*

✿ ✿ ✿

Praise for Forever in Darkness

"Stephanie Rowe has done it again. The Order Of The Blade series is one of the best urban fantasy/paranormal series I have read. Ian's story held me riveted from page one. It is sure to delight all her fans. Keep them coming!" ~ *Alexx Mom Cat's Gateway Book Blog*

✿ ✿ ✿

Praise for Darkness Awakened

"A fast-paced plot with strong characters, blazing sexual tension and sprinkled with witty banter, Darkness Awakened sucked me in and kept me hooked until the very last page." ~ *Literary Escapism*

"Rarely do I find a book that so captivates my attention, that makes me laugh out loud, and cry when things look bad. And the sex, wow! It took my breath away... The pace kept me on the edge of my seat, and turning the pages. I did not want to put this book down... [Darkness Awakened] is a must read." ~ D. Alexx Miller, Alexx Mom Cat's Gateway Book Blog

☙ ☙ ☙

Praise for Darkness Seduced

"[D]ark, edgy, sexy ... sizzles on the page...sex with soul shattering connections that leave the reader a little breathless!...Darkness Seduced delivers tight plot lines, well written, witty and lyrical - Rowe lays down some seriously dark and sexy tracks. There is no doubt that this series will have a cult following. " ~ *Guilty Indulgence Book Club*

"I was absolutely enthralled by this book...heart stopping action fueled by dangerous passions and hunky, primal men...If you're looking for a book that will grab hold of you and not let go until it has been totally devoured, look no further than Darkness Seduced."~*When Pen Met Paper Reviews*

☙ ☙ ☙

Praise for Darkness Surrendered

"Book three of the Order of the Blades series is...superbly original and excellent, yet the passion, struggle and the depth of emotion that Ana and Elijah face is so brutal, yet is also pretty awe inspiring. I was swept away by Stephanie's depth of character detail and emotion. I absolutely loved the roller-coaster that Stephanie, Ana and Elijah took me on." ~ *Becky Johnson, Bex 'n' Books!*

"Darkness Surrendered drew me so deeply into the story that I felt

Ana and Elijah's emotions as if they were my own...they completely engulfed me in their story...Ingenious plot turns and edge of your seat suspense...make Darkness Surrendered one of the best novels I have read in years." ~*Tamara Hoffa, Sizzling Hot Book Reviews*

Praise for Ice

"*Ice*, by Stephanie Rowe, is a thrill ride!" ~ Lisa Jackson, #1 *New York Times* bestselling author

"Passion explodes even in the face of spiraling danger as Rowe offers a chilling thrill-ride through a vivid--and unforgiving--Alaskan wilderness." ~ Cheyenne McCray, *New York Times* bestselling author

"*Ice* delivers pulse-pounding chills and hot romance as it races toward its exciting climax!" ~ JoAnn Ross, *New York Times* bestselling author

"Stephanie Rowe explodes onto the romantic suspense scene with this edgy, sexy and gripping thriller. From the very first page, the suspense is chilling, and there's enough sizzling passion between the two main characters to melt the thickest arctic ice. Get ready for a tense and dangerous adventure." ~ *Fresh Fiction*

"Stephanie Rowe makes her entry into Romantic Suspense, and what an awesome entry! From the very first pages to the end, heart-stopping danger and passion grab the heart. ... sends shivers down the spine... magnificent... mind-chilling suspense... riveting... A wonderful romance through and through!" ~ *Merrimon Book Reviews*

"[a] thrilling entry into romantic suspense... Rowe comes through with crackling tension as the killer closes in." ~ *Publisher's Weekly*

Praise for Chill

"*Chill* is a riveting story of danger, betrayal, intrigue and the healing powers of love… *Chill* has everything a reader needs – death, threats, thefts, attraction and hot, sweet romance." ~ Jeanne Stone Hunter, *My Book Addiction Reviews*

"Once again Rowe has delivered a story with adrenalin-inducing action, suspense and a dark edged hero that will melt your heart and send a chill down your spine." ~ Sharon Stogner, *Love Romance Passion*

"*Chill* packs page turning suspense with tremendous emotional impact. Buy a box of Kleenex before you read *Chill*, because you will definitely need it! …*Chill* had a wonderfully complicated plot, full of twist and turns. " ~ Tamara Hoffa, *Sizzling Hot Book Reviews*

A Real Cowboy Rides a Motorcycle

ISBN 10: 1940968151

ISBN 13: 9781940968155

Copyright © 2015 by Stephanie Rowe.

Cover design ©2015 MJC Imageworks. For more info on the cover artist, please visit www.mjcimageworks.com.

Acknowledgements

Special thanks to my beta readers, who always work incredibly hard under tight deadlines to get my books read. I appreciate so much your willingness to tell me when something doesn't work! I treasure your help, and I couldn't do this without you. Hugs to you all! Thanks also to the Rockstars, the best buzz team ever!

There are so many to thank by name, more than I could count, but here are those who I want to called out specially for all they did to help this book come to life: Malinda Davis Diehl, Donna Bossert, Leslie Barnes, Kayla Bartley, Alencia Bates Salters, Alyssa Bird, Jean Bowden, Shell Bryce, Kelley Daley Curry, Ashley Cuesta, Denise Fluhr, Sandi Foss, Valerie Glass, Heidi Hoffman, Jeanne Stone, Rebecca Johnson, Dottie Jones, Janet Juengling-Snell, Deb Julienne, Bridget Koan, Felicia Low, Phyllis Marshall, Suzanne Mayer, Erin McRae, Jodi Moore, Ashlee Murphy, Judi Pflughoeft, Carol Pretorius, Kasey Richardson, Caryn Santee, Summer Steelman, Regina Thomas, and Linda Watson.

Special thanks to Michael James Canalas at MJC Imageworks for a wonderful cover. Mom, you're the best. It means so much that you believe in me. I love you. Special thanks also to my amazing, beautiful, special daughter, who I love more than words could ever express. You are my world, sweet girl, in all ways.

Dedication

For Donna Bossert. Thank you for all your support and friendship. I treasure you!

A Real Cowboy Rides a Motorcycle

A *Wyoming Rebels* Novel

Stephanie Rowe

Chapter 1

Taylor Shaw peered through the torrential rain hammering her windshield, inspecting the somewhat grand ranch house stretched out in front of her. It was a single story, but the huge porch and the massive picture windows gave the impression of grandeur and luxury that made her smile. This was the home of her best friend, Mira Cabot, and it was perfect.

For a brief moment, tears burned in her eyes and her throat tightened, as she recalled how hard Mira's path had been for so long. And now…she'd found her place. *You go, girl.*

God, she couldn't wait to hug Mira, and to hear about the life she'd been brave enough to tackle. Taylor knew she'd never have been as courageous as Mira, and she was so damn proud of her. Unable to keep the grin off her face, Taylor shoved open the door of the tiny rental car she'd managed to procure at the airport and almost dove out of the car in her eagerness to see Mira.

Dodging the flood of raindrops pummeling the Wyoming ranch, Taylor bolted across the muddy driveway, and vaulted up the steps to the front door. She rang the doorbell, and hopped back and forth, trying to keep warm as she waited for Mira to open the door.

She was drenched within seconds, but she didn't care one bit that she'd left her coat in the car. Who needed a coat when she was going to be hugging her best friend after months of being apart? She waited eagerly, barely even noticing how the rain was driving the coldness right through to her bones. In seconds, she would be hugging Mira. *Seconds!*

Footsteps thudded inside, and she grinned wider as she saw the door begin to open. She flung out her arms with a squeal. "Surprise—!" She cut herself off, startled to see a tall, well-muscled cowboy staring at her like she was some crazed, bedraggled freak. His blue plaid shirt was unbuttoned, revealing an amazing chest, and his dark hair was tousled, as if he'd been climbing into bed just before she'd rung the doorbell.

Whoops. She immediately dropped her arms and tried to appear harmless and sane. "Oh, sorry. I thought Mira would answer. Is she here?" She tried to peek past him, but he was big and muscular, blocking the door.

"She's asleep." He looked her up and down. "Can I help you?"

"Asleep?" She stared at him, horrified at his comment. "What time is it? Is it late?" She knew she'd gotten lost a couple times on the way there, but it couldn't be that late, could it?

"It's nine o'clock, but she gets tired easily." He narrowed his eyes, and there was no doubt of his protectiveness of Mira, which, of course Taylor appreciated, except for the fact that Mira didn't need protection from her.

There was only one man who would defend her friend so determinedly, and that would be the man who Mira had traveled cross-country to shack up with, Chase Stockton. Taylor smiled and held out her hand to shake his, realizing belatedly that introductions would probably be appropriate before barging into his house. He couldn't be expected to know how to handle their typical interactions. "You must be Chase. I'm Taylor Shaw, Mira's best friend from home."

"Taylor!" His frown disappeared into a welcoming smile that made him devastatingly handsome, and he swung the door open. "Come on in. I didn't know you were coming today. I thought it was next week. The wedding isn't for ten days."

"Thanks." Ah, yes, being invited indoors was way better than having her path blocked. Inside was definitely preferable to standing in a torrential downpour. "I wanted to surprise her, so I didn't call ahead. We like to do that to each other sometimes." She didn't mention that she'd also been desperate to escape from work. It was sucking the life out of her, and she needed to regroup and figure out what to do. What better place to regroup than with her best friend and a pint of ice cream, like they'd done countless times over the years?

As uninspiring as her work was, the problem wasn't that simple. As it turned out, having Edward become her ex-boyfriend, while still being her boss, was making work almost intolerable. Every time she saw him, a thousand emotions came flooding back, none of which were ones that made her want to jump for joy and dance on top of her desk in celebration.

So, she'd come here to support Mira in her upcoming wedding, as planned, but she'd come early because she needed her friend's advice and support. She and Mira had always been there for each other, especially when neither of them had anyone else to turn to, which had been the situation for both of them for a long time.

"Well, come on in," Chase said, gesturing her inside. "Get out of the rain."

Whoops. She'd forgotten to actually accept his invitation and go indoors. Oy. She was more stressed than she'd even realized. "Right. I'm on it." She stepped inside, and her flats squelched on the floor. They both looked down at the pool of muddy water spreading out from her feet and across the gorgeous stone floor. Heat flooded her cheeks. "Oh… I'll just wait outside—"

Chase snorted. "It's a ranch, Taylor. It's made for mud."

"Yes, but it's a really lovely ranch." The entry was paved with stone, but gleaming hardwood floors stretched across the rest of the house. She could see into a sleek modern kitchen, and a comfortable, rustic living room was just off to the right. The house was beautiful and homey, and a little bit of envy trickled through her when she thought of the stark apartment that she slept in on the rare occasion she wasn't traveling for work.

He grinned. "Thanks. We've put a lot of work into it." The pride was evident in his voice, making Taylor smile. She could tell already that Chase was a good man. Mira had been right to believe in him.

"I'll go see if she's awake. Help yourself to anything in the kitchen. I'll be right back." Chase indicated the kitchen, and then strode down the hallway, his cowboy boots clicking on the beautiful floor, his Wranglers faded like a real cowboy's should be. There was no doubt Mira had found herself a genuine cowboy, one that was every bit the man Mira had thought he was.

He disappeared through a closed door at the end of the hall, leaving Taylor alone. She let out a sigh as her stomach rumbled with hunger. She glanced longingly at the kitchen, but made no move toward it. Normally, she wouldn't hesitate to raid Mira's cabinets in search of sustenance, but this was Chase's house, and she was a stranger.

She shifted restlessly, afraid to walk around and drip all over everything. Hugging herself against the encroaching chill while she waited, she heard low, intimate murmurings from down the hall, whispers that weren't for her, whispers that she'd expected to be a part of when she'd decided to come here.

Wow. Right. She wasn't Mira's number one anymore. She hadn't thought of that.

She took a deep breath. That was okay. She was ecstatic Mira had found Chase. There was still room for best friends even when a man was in the picture.

"Taylor?" Mira's sleepy voice echoed down the hall, and Taylor's heart leapt.

She spun toward her friend, and then her mouth dropped open when she saw Mira waddling toward her, her massive belly barely covered by her pale pink robe. Her dark blond curls were longer now, and she was no longer sporting the too-skinny look that had worried Taylor for the last few years. Her breasts had tripled in size, and she looked radiant, gorgeous, and healthy, everything Taylor had hoped for with all her heart, everything that Taylor had never been able to do for her. "Wow. You're huge, girl. It's like you have half the kitchen tucked up under there." Of course she'd known her friend was pregnant, but seeing her that way was a shocking reality. Chase was walking beside her, his arm over her shoulders, as if he couldn't bear not to be touching her, and Taylor's sense of exclusion grew stronger.

Mira grinned and put her hand on her belly. "Only a few more weeks until you can call me mama."

"I call her mama already." Chase's voice was affectionate and warm, and he looked at Mira as if she was his entire world.

It was so intimate between them, with no room for a third party. Taylor stepped back, her hands falling down to her sides as she abandoned her hug. What had she done coming here? Why had she thought nothing would change now that Mira had found Chase?

But Mira didn't hesitate, throwing her arms around Taylor and hugging her just as tightly as she ever had.

Tears filled Taylor's eyes and she hugged Mira back just as fiercely, all her fears melting away. "I missed you," she whispered, her throat tightening up. God, she hadn't realized how lonely she'd been since Mira had moved away, but being with her friend again made her viscerally aware of how empty her life was when she wasn't burying herself in her work.

"I missed you, too, Taylor," Mira replied, pulling back.

Reluctantly, Taylor released her. "How are you doing? You feeling okay?" She glanced at Chase. "Is he being good to you?" she asked in a mock stage whisper.

Mira laughed, her eyes lighting up with happiness. "Everything is great. What about you?"

Taylor glanced at Chase with his arm around Mira again, and she knew now wasn't the time for her to start crying on Mira's shoulder. So, she managed a flippant smile. "Everything is awesome. I finished my latest assignment early, so I wanted to come early to help out. I figured you could use another hand getting things ready for the wedding and the baby."

"Of course! You're always welcome." The genuine warmth in Mira's voice eased some of Taylor's rising tension and sense of isolation. "I'll put you to work in the morning. Where are you staying?"

"Where am I—?" Taylor felt heat rush to her cheeks. It hadn't even occurred to her to find a hotel. She'd just assumed that she'd stay here, but she quickly realized what a mistake that had been. "I—"

"Oh, stay with us," Mira said quickly, her face softening as she astutely picked up on Taylor's situation. "Our basement guest room is full of boxes we retrieved from my parent's house and haven't unpacked yet, and the first floor bedroom now has a crib in it, but you could sleep in the living room."

Taylor felt her heart sinking. Sleep on the couch? In

their space? She knew she'd feel like she was intruding every second she was there. "That's okay. I'll just—"

"Or the bunkhouse," Mira interrupted, her face brightening as she thought of it. She and Chase exchanged a special smile that once again made Taylor feel like she was standing on the periphery. "Is it ready for her, Chase?"

He nodded. "I had it cleaned after Steen and Erin moved out. It's all set."

Taylor frowned, trying to follow the conversation. "Steen and Erin? Who are they?"

"Oh, you'll love them," Mira said, her eyes sparkling with happiness. "Steen is Chase's brother, and Erin is his fiancée. They're building a house and a vet clinic on the south side of the property. They were living in the bunkhouse, but they moved to a trailer home next to their house so they have a little privacy while it's being built. Erin is such a doll. You'll love her."

"Oh." Taylor cleared her throat at the obvious affection in Mira's voice. Clearly, she and Erin had become close friends, and they were almost sisters now if Erin was engaged to Chase's brother. Taylor clasped her hands behind her head, suddenly wishing that she'd arranged for a hotel room. This wasn't what she'd envisioned at all. "I'm sure we'll get along great," she managed.

"Of course you will." Mira yawned, and Taylor realized she was overstaying her welcome.

"So, I'll just let you guys do your thing," she said, taking her cue to leave. "If you can point me to the bunkhouse, I'll go set up there."

"I'll take your bags down there," Chase said, reaching for a weather-beaten trench coat that looked like it was built for storms like the one howling outside.

"Oh, no. I'm all set. I don't have much—"

"You're not going out alone," Chase said, his voice mellow but unyielding. "I've got you covered."

Taylor's throat suddenly tightened, and she had to look away and blink several times. God, how long had it been since someone had done something as simple as heading outside in a driving rainstorm to help her with her bags? She didn't even know Chase, but he made her feel like she mattered. How had

Mira found someone this wonderful? She hadn't even realized men like Chase existed.

"Do you want to snag some food to take with you?" Mira asked. "I don't think there's anything there." Before Taylor could answer, she was already heading to the kitchen. "I think I have some coffee you'll like," she called out as she opened cabinets. "And of course, your oatmeal for breakfast. And I have some leftover chicken that Chase grilled tonight," she said, yawning again. "I'm so sorry that I can't stay up with you. I just get so tired."

"It's totally fine," Taylor said. "I should have called first." God, she should have called. She'd had visions of sitting up on the couch for hours with ice cream and hot chocolate while they caught up. She hadn't thought about how things would be different, and she should have.

Chase shoved a cowboy hat on his head while Mira handed Taylor a grocery bag. She hugged Taylor again, a fierce hug that soothed some of Taylor's tension. "I'm *so* glad you're here, Taylor."

"Me, too." The tightness around her chest loosened slightly at Mira's sincerity. "I'll see you in the morning. You can come grab me when you're ready for company, okay? I don't want to barge in on you twice."

Mira smiled. "Deal."

Chase walked over to Mira, locked his arm around her waist, and pulled her close for an almost unbearably sweet kiss. "I'll be right back. Don't have the baby while I'm gone."

Mira laughed and lightly swatted his chest. "You'll have to take it up with the baby, not me."

He leaned forward and put his ear to her belly, as if he were listening. Then he nodded. "The baby says that I'm in charge. He says he'll wait."

Mira's eyebrows shot up. "*She'll* do what *she* wants."

He shot her a cocky look. "We'll see."

A part of Taylor wanted to put her ear to Mira's belly and listen to the baby as well, but another part of her wanted to slink away from the intimacies that she wasn't a part of and hop on the next plane out of town. She did neither. She was too tired to leave, and too uncertain to reach out and slap her palm across her best friend's belly. So she just smiled. "See you in the morning, Mira."

"You bet!" At Mira's wave, Taylor ducked out into the rain, no longer caring that she was soaked and covered in mud. She just wanted a moment to regroup and figure out where she could fit into her best friend's new life.

There had to be a place, right? Because if there wasn't, she had no one else.

God, that was a great thought. Surely she could muster up a more positive attitude. She could get a cat. Or a goldfish. A fish would be a good listener, right?

But as she slogged through the mud, following Chase to her car, she knew there was no way to deny the truth: fish were slimy, and if she had to rely on one to be her dearest friend… well…that was just not a good solution.

She shook her head, unable to shake the isolation that was beginning to grip her. What was she going to do?

He was tired.
He was cranky.
He was wet.

Zane Stockton idled his motorcycle outside his brother's ranch house, narrowing his eyes at the darkened windows. Gone was the time when he'd let himself in and crash. There was a woman in there now, and that changed all the rules, especially when it was two in the morning.

He probably shouldn't have come tonight, but he was here, and he was done being on the road for now. Rain had been thundering down on him for hours, and he was drenched. He just wanted to sleep and forget about all the crap that had gone down today. Grief was gnawing at him, the kind of grief that he had to escape, the kind that would destroy him if he let it.

Which was why he'd come to the ranch. It was the only place in his life, besides the open road, where the noise in his head quieted long enough for him to think.

Trying not to rev the engine too much, he eased his bike down the driveway and turned right into the lean-to beside the bunkhouse. He settled his bike and whipped out a couple towels to clean it off, making sure it was mud-free before calling it a night.

Task accomplished, he grabbed his bag from the back of the bike, scowling when he realized it had gotten wet. Not that it mattered. Nothing mattered now except crashing. He sloshed through the puddles toward the front door of the bunkhouse, retrieved the key from the doorframe, and pried the thing open.

It was pitch dark inside, but he knew his way around and didn't bother with a light. He dropped the bag, kicked off his boots and his drenched clothes, then headed for the only bed that was still set up in the place after Steen and Erin's brief occupation of it. Zane was damn glad they'd upgraded their lodgings to a temporary mobile home so the bunkhouse was now available again for use by the family vagrant.

Zane jerked back the covers and collapsed onto the bed. The minute he landed, he felt the soft, very real feel of a body beneath him, including the swell of a woman's breast beneath his forearm. Shit! "What the hell?" He leapt to his feet just as a woman shrieked and slammed a pillow into the side of his head.

"Hey, I'm not going to hurt you! I'm Chase's brother!" He grabbed the pillow as it clocked him in the side of the head again. "Stop!"

There was a moment of silence, and all he could hear was heavy breathing. Then she spoke. "You're Chase's brother?" Her voice was breathless, and throaty, as if he'd awakened her out of a deep sleep, which he probably had. It sounded sexy as hell, and he was shocked to feel a rush of desire catapult through him.

Shit. He hadn't responded physically to a woman in a *long* time, and now he'd run into a woman who could turn him on simply by *speaking* to him? Who the hell was she? "Yeah," he said, sounding crankier than he intended. "Who are you?"

"You're Steen?" He heard her fumbling for something, and he wondered if she was searching for a baseball bat, pepper spray, or something that indicated she hadn't been nearly as turned on by his voice as he'd been by hers.

"No, a different brother," he replied, his head spinning as he tried to figure what was going on, and why he was reacting to her so intensely. "I'm Zane. Harmless. Good guy. No need to decapitate me."

There was a pause in her movements. "I wasn't going to decapitate you. I was looking for my shirt."

"Your shirt?" he echoed blankly. "You're not wearing a shirt?" He hadn't noticed that much bare skin for that brief moment he'd been on top of her. How had he missed it?

"I'm wearing a camisole, but it's not exactly decent. Give me a sec." A small laugh drifted through the darkness. "You're such a guy. Of course you'd fixate on the possibility of me being naked. Do all men think only of sex?"

He grinned, relaxing. He'd startled her, but she'd regrouped quickly, and he liked that. She wasn't a wimp who was running to the door screaming. "What's your name?" he asked.

"Taylor Shaw. I'm Mira's best friend from home. I surprised her for a visit, but it turns out, there's no space in the house."

"Nope. Not anymore. I'm displaced too." He suddenly wanted to see her. "You decent yet?"

"Yes, but barely—"

He reached over and flicked on the small light by the bed. The soft yellow glow was less harsh than the overhead light, but it still took his eyes a moment to adjust to the brightness. When they did, he saw Taylor sitting on the bed, curly blond hair tumbling around her shoulders in a disheveled mess that made her look completely adorable. Her eyes were a deep blue, fixed on him as she squinted against the sudden light. He could see the curve of her shoulders beneath her light pink, long-sleeved shirt. The faint outline of a white camisole was evident beneath her shirt, not quite obscuring the fact that she wasn't wearing a bra. Her gray yoga pants were frayed at the knee and cuff, but they fit her hips with perfection. She looked like she'd just tumbled right out of a bed, and she was sexy as hell.

But it was her face that caught his attention. Her gaze was wary, but there was a vulnerability in it that made him want to protect her. He had zero protective instincts when it came to women…until now, until he'd met this woman who'd tried to defend herself with a pillow.

Then her gaze slid down his body, and his entire body

went into heated overdrive. It wasn't until her eyes widened in surprise when her gaze was at hip level that he remembered something very important.

He was naked.

Chapter 2

Taylor blinked in surprise as her gaze stopped just below Zane's navel. He was *naked*.

"Shit. Sorry." Zane grabbed the pillow she'd used on his head and slammed it in front of his crotch a split second before she managed to get a full eyeful. "I forgot."

She jerked her attention off his muscular body, and back to his face, horrified that he'd caught her staring at him. She hadn't *meant* to check him out. It was just that he was standing there, and he had amazing shoulders and her gaze had wandered, because what woman's wouldn't have, right? "It's okay," she said quickly. "Not a big deal." Not a big deal. It wasn't, of course, in the grand scheme of things. A naked man was a naked man, right? They all had the same body parts.

Except that Zane Stockton had taken the definition of man to an entirely new level. He was rippling with muscle, there were crisscrossed scars across the front of his right shoulder, and the dark hair on his chest angled down to a V where his hips narrowed. He was sculpted masculinity, and there was no way for her to lie to herself and pretend she hadn't noticed.

"No?" He cocked a dark eyebrow at her. "Not even a little bit of a big deal?"

"Of course not." She tried to keep her voice even, and her eyes on his face, but it was difficult. She'd never been around a man who exuded so much maleness. She could easily believe he was Chase's brother after seeing how utterly masculine Chase had been. Unlike Chase, however, Zane felt dangerous and wild, a man who had never sat behind a desk or in a boardroom. The wolf tattoo on his right biceps looked like it had come from within him, instead of being penned on by someone else.

"Then you can have your pillow back." He tossed it at her, and she caught it as he sauntered across the room toward a duffel bag on the floor.

She tried, she really *tried*, not to notice the way his back rippled with muscles as he walked away from her, and she *really* tried not to check out his butt. She almost succeeded, managing to sneak only a quick glance before finding a place on the wall to stare at blankly.

"I don't care if you stare." There was definite amusement in his voice as he grabbed a pair of boxer briefs from his duffel.

"I'd care if you were staring at me naked," she pointed out, trying to justify her laser-like focus on the knot in the wall.

"Interesting thought." His voice was low and husky, shivering across her skin like an invisible caress.

She shot an annoyed glare at him, and then relaxed when she saw that he was wearing his boxer briefs. The dark blue hid enough detail that she could face him. "Clearly, I have more manners than you do."

Zane walked over to her, and she scrambled to her feet as he neared. He was barely dressed, and she didn't want to be sprawled on the bed as he approached. "I have no manners at all," he said. "I was raised in a shit hole, and I don't clean up well."

His tone was hard, daring her to challenge him, but she saw a spark of defiance in his dark eyes that made her heart soften. She had no doubt that he was raised exactly as he'd just claimed. "I'm sorry."

He narrowed his eyes. "Sorry for what?"

"That you were raised in a shit hole. No one deserves that."

He stared at her for a long moment, so long that she wanted to squirm. She didn't, however. Instead, she simply raised her chin.

Silence hung between them, suspended in the dimly lit cabin. Finally, he shrugged. "You want the wall side?"

She blinked. "What?"

He gestured at the bed. "Which side you do want?"

Her gaze snapped to the double bed, which was far smaller than the queen-size bed she had at home, or the king-size beds she always requested in her hotel rooms. "You're going to sleep with me?"

"Yeah."

She let out her breath, ignoring the warring factions inside her of joy and delight versus outrage and fury. "Why would you think that is a good choice?" Wow. She was impressed with how diplomatic she'd managed to sound. One might think she had years of experience with hellish bosses and nightmarish clients. Oh, wait, she had.

He ran his hand through his hair impatiently, drawing her attention to how damp it was. The dark hair was curling around the base of his neck, too long to be a cowboy or a corporate exec, but just long enough to belong to a troublemaker or a rebel. "Because I've been riding for hours. I'm wet. I'm tired. This is the only bed left in the bunkhouse or anywhere on the ranch. I'm getting in it, and you can sleep on the hard floor by yourself, or with me in the bed."

And with that, he moved past her, flipped back the covers, and dropped onto the mattress.

For a moment, she stood there in shock, staring at him as he made himself comfortable in the bed she'd been occupying only moments before. "You're kidding, right?"

"I don't have a sense of humor." He rolled onto his side, facing her. The bed seemed to have shrunk to half the size now that he was in it. His shoulders were broader than she'd realized, and he seemed to literally possess the area he was in. His eyes were dark and unfathomable, so intense she felt as though he were prying away all her haughty facades and seeing her for the broken, exhausted woman she really was. "I'm not a good guy, but I have a sense of honor I'd never break. We could both be naked in this bed, and I'd never touch you unless you asked me to. You're safe with me."

He never broke eye contact when he spoke, and Taylor knew he meant every word. "You're a cowboy? Like Chase?" She knew it was silly, but she'd always associated cowboys with a sense of honor and morality. They were the men who knew how to be polite to a woman, who wouldn't hesitate to defend his girl, no matter who came after her.

Zane, however, didn't offer himself up as her fantasy man. "I was once. Not anymore." He offered no further explanation. Instead, he rolled onto his back and draped his arm over his face, shielding his eyes. "Turn out the light when you decide where you're sleeping. The floor sucks, though."

Taylor glanced around the bunkhouse. There was a small kitchen area, the door to the tiny bathroom, and the bed. Nothing else except another door tucked against the far wall. "What's in there?"

"Everything that Steen and Erin rejected." He didn't move his arm from his face. "Chase used to have this place set up with a bunch of bunks so that he could accommodate all the vagrants who showed up to stay, but we never came, and Erin and Steen redecorated. Now we have one bed."

Taylor quickly walked across the room and opened the door. It was pitch-black inside, but she found a light switch by the door. Piled from floor to ceiling were bunk bed frames and mattresses, packed in the tiny room. No bedding, and the room smelled musty and old. There was no way anyone was going to sleep in there tonight. It would take days to get it cleared out.

Grimly, she pulled the door shut and leaned against it, staring at the bed. Zane was stretched out across it, taking up almost the whole thing, except for a small area against the wall. She'd have to climb over him to get to the free space. With a sigh, she ran her hand through her hair. How could she kick him out? She could hear the rain hammering on the roof, and she knew there was no space up at the main house.

But how could she just climb in there with him? She didn't know him, he was mostly naked, and he was...well...a man. Not just a man, but a man she was viscerally aware of as a woman. She'd spent a long time convincing herself that she didn't need a man, but there was something about Zane that had awakened a part of her that had been long dormant. Yes, of course, seeing him in the flesh was riveting, but there was something more to him, something that called to a part of her that had been broken so badly that she'd never thought it would work again. She'd never wanted it to work again, because to feel things meant heartbreak she wouldn't survive. Somehow, Zane had touched those chords inside her, and she didn't want them to wake up.

He moved his arm off his face and lifted his head to study her.

She lifted her chin, folding her arms to ward off the chilly, damp air that was beginning to settle in her bones. "I can't share a bed with you. I don't even know you."

He said nothing. He simply held out his hand to her.

She stared at his hand, and part of her wanted to just take what he offered and crawl into bed with him, to fall asleep hearing someone else's breathing for the first time in a very long time. The other part of her wanted to grab her bags, run back to the airport, and get on the first plane back to the life she was used to...the one that was slowly killing her.

"You're tired," he said. "I'm tired. Come on."

She sighed, fighting the urge to capitulate, even as her teeth began to chatter. Her feet were ice cold, and she was shivering. "I don't think—"

"The heat's not working in this place anymore," he said. "Unless you have an electric blanket, you're going to need me anyway."

She barely stifled a giggle. "You're trying to convince me by presenting yourself as an electric blanket?"

"For hell's sake, woman, get your ass in this bed before I make you." He held up the blanket to make space for her to slide in with him. "Martyrs are fools, and I can't stand fools. Are you going to wimp out and spend the night freezing, or are you going to get your ass in here?"

"I'm not a wimp," she snapped, even as she gave in. She wanted to be in that bed with him, and there was no way to deny it. With a sigh of resignation, she darted across the room to the bed. He was still on the outer edge, and he didn't move over.

His eyebrows rose in a challenge, and she thought she saw the smallest hint of amusement twitching at the corner of his mouth.

"Oh, for heaven's sake." She yanked the blanket out of his hand and climbed across him. There was no way to avoid touching him, and her belly tightened at the feel of his body beneath hers as she crawled over him. It just felt good, so crazy good, to feel another human being's body against hers.

As she settled into her corner of the bed, she realized that she'd had no idea how much she'd missed physical contact. Just being beside Zane made her want to burrow up against him and breathe deeply.

Zane moved beside her, and she heard him click off the light on the nightstand, plunging them into total darkness. He shifted again, and the bed creaked beneath his weight as he settled into the mattress, pulling the covers up over both of them.

"You think this bed will hold both of us?" she asked. She knew it would, but she felt awkward lying in the silent darkness with him, a stranger. She needed to connect with him so it wouldn't feel so weird.

"Given what Steen and Erin probably did here, I'd say it's plenty strong for sleeping."

Awareness swirled through her at the implications of his words. "It's always about sex with guys, isn't it?" They weren't touching, but she could feel the heat from his body filling the space they shared beneath the blankets. He was such a strong presence, he made her feel warm and safe. She liked the fact he was between her and the rest of the room. If anyone came in, they'd have to go through Zane to get to her, and she suspected that wouldn't be an easy task.

He laughed softly at her question. "Darlin', it's never about sex with me. Been there, done that. I got no time for that these days."

She snorted. "Give me a break. Every remark you've made tonight has had sexual innuendoes." Well, maybe not *every* one, but it had been a high percentage for sure...then, as she thought about it, she realized that maybe he hadn't actually made any sexual references. Maybe she'd just interpreted them that way because *she* was the one with sex on the brain? She felt her cheeks begin to heat up with embarrassment, and she wanted to sink into the mattress.

"Is that so?" Zane sounded thoughtful. "You might be right. If you are, then I'd have to revise my answer and say that it's never about sex with me anymore, unless a certain Taylor Shaw is in my bed."

His answer seemed to ignite the darkness, and Taylor caught her breath. So, the chemistry humming between them wasn't just her being delusional? It was mutual. Oh, *wow*. "You don't even know me," she whispered, rolling onto her side to face him. Of course, she couldn't see him at all, just darkness. She wanted to reach out and touch him, just to see where he was, but she didn't. How could she? This weird, middle-of-the-night intimacy wasn't about getting real with actual touching.

"Nope, I don't, but I got some things figured out already." The bed shifted as Zane turned, and she wondered if he was facing her. "I know you're a little scared of being in this bed with me, but you did it anyway. Not only is that endearing as hell, but I also appreciate the fact you didn't tell me to get my ass out into the rain so you could have your privacy. You hit me in the head with a pillow to protect yourself. What guy doesn't admire that kind of attitude? Vulnerable, empathetic, and a little bit bad ass? And you surprised your best friend with a visit, but didn't say one bad thing about the fact you got booted to the bunkhouse upon your arrival. That says loyalty to me, and loyalty is damned important. Plus, you look smoking hot in that getup you've got on, so yeah, you got me thinking about things I haven't had time for in a long time."

Her heart began to race, and desire curled through her. A part of her wanted him to reach for her and draw her into his arms. Somehow, in this darkness, in this intimacy, it felt like she could do things that she'd never do in real life...like get naked with a man she didn't even know?

Oh, God. Really? She rolled onto her back, clutching the blankets to her chest. What was she thinking? Just because Zane was the brother of the man her best friend was going to marry didn't change the fact he was a complete stranger.

"And what man wouldn't fall for that look of absolute vulnerability in those eyes of yours? So bold, and yet soft at the same time. It's compelling." Zane said softly, almost so quietly that she didn't hear it. But she did, and she knew she was meant to.

"Are you trying to seduce me?" she asked, her voice equally as quiet.

He was silent for a moment. "Would it work?"

"It might," she said honestly. "There's something about you."

"Yeah. I know what you mean."

Again, neither of them spoke for a moment, and she waited, nervous, afraid he would break his promise and try to seduce her, afraid that she would say yes. She'd never had a one-night stand in her entire life. She wasn't cut out for it emotionally, and she didn't like sex enough to need a quick fix of hot and sweaty to get through the day. But with Zane... something seemed to come alive inside her, something that was powerful and dangerous and made her tread too close to an edge she'd battled against for so long.

"You dating anyone?" he asked, his voice startling her when he spoke.

"No. You?"

"No."

Again silence, then he spoke again. "I don't get involved with women," he said. "I don't have time for a girlfriend or anything serious. You should know that about me. I don't want you to think I'm something I'm not. I'm in town to run the ranch while Mira and Chase have the kid, then I'm out of here. I'm not sticking around."

She bit her lip and closed her eyes. "You're not a family guy? No dreams of a white picket fence and little munchkins running around the yard?"

He stiffened beside her, as if she'd just tried to shoot him in the head with a gun. "Shit, no. You've got to be kidding."

She heard the absolute truth of his words, and her entire body shuddered with relief. Zane wasn't lying to her. He wasn't a family guy...which meant he was safe.

"Why?" His voice was wary now. "Is that what you're looking for?"

She shook her head, giving the answer she always gave now, the one that she had almost convinced herself was the truth. "Absolutely not. Settling down isn't in my nature."

He moved then, and suddenly, she felt his breath warm against the side of her neck. "No?" he whispered.

She went still, afraid to move, afraid to face him, afraid that if she turned toward him, if her lips accidentally brushed his in the dark, that it would start a cascade of chain-reactions she wasn't prepared for. "No," she said.

"How long are you here for?" His words sent shivers down her spine. "In town?"

She could barely breathe through the tightness in her lungs. "Until the wedding, and the baby. Two weeks, probably."

"Two weeks." He said the words like a seduction that caressed along her spine. "Could be an interesting two weeks, Taylor."

She swallowed hard. "Go away, Zane. I need to sleep."

He laughed softly, a deep rumble that seemed to echo through her body and settle low in her belly. "Good night, darlin'. I'll see you in the morning. Let me know if you get cold." He moved away, back to his own side of the bed, which was still dangerously close to her.

Taylor let out her breath in a shuddering exhale. She was still cold, and she knew he was well aware of it. Not that she would *ever* ask him to warm her up. She wasn't that foolish. Or brave. Or whatever you wanted to call it.

She might have climbed into bed with him, but that was as far as it was going, end of story.

Chapter 3

Zane awoke to the scent of a woman. It drifted through him, enveloping him in a sense of primal satisfaction he hadn't felt in a long time. Then, he became aware of not only the scent of a woman, but the feel of one wrapped intimately around him.

His eyes snapped open, and he lifted his head. In the dim light of morning, he could see the woman from what he'd thought were his dreams wrapped around him. It hadn't been a dream. *She was real.*

Taylor was using his chest as a pillow, and her blond curls were tumbling across his bare skin. Her feet were tangled with his, and his arm was wrapped around her shoulders, holding her close against him. Her belly was snug against his hip, and her thigh was resting directly on top of his cock, which was hard as rock.

But what he noticed most of all was that her fingers were wrapped around his wrist, holding on tightly to him in her sleep, as if she were afraid he would leave her. He stared at her hand, amazed by how delicate it looked compared to his wrist. She was all woman, with curves that made him hunger for more.

He let his head drop back to the pillow, contemplating. He couldn't remember the last time he'd slept with a woman. Yeah, he'd had a few nights of fun, but he always made sure that when it came time for sleeping, he was alone. He didn't like people in his space, and he certainly didn't want to wake up in the morning and owe someone else his time and energy, or even coffee.

And yet, here he was, so tangled up with Taylor that there was no way he'd be able to extricate himself without waking her up. He was completely trapped by her, and it should feel like a noose was around his throat.

But it didn't.

He was actually damned comfortable right where he was. He liked having her against him, and he really liked the way she was gripping his wrist in her sleep. Was it because he hadn't had sex with her? He owed her nothing, and she would expect nothing, so there was no pressure to be anything other than who he was. Hell, he'd already made it clear that he had no manners, right?

A small smile played across his lips as he tightened his arm around her, tucking her even more securely against his side. His hand was on her hip, and he left it there. He had a sudden urge to trace circles on her hip, to tease his fingers across her skin, but he didn't move.

Staying where he already was felt like it was within the parameters of acceptable. Doing something else, like running his hand over her thigh where it was draped across his cock, was not, but there was no way to deny he was thinking about it.

He thought back to how she'd whacked him in the head with a pillow, and his grin widened. She had spunk, and she hadn't wanted anything from him. He was used to women wanting him for his body or his name, and it was damned refreshing to have Taylor see him completely naked, but then not want to have sex with him. She'd treated him like he was a regular human being, and he liked it. A lot.

She stirred against him, mumbling something in her sleep, and he went still, trying not to wake her up. He wasn't ready for reality to intrude. He wasn't ready for the yelp of horror or an insulting accusation that he'd tried to assault her during the night. He wasn't ready for that predatory gleam in her eyes when she realized that the man she'd spent the night with wasn't only the brother of her best friend, but a man who many women had tried to claim.

His good mood faded, and he tensed, waiting for that same crappy experience of being recognized as the three-time bull riding world champion and all the shit that came with it.

She yawned, and nestled closer against him, tucking herself against his side so intimately that his jaw clenched. It felt fantastic, like the calm before the storm. He probably should get up, shove her aside, and hit the road before she realized her good fortune in who she'd slept with, but he didn't.

He waited.

For some stupid-ass reason, he waited.

It didn't take long. He knew the moment she woke up and realized where she was. Her body tensed against his, and her breathing changed. She didn't move for a long moment, and he knew that she was trying to figure out whether he was awake. He realized, then, that he should probably have moved his hand off her hip. Now that he was awake, there was no excuse for leaving it there.

Shit. What was she going to pull on him? Was she going to accuse him of manhandling her? He should have gotten up the minute he'd woken up, and at least given himself a chance to get out of bed before she realized what position they'd ended up in.

"Zane?" Her voice was thick with sleep, and desire raced through him.

He gritted his teeth, debating whether to pretend he was asleep, but he quickly dismissed it. He'd never run away from anything, and he wasn't going to now. "Yeah?" He waited for the words, for the challenge, for the accusation, for whatever would be coming.

She yawned again, making him wait for her response. "Thanks for not getting up," she finally mumbled.

He frowned, trying to process what she'd just said. "What?"

"You didn't get up." To his shock, she burrowed even more tightly against his side. She didn't jerk her leg off his cock, but she also didn't try to grind it against him either. She made no reference to the sexual potency of their position at all. "I haven't woken up with someone in a long, long time, and I forgot how good it feels."

He thought about it, waiting for the next words, the ones that would condemn him. "But?"

"No buts. It's just nice." She sighed again, a deep sigh of

such contentment that he started to relax. "There's no baggage, you know? Since we don't know each other and didn't have sex or anything. It's just...nice. No pressure. Just nice."

The tension vanished from his body, and he tightened his arm around her. "Yeah, I know what you mean." He hesitated, and then brushed his finger over her hair. He'd been dying to touch it, but he hadn't dared.

She didn't object, and he moved his hand, trailing it down her head and over her hair.

"That feels good," she said softly. "I haven't been touched like that in a long time."

He relaxed further, tangling his fingers in her hair. He couldn't remember the last time he'd touched a woman without having to watch his back. He was always moderating his comments and his actions, unwilling to do or say anything that could get him into trouble or make her think he was promising things he wasn't, so he never had the luxury of simply experiencing the moment. "Why not? Seems like you'd have a posse of guys after you."

She shrugged, and released his wrist to splay her fingers across his chest. Her touch was so soft that his gut clenched. He was used to women who touched him with the purpose of seduction, but Taylor's touch was simple and innocent, and completely erotic. "Dating men is so complicated," she said. "I've been taking a break for a while. I don't mind being alone." She drew a circle on his chest. "I forgot about this kind of intimacy, though," she said. "Just being held, you know?"

"Yeah." On a whim, he lifted his head and pressed a kiss to the top of her head. She sighed with contentment, making him grin. "I haven't been in a relationship in a long time. I don't have the time or energy for it. Women..." He paused, not wanting to insult her gender.

"Women what?" She yawned again, still tracing lazy circles across his chest. She didn't sound like she was about to take offense, so he decided to answer the question.

"Women can be mercenary."

She laughed softly. "Yes, they can." She looked up at him, her blue eyes clear now. He was shocked by how blue they were. In the night, he hadn't had a sense of exactly how vibrant they were, but now...they were vivid and intelligent, and absolutely riveting. "Tell me, Zane, what do they want from you? Is it because you're hot?"

He grinned. "Am I hot?"

She smiled back at him, and lightly punched his chest. "You know you are. I can see it in your eyes."

His smile faded, and he realized that she had no idea about his past. He didn't want to tell her. He liked that she looked at him like he was just a guy. He lived in a world where he hadn't been just a guy for a long time, perhaps ever. He'd once been the troublemaker from the wrong side of the tracks, and then he'd become the tour's most eligible bachelor, and all of it had sucked. So, he just shook his head. "It's nothing—"

There was a sudden sound from the front door, but neither of them had time to move before the door flew open and Mira walked in. She took one look at the two of them in the bed, and her jaw dropped. "Zane? Taylor? What's going on?"

Zane's first instinct was to haul ass out of the bed and explain that nothing had happened, to establish that he and Taylor were not together...but he didn't. He actually, without meaning to, slid his fingers around to the back of Taylor's neck and lightly clasped her. "Good morning, Mira. The house was dark when I arrived, so I didn't want to bother you. I crashed here."

"But—"

"Oh, stop, Mira." Taylor patted his chest affectionately, and then sat up, her long-sleeved shirt sliding off one shoulder in a dangerously sexy move. "You know perfectly well nothing happened here. Zane barged in, completely soaked, and claimed half the bed."

Zane realized that all hell wasn't going to break loose. Taylor wasn't going to fall over herself trying to pretend that they'd had sex, and she wasn't going to freak out and dive out of the bed. She was relaxed, and utterly unconcerned. Slowly, he clasped his hands behind his head, amusement beginning to build deep inside him as he watched the interplay between the two women. He liked the fact Taylor was in his bed and not getting up. Yeah, he liked it a lot.

Mira's gaze slipped to Zane. "He's naked. And in bed

with you."

Taylor's smile slipped. "You really think I had sex with him?" Her voice was hurt, and she sounded confused. "Why would you think that?"

Zane was surprised at the question. Why *wouldn't* Mira think that? She'd walked in while they were entwined around each other in bed, and, as far as she knew, he was naked.

But when Mira looked at Taylor, her face softened. Then she smiled, her face so full of warmth that jealousy actually twitched inside Zane. "I'm sorry. You're right. I know you better than that." She walked across the room and sat down on the bed, next to Zane. "I missed you, Taylor."

"I missed you, too." The women reached across him and hugged each other, and Zane's ease with the situation vanished. He wasn't into hugs and tears and all that stuff. He held up his hands, not sure where to put them with the women hugging across him the way they were. "Okay, ladies, I'm generally up for threesomes, but when one of the women is pregnant and about to marry my brother, I draw the line."

The women broke apart with a burst of laughter, and Zane used the opening to extricate himself from the covers, whipping his feet around Mira and hitting the floor. He grabbed his still-damp jeans and a shirt, yanked them on, and pulled on his boots, all in about five seconds. He grabbed his duffel. "I'm going to dry my clothes—" He realized then what he'd said. "I mean, is it okay with you if I use your dryer, Mira?" Shit, it annoyed him that he had to ask that. This ranch was for the Stockton men, not for the women. He knew it had changed, but that didn't mean he had to like it.

She smiled, that same warm smile she'd always given him, as if she didn't care one bit that he didn't like her there. "Zane, you don't have to ask. You're always welcome. Breakfast will be ready in ten minutes, if you want to join us."

"Yeah, maybe, thanks." He ducked out of the bunkhouse, leaving behind the sound of the women's laughter. He wondered how long it would take for them to start talking about him, and irritation slid down his spine. Mira would tell Taylor all about him, and the next time Taylor looked at him, she'd see what everyone else saw.

He felt like snarling as he stepped out into the bright sunlight, squinting against the light. With a low growl, he walked over to his bike and opened the case on the back. Inside was his cowboy hat. He never wore the damn thing anymore, but if he was running around the ranch for two weeks, he'd need it. He pulled the old thing out and jammed it on his head.

It felt weird, and he didn't like it, but at the same time... something about it called to him. He ran his finger over the brim, instinctively wiping off the bit of dust that had tried to claim it. He brushed his hand over the soft leather of his bike seat, so slick compared to the feel of his hat. The urge to climb onto his bike and leave was so strong, he actually wrapped his fingers around the cool metal handlebars. He'd never stayed here more than one night at a time. He never stayed anywhere for long.

But he'd made a promise to his brother, and he wasn't going to let him down. He was going to stay to help with the ranch until the baby was born. His brother had never asked him for help before, and Zane wasn't going to turn him down. That's what Stockton men did: they always, *always*, stood by each other, no matter what.

With a grim sigh, he turned away from his bike, and headed for the barn. But as he walked, he couldn't help but glance over his shoulder at the bunkhouse. The small, flat-roofed building looked like nothing, but he could still hear the whisper of women's voices. He paused for a moment, trying to separate Taylor's voice, but he was too far away.

The moment with her was over.

It was what it was, and he was moving on.

But as he headed down the dirt driveway toward the barn to do a quick assessment of his responsibilities before breakfast, he couldn't help but think about the fact that both he and Taylor were going to be on the ranch for the next two weeks.

Two weeks was a long, damned time. Long enough that he'd considered it a rare, specialized torture designed just for him...until he'd met Taylor. Now, two weeks was still a long, damned time...long enough that interesting things could happen. Really interesting. With a slow smile, his irritation faded, and by the time he'd reached the barn, he was whistling.

Chapter 4

"When was the last time you had sex?"

Taylor grinned at Mira's question, shouted unabashedly from the other side of the bathroom door. She turned off the hairdryer, amused that Mira had managed to restrain herself that long before interrogating her. It felt so good to be harassed by Mira again. She'd missed having her privacy invaded by her. "It's been a while," she admitted, running a brush through her still-damp hair.

"Tony? Was it Tony?"

Taylor's smile faded, and that familiar ache settled in her heart, the ache that she was beginning to think would never fully go away. "I've dated since my ex-husband," she said.

"Have you? I mean, really?" The door opened, and Mira stuck her head in the bathroom. Her brow was scrunched in worry.

Taylor picked up her foundation and opened it. With Zane wandering around the ranch, a part of her was tempted to put on makeup and turn herself into the corporate Taylor who never showed her flaws. She studied herself in the mirror, at the face she always covered up with makeup when she was at work. She was so used to wearing foundation and smoothing over her skin so she was always perfect. But today, her cheeks were flushed, and she looked...alive.

Suddenly, she didn't want to plaster foundation over her face, and she didn't want to shove her hair up in a tight bun. She dropped the foundation and picked up her mascara instead.

A brush over her lashes was all she felt like doing, and it was liberating. "I dated Edward for six months."

Mira leaned against the doorway, her arms folded over her chest. "Your boss? That Edward?" She frowned, looking confused, for good reason, since Taylor had never told her.

Taylor glanced at her. "Yeah, but he wasn't my boss when we started dating."

Her friend's mouth dropped open. "You never told me about him. How could you not tell me about him?"

Taylor turned to face her. "Mira, you were so buried in taking care of your mother, I was afraid to tell you. I didn't want you to feel bad that I had someone and you didn't. You were struggling so much, and I just couldn't do that to you."

Mira's eyebrows shot up. "*And* you didn't want me to interfere."

Taylor smiled. "Yeah, well, you do like to stick your nose in my social life." She turned back to the mirror and finished up with the mascara. "It doesn't matter. It's over."

"When did it end?"

Taylor bit her lip. "A while ago. Once he became my boss, it got awkward. You know, he got more responsibility and had different priorities."

Mira said nothing, and Taylor glanced over at her. Her heart tightened when she saw the knowing look on her friend's face. "Don't say it."

"He wanted to settle down with you, didn't he? He wanted more from the relationship?"

Taylor didn't answer right away, busying herself with putting her makeup back into her travel bag. "It just wasn't a fit," she finally hedged.

"So, that's why you like Zane, right? Because he's a perennial vagabond, and you know he'll never want to settle down with you. He's as afraid of commitment as you are."

Taylor glared at her friend. "I'm not afraid of commitment. It just wasn't right with Edward."

Mira put her hands on her hips. "Did you love Edward?"

"I don't know. I—"

"Did he ask you to marry him?"

"No. Not in so many words, exactly." Taylor pushed past

Mira and walked back into the main room of the bunkhouse. Her bag was on the floor against the wall, and she grabbed a pair of jeans from it.

"Did he ask you to move in with him?" Mira pressed.

Taylor yanked on her jeans. "Maybe, but just because I didn't want to move in with him doesn't mean I have commitment issues—"

"It's been six years, Taylor. You can't keep hiding from men—"

"I'm not hiding," she snapped as she grabbed a long sleeved tee shirt and yanked it over her head. "I work hard. My career is important to me, and I don't have extra time to give to a guy who wants more from me." She sat down on the bed to pull her socks on, and she made the mistake of looking at Mira.

Her friend's face was filled with sadness, making Taylor's heart ache. "Don't look at me like that, Mira," she whispered. "I'm okay."

Mira walked over and knelt in front of her, putting her hands on Taylor's knees. "I didn't think I had time for anyone either," she said softly, "but Chase has accepted me for who I am. He doesn't want anything, except what I can give him."

Tears suddenly burned in Taylor's eyes, but she blinked them away. "I'm happy for you, Mira. I can't even tell you how happy that makes me. You deserve it."

"But I didn't want to try either, any more than you do. I was forced to put myself out there, and I never would have if I hadn't had to. You and I have been hiding for years. It's time to stop. It's really, really good out in the sunshine."

Taylor managed a smile. "But you're amazing, sweetie. Chase would be an idiot not to love you."

"And you're not amazing, too?"

Her smile faded. "We both know what I am." There was no need to spell it out. Her best friend knew all her secrets.

Mira's chin jutted out, refusing to accept Taylor's claim. "The right guy won't care."

"He won't care, until he does." She met Mira's gaze. "They always eventually care, and I'm not going to wait around for him to realize it. My work gives me the independence to live my life the way I want. I fit in relationships when I can, and get out in time."

"That's no way to live." Mira sighed. "Don't go down this road with Zane. It has no future. He's not the kind of guy who even has the capacity to realize how amazing you are, let alone decide you're worth investing in."

A little part of Taylor ached at Mira's words, a longing that she worked so hard to keep buried. "Then he's perfect for me, right? Some fun for a couple weeks, and then back to the grind for both of us."

"No." Mira's fingers tightened on Taylor's knees. "Don't sell yourself short. At least pick a guy who might be able to step up. Choose someone who at least has the chance of surprising you."

"In my experience, the surprises that men have to offer are never, ever good." Taylor sighed. "Listen, sweetie, this isn't about me. This is your time. I'm here to help you get ready for the wedding, or do your laundry or whatever you need." She nodded at Mira's massive belly. "You should be sitting around with your feet up, not worrying about me."

Mira raised her brows. "I live on a ranch. No one sits around with their feet up. There's work to be done, my friend."

Taylor finished tying her boots and stood up. "Then show me what to do. I'm ready to get busy." She held out her hand. Mira grasped it, and she hauled Mira to her feet. "Damn, girl, you're getting heavy. What do you have in there? A set of gym weights?"

Mira laughed, her voice lifted in genuine happiness. "Feels like it sometimes. You want breakfast? I made muffins."

"Your famous blueberry ones?" Taylor's mouth started to water.

"One and the same."

"I'm in." Taylor tucked her arm through Mira's as they walked toward the door. Despite their heavy conversation, her heart was lighter now than it had been. Even if Mira was about to become a wife and a mom, their bond was still the same. The only difference now was that Taylor didn't have to worry about Mira whenever she was traveling.

And of course, there was the fact that whenever she went home, Mira was no longer there. She lived in Wyoming now, a thousand miles away from the town where Taylor called home. That was another difference, a huge one.

This time with Mira wasn't real life anymore. This was just a quick vacation. No more girls' nights together, just brief visits that would be all they had to maintain their bond.

Mira looked over at her as she pulled open the screen door. "What's wrong?"

Taylor managed a smile. "Nothing at all. I'm good." She stepped back to allow Mira to waddle through, refusing to acknowledge her sadness about leaving the ranch. She was here for two weeks, and she was going to enjoy every minute of it, not worry about a future that wasn't here yet.

And, as she followed Mira outside, she couldn't help but look around for Zane, to no avail. He was nowhere to be seen. She sighed, all too aware of the flash of disappointment that he wasn't around. Yes, she knew he wasn't the kind of man a girl would build a future with, but that was why she liked him. Zane was safe, as safe as a man could ever be for her. She knew that was why she was attracted to him, but she didn't care.

It had been a long time since she'd had a morning as nice as the one she'd had, waking up in his arms.

"Do me one favor?" Mira said as they headed toward the house.

"You bet. What's that?" Taylor noticed a huge motorcycle tucked up next to the bunkhouse. Was that Zane's? Was he a biker? A biker cowboy? Wow. That was like a double dose of testosterone right there.

"Just don't have sex with him."

Her gaze jerked back to Mira. "What?"

"With Zane. Sex complicates things. You're a woman, and no matter how much you deny it, if you have sex with him, it's going to complicate things. You're not made of steel, Taylor, no matter how much you wish you were." Mira raised her brows. "Promise me, Taylor."

The promise was easy. "Of course I won't have sex with him." Attraction and innocent snuggling was one thing. Sex? That was different. Mira knew her too well. "I promise not to have sex with Zane. Ever." And she meant it.

She wasn't going to have sex with him? Ever?

Zane stopped dead in his tracks, his hand suspended in the air just above Taylor's shoulder, her words stopping him in mid-motion. Sex? She and Mira were talking about whether she was going to have *sex* with him?

Yeah, he thought she was appealing and intriguing, and he'd thought more than once about what it had felt like to have his hand on her hip while he'd been at the barn, but to be discussing it in broad daylight took all the spontaneity out of it.

Plus, she'd said *no*.

His brother's low chuckle jerked him out of his stupor, and he glared at Chase, who had stopped next to him. "Shut up," he growled.

"Don't mess with my fiancée's best friend," Chase said in a low voice, as the women kept walking, so caught up in their discussion that they hadn't even noticed the men approach from behind. "She wants your hands off Taylor, so keep them that way."

Zane shoved his hands in his pockets. "Since when do women define the rules between us, bro?"

Chase's eyes narrowed. "Don't try to bring Mira between us. It's about basic human respect. This place is yours, and you know it. You've got a hundred and twenty acres waiting for you any time you want to claim it."

Zane watched Taylor walk up the driveway. Her jeans were snug and fit her curves just right, and she looked like sin and temptation in her hiking boots. In his youth, cowboy boots would have been even hotter, but he'd had enough of women in cowboy boots. "I'm not staying around," he said. "Give that part of the ranch to someone else."

"Everyone has a part. That one's yours." Chase slammed a hand down on his shoulder. "Someday, you need to give me a different answer, and tell me you're staying."

Zane jerked his eyes off Taylor and looked at his brother. "You got it all now. You got a woman and a kid, you've got Steen and Erin setting up roots. You don't need me or any of the rest of us here. Let go of the fantasy."

Chase met his gaze. "We went through hell as kids. The only thing that got us through it was each other. Those roots are important. Life is going to get shitty again sometime, for all of us, and it matters to me that we can count on each other. This place is the Stockton ranch, which includes all the brothers, even you."

"You want to know why I don't come around more?" Zane's bad mood from yesterday came back with a vengeance. He'd come to the ranch to get away from stuff he didn't want to deal with, but he was right back into the full pressure situation with Chase. "Because every time I set foot on this property, you ride my ass to move back here. I'm not coming back. I haven't lived with you guys since I was a baby. It's not my thing. Stop pushing it on me, or at some point, I'm not going to come back at all. Just back the hell off. This is what I am. Nothing more. I can't play house with you and the rest of them. It's just not my thing, so let it go."

Chase dropped his hand from Zane's shoulder. His jaw tightened, but he inclined his head. "Understood. I won't ask again. You know the deal, if you ever change your mind."

"Yeah, I know it." Relief settled through Zane at Chase's capitulation. No more pressure from Chase about setting up shop at the ranch.

Silence settled between the brothers for a moment, and Zane felt a twinge of guilt at shutting his brother down. But at the same time, he couldn't go there, and he knew it. "We good?" He held out his hand.

Chase grabbed and shook it. "We're good." He yanked Zane over for a brotherly hug that Zane managed to endure, and then released him. "You want some grub? We have a lot to do today. I want to ride out to the far pastures and show you some fence work that needs to be done."

"Yeah, you got it." Zane fell in beside Chase as they headed up toward the ranch house. As they walked, he couldn't help but contemplate the fact that Mira and Taylor had disappeared through the front door a few moments ago. He didn't like women in his space or on the ranch, but having Taylor at the breakfast table made it a hell of a lot more interesting. He was actually kind of looking forward to it.

"I don't think she's going to make it to the wedding," Chase said as they neared the house.

Zane shot a sharp glance at his brother. "What are you talking about?" Did he think Mira was going to bail on him?

"The baby. I think he's going to come early. I'm going to be counting on you to hold down this ranch while we're at the hospital, and the first few days." Chase looked at him. "I want to be a good dad. A real dad. I want to be there from the first minute. I don't want to be running out to deal with a sick horse when my kid needs something. I want to be there."

Zane tipped his cowboy hat at his brother. "I got you covered. I'll take care of everything until you're ready."

Chase nodded, tension flexed in his jaw as he looked toward the house again. "It scares the shit out of me that this kid is going to count on me," he said softly. "What do I know about being a good dad? Or a good husband? All I know is hell."

Zane didn't have a lot of words of advice for his brother. He knew exactly what Chase's childhood had been like, what all their childhoods had been like. But Chase was waiting, and he had to say something. "You took care of all of us as kids. Just do the same thing and it'll be good."

Chase glanced at him. "Same thing? That's it?"

"Same thing, bro. You did good."

"I can do that, I guess." Chase let out a deep breath that Zane hadn't realized he'd been holding. "Okay, let's go eat."

"You got it." As Zane followed Chase up the stairs, he considered Chase's confession. He'd never really thought about being a dad or a husband. It was so far from his realm of possibility, that he'd never bothered to waste a thought on it. But Chase was facing it now, and Zane had to admit that if he were in Chase's boots, he'd be pretty damn terrified too.

In a way, he already was in Chase's boots, and he'd already failed, and the funeral he had to attend in three days was damning proof of it.

Chapter 5

Taylor had never realized exactly how pathetic she was until spending a day with her hugely pregnant friend, who had completely shamed her with energy and cheerfulness. Taylor was fit, healthy, and wasn't packing around a watermelon under her sweatshirt, and she hadn't been remotely capable of keeping up with Mira's frenzied activity. By the time dinner was over, she was toast.

With a groan, Taylor flopped face-first onto the bed in the bunkhouse, not even bothering to take off her boots. She'd always known Mira was tireless as a caretaker when her mother was so sick for so long, but she'd had no idea exactly what a powerhouse she was.

The woman was weeks away from giving birth, and it hadn't slowed her down one bit. She'd been on a relentless mission in the basement, unpacking all the boxes of stuff she'd brought back from home. Mira had unpacked like a woman possessed, claiming it was the nesting instinct of a pregnant woman. Whatever it was, it had turned the day into a whirlwind of heavy lifting that had made every muscle in Taylor's body ache.

"I think I liked her better when she sat around on the couch and ate ice cream with me," she muttered to herself, not even bothering to open her eyes. It was only nine o'clock, but she was completely done for the night. She was pretty sure she was going to fall asleep in her boots. Even the mere thought of peeling them off her feet was exhausting.

She'd hoped to catch glimpses of her favorite eye-candy on the ranch, but she'd been buried in the basement all day and seen nothing but boxes, family heirlooms of dubious value, and Mira. According to Mira, Chase and Zane had been riding the pasture fences all day and had taken lunch with them. The men hadn't even appeared for dinner, which, in retrospect, was probably a good thing.

A day with Mira had reminded her that she was here to support her friend, not to indulge in stupid fantasies with short-term men. She'd met Erin, Steen's fiancée, briefly when she'd stopped by to steal some coffee filters, and Taylor had liked her immediately. She'd been a little jealous of the apparent friendship between Mira and Erin, a bond that had once included only Taylor and Mira, but Erin had been so lovely that Taylor hadn't been able to stay cranky and feeling sorry for herself.

Steen and Erin were apparently wrapped up in the construction of their new home and Erin's vet clinic on the south side of the ranch, but she'd invited Taylor by to see the progress. She'd been glowing with happiness, just like Mira, and their excitement had been contagious, but it had also made Taylor feel like a crotchety spinster aunt.

Either way, she was glad for the privacy of the tiny bunkhouse and a night off from having to socialize in a world she didn't quite fit in.

"Nice view." Zane's low voice slid over her as the door creaked open. "Is that an invitation?"

Excitement rushed over her, and she scrambled to a sitting position, depriving Zane of the view of her backside sprawled across the bed. As she righted herself, Zane strode into the tiny bunkhouse, using the heel of his boot to kick the door shut. He was covered in dust and grime, and he was wearing leather chaps over his faded jeans. His cowboy hat was tipped back, and his cowboy boots thudded on the wooden floor. Whiskers shadowed his jaw, and he looked every bit the rugged frontier cowboy, and *nothing* like the clean-cut starched-shirt businessmen she worked with every day. Zane was dangerous, elemental male, and just the sight of him made her stomach do flip-flops. "Of course it's not an invitation," she said, "I didn't think you were coming back here."

He unfastened his chaps and hung them on a hook by the door, showcasing exactly how well his jeans fit over his narrow hips. "Where else am I going to stay? The house is full, my bike isn't great for sleeping, and I'm too old to sleep in the barn with the horses."

"You're sleeping here? Again? With me?"

Zane looked over at her, his eyes dark and moody as he took off his hat and hung it on the wall. He ran his fingers through his hair, fluffing the indent from his hat as he strode across the room toward her.

Taylor stiffened as he bent over her, setting one hand on either side of her hips. His face was inches from hers, and the scent of leather and man slid through her like an intimate caress. "Darlin', I've spent the entire day working on a ranch doing things I swore I'd never do again, and all day, the only thing that's kept me going was the thought of wrapping myself around you in that bed all damned night. So, yeah, I'm sleeping in that bed, and if you drag out one of those old mattresses from the back room, I'm going to burn the damn thing up so you have nowhere else to sleep."

Her heart leapt, and she lifted her face to his. "Nothing's going to happen if you sleep here," she said. "I'm not going to have sex with you."

A lazy, dangerous smile drifted across his face. "I know you're not. I heard you guys talking. But you never said a damn thing about wrapping that fine little body of yours around me all night."

She blinked at the image of being wrapped around him all night, and tried to force it out of her head. "You heard us talking?" She quickly replayed their conversations from the day, trying to figure out what else he might have heard. "When?"

He winked at her as he stood up and began unbuttoning his faded plaid shirt. "Can't remember." He stripped off the shirt, revealing a tight, black tee shirt that showcased biceps and pecs that strained against the fabric. "But I remember admiring your butt in those jeans." He tossed the shirt on his duffel bag, and then ripped off his tee shirt.

She knew she should avert her gaze, not simply because he was trying to get her to look at him, but also because, well, she *wasn't* going to do anything about the fact that she was completely captivated by everything about him. She tried, she *really* tried not to gawk, but when he walked over to the bed and stood in front of her, there really wasn't anywhere else to look except at him.

She cleared her throat and pinned her gaze to his face, trying not to gape at his bare chest or the washboard abs, or the scar on the front of his right biceps. "What?"

He narrowed his eyes, and said nothing. It was as if he were waiting for something.

She held up her hands in a gesture of confusion. "I'm sorry, Zane, but you're kind of like a dog, staring at me like you want something and expect me to read your mind. You want a walk? A bone? What?"

The corner of his mouth twitched. "That's it? That's all you have to say?"

Did he have a dimple? He almost had a dimple. How could a rugged cowboy biker with five o'clock shadow and layers of ranch dust have a dimple? That was just too endearing for a man like him. "I have a lot to say as a general rule. I just have no clue what it is that you're expecting me to say."

"She didn't tell you?"

"Who didn't tell me what?"

"Mira didn't tell you who I am?"

She frowned. "Aren't you Chase's brother?"

"Yeah, not that." He gestured impatiently. "The whole bull riding thing. That."

"You ride bulls?" Wow. He'd just gone from rugged to hardcore. "Is that what the scar on your arm is from?"

"I used to ride. Not anymore." He narrowed his eyes. "I was the world champion for three years in a row."

"Um…congratulations? Is that what you want from me?" Tension was vibrating fiercely through his body, making his muscles strain beneath his taut flesh, making her pretty sure that kudos wasn't what he was waiting for. "Seriously, Zane, I'll be honest, I have no clue where you're going with this, and I'm too tired to guess. I can tell you're upset, but I'm totally clueless about what's going on. So, great job on the championship. I'm impressed." She held out her hands in a gesture of surrender.

"Or...should I ask to see your trophy? I don't know what you're getting at, or why you look so angry with me." She supposed she should be nervous with all his simmering hostility, but she wasn't afraid of him at all. She somehow knew he'd never hurt her. She *was* confused, however.

He stared more intently at her. "You don't care," he said softly. "You don't care, do you?"

She sat up straighter. "That's a little harsh, don't you think? I mean, yes, I barely know you, but I'm not callous enough not to care when someone accomplishes their dream. Seriously, what do you think I am—"

"No." He crouched in front of her, his hands on her knees. It was the exact same position that Mira had been in with her, but it was a completely different experience when Zane did it. He seemed to take over the space between them, trapping her. She didn't want to run, though. He was dangerous and irritated about something, but she wanted to stay right where she was. The same feeling of rightness filled her, that same wonderful sensation of awakening in his arms. There was simply something about him that made her want to stop running and stand still, not forever, but for a little bit. "You still see me, don't you?" he said softly.

She narrowed her eyes, searching his face as she tried to understand what he was saying. His eyes were turbulent, and his jaw was tense. His hands were warm on her knees, dwarfing her leg. "Yes," she said slowly, trying to figure out the issue.

He moved closer to her. "I want to have sex with you tonight," he said, his voice a low rumble that seemed to ignite everything inside her. "I want to kiss every inch of your body, and give you the best damned night of your life."

Heat flooded between her legs, and her heart started to pound at the completely unexpected change in topic. "Seriously?"

"Yeah." He slid his hand behind the nape of her neck. His touch was seductive and amazing, sending chills down her arms. "Kiss me, Taylor. Just one kiss."

Oh, God. This was way out of control, especially given the fact that she wanted desperately to say yes and lose herself to him. But there was no way. She'd made a promise to Mira, and it had been the right promise. "I can't." She put her hand on his

chest to push him back. "Don't get me wrong. I think you're…
um…well, you tempt me and no one else has tempted me for a
long time, but I can't do that with you."

He didn't back up, or let her go. "One kiss, Taylor. Just
one." He moved closer, and for a split second, she considered
letting him kiss her. It would be so incredible to be kissed by
a man she was so entranced by. How wonderful would it be to
once, just once, let herself go with a man and not worry about
the consequences.

Except there were always consequences. "I can't." She
pulled her legs back from between his knees, swung them to
the side, and vaulted off the bed. By the time she'd landed on
her feet and managed to get her hands in a position of sufficient
defiance on her hips, Zane was standing as well, staring at her
with an expression of absolute disbelief.

His shocked expression irritated her. "What? Are you
that surprised that I could turn down a bull riding champion?
Did you think that just because you're some famous hottie
that all the women want, that I'd fall for it too? That's why you
told me, wasn't it? So I'd have sex with you?" God, she was so
disappointed. She hadn't expected that of him at all. "I can't
believe you used that ploy with me." She pointed at the door
to the back room. "You can get yourself an old musty mattress,
because there's no space in that bed tonight." Suddenly, she
didn't feel safe with him. Last night had been perfect, and he'd
made no move to seduce her. She hadn't expected that to change,
and now that it had, she felt uncomfortable. She was also kind of
crushed. He'd seemed like such a good guy, dangerous and sexy,
but honorable. And now he'd tried to use his bull riding thing to
get her to have sex with him? She was so bummed. She'd totally
misjudged him, as well as her ability to see who she should have
faith in. "Or sleep on your bike. Not here."

"Hey." He caught her shoulders as she tried to spin
away. "Wait a sec."

She tried to knock his hand away. "Let me go, Zane.
Seriously. You crossed a line there, and—"

"I had to see," he said, his voice urgent. "Let me explain."

There was something about the tone of his voice that
got her attention. She paused, eyeing him warily. "What?" She

seriously doubted there was a reasonable explanation, but for some inexplicable reason, she wanted him to have one. Until now, he'd made her feel safe. She'd trusted him. It had felt good, and she wanted it back.

"When I was on the tour, women were always all over me," he said, not releasing his grip on her shoulders, forcing her to stand and listen. "They wanted a chance to be with the superstar. I had one woman claim that I'd gotten her pregnant, even though I'd never even had sex with her."

Taylor blinked, startled by the unexpected revelation. "Really?"

"Yeah. Her friends all swore she'd gone back to my hotel room with me. The only thing that saved me was a video in the hall outside my room that showed me going in there alone that night. These women were the type who hadn't given me the time of day when I was a dirt-poor kid with no home. Now that I was famous, they all wanted to have sex with me. I had to know if you were like that. I thought—" He shrugged. "I heard you tell Mira how there was no chance you were going to have sex with me. I needed to know if that would change once you knew who I was." He searched her face. "I'm sorry," he said softly. "I just can't deal with women like that anymore. I didn't want to get in that bed with you tonight if you were going to twist it to your advantage in the morning, regardless of what actually happened."

He didn't try to hide his exhaustion, and her heart tightened. She could tell he was being honest, and she doubted he was a guy who revealed his vulnerabilities very often, if ever. His explanation made sense. Her fear and distrust of him dissipated, but at the same time, she felt a vague sense of disappointment. "So, you actually have no interest in getting me naked? Is that what you're saying?"

He stared at her, and then a slow grin appeared. "I gotta be honest, Taylor, getting you naked has been on my mind since last night."

Heat coiled around her. "So what would you have done if I'd said yes?"

"I would have walked away." His response was so automatic that she knew he spoke the truth. As much as he wanted her, his emotional baggage was so heavy that he would have gotten out of the bed and left if she'd been the type of woman he was accustomed to.

She lifted her chin. "So, you want me only as long as you can't have me. Is that what you're saying?" She met his gaze. "I hate games, Zane. I really do."

"No, that's not what I'm saying." He released her shoulder and lightly clasped her chin. "I'm attracted to you. But my aversion to being used trumps everything else. But since we have that cleared up, I can now go about trying to seduce you and actually mean it."

Her heart began to hammer again, just like it had on the bed. "Don't kiss me. I mean it. I can't climb in that bed with you if I'm going to have to worry about what might happen once you get in there." She searched his eyes. "I'm not a one-night stand, Zane. Don't treat me like one."

He paused, his tempting lips only inches from her mouth. "You said you don't like commitment."

"I know, but...I mean..." God, how did she put it into words? "I don't do sex without commitment, but I don't want commitment." As she said the words, she realized how stark it made her sound, how empty it made her life sound. "I just—" She touched his chest. "Last night was wonderful," she said softly. "I didn't worry about anything. It was just us, and it was safe and sensual and..."

"You felt safe with me?" He sounded surprised.

She nodded, sort of embarrassed by her comment. "I mean—"

"No. It's perfect. I want to give that to you." He lightly pressed a kiss to her forehead. "You don't need to say anything else. Go to bed. I'll be there in a few minutes. I just need to shower." He pulled back and winked at her. "Unless you want to join me in the shower?"

She had a sudden image of water cascading over his chest. "Stop."

He grinned. "Harmless teasing, darlin'. I'm not going to do a single thing to that sexy body of yours until you beg me to." He turned away and headed toward the bathroom, unfastening his belt as he walked. "I'll leave the door unlocked in case you change your mind, though." He gave her a cheeky grin, then toed the door shut, leaving it ajar ever so slightly.

Taylor let out a breath and leaned against the kitchenette stove. Zane was trouble. She had no doubt about that whatsoever. He was sexy as sin, and he knew it. But at the same time, his vulnerability about being used for his fame had been genuine and endearing. He was still fit and strong, clearly in condition to be riding bulls, but he'd referred to it in the past tense. Why had he walked away when he was at the top of the game?

The shower turned on, drawing her attention back to the present. She stared at the wooden door, sort of shocked by how tempted she was to take him up on his offer. She needed a shower, too. It had been a long time since she'd showered with a man. Bathing with a guy wasn't just about sex. It was more intimate than sex, a sharing of personal space, kind of like how snuggling in bed had been, only with nakedness and streams of water cascading over bare flesh.

She closed her eyes. Why was he tempting her so much? As she'd told Mira earlier, she was fine being alone. She didn't miss having a man in her life, and she didn't need someone else to love her in order to feel complete. But Zane, with his vulnerability, his cockiness, his potent sexuality, and his tenderness, was making her crave the kind of physical and emotional intimacy that she'd worked so hard not to need.

She wanted him to make love to her. There was no way to deny it. If he tried tonight, she didn't know if she could say no. But Mira was right. If she had sex with him, it would complicate things for her emotionally, and she couldn't go through that again. She would regret it in the morning if she gave in tonight.

With a sigh, she walked across the room to her suitcase, which was tucked in the corner. After making sure the shower was still running, she quickly stripped out of her boots and clothes. She pulled on the same camisole and leggings she'd slept in last night, but paused with her long-sleeved tee shirt in her hand. If she were sleeping alone, she wouldn't be wearing it. But it made her feel safer, not from Zane, but from herself.

The shower went off, and she jumped, quickly dragging the shirt over her head. By the time Zane walked out of the bathroom, wearing nothing but a pair of boxer briefs, she was waiting by the door, toothbrush in hand, fully covered from her neck to her ankles.

But when Zane walked out and his gaze burned over her, she suddenly felt like she had absolutely nothing on whatsoever.

"Love those stretch pants," he said, his voice just the tiniest bit rough.

She swallowed. "They're comfortable."

His gaze went to her tee shirt. "You going to be hot in that, darlin'?"

"Probably. Are you going to be cold wearing only your underwear?" She couldn't fail to notice that he had an erection, and the realization made heat pool between her legs, but she refused to look anywhere but into his eyes, which were smoldering with so much heat that it didn't really help matters.

He grinned. "No chance of that. Body heat is a powerful thing. I promised no sex, but I also promise you that I'll be wrapped around you all night long." He cocked an eyebrow. "If that's okay?"

She smiled, touched by his hesitation. "Yes, that's okay."

His grin widened. "Well, then, brush those pearly whites and get that hot little ass of yours into my bed soon, will you?"

She laughed, and poked him in the chest with her toothbrush. "I was here first. It's my bed."

He caught her hand and pressed a searing kiss to her knuckles. "Our bed, then. Be quick. I miss your body." His gaze was burning into her. "And I mean that."

She swallowed. "I can tell."

Neither of them moved, his hand still wrapped around hers. For a moment, she thought he was going to kiss her, then he dropped his hand and turned away, releasing her.

She took a deep breath and fled into the bathroom, but it took several minutes for her heart to stop pounding. How on earth was she going to sleep with him all night and keep saying no?

But she had to. She knew she did.

Chapter 6

Her hand was on his cock, and his self-control was just about at its limit.

Zane clasped his fingers more tightly behind his head, his biceps taut as he stared at the ceiling of the bunkhouse. The faint light of the moon illuminated the knots in the ceiling as he counted the small wooden circles, trying to think about anything other than the woman sleeping on top of him.

He'd woken up an hour ago in the middle of the most erotic dream he could recall having, one that involved him, Taylor, and a whole lot of nakedness. He'd found himself on top of Taylor, his cock hard as rock, his face buried in the curve of her neck. Her hands had been tangled in his hair, and her nipples had been hard against his chest, but her steady breathing had told him that she was still deeply asleep. Her body had been soft and incredible beneath his, and it had taken several moments for him to wake up enough to realize what was going on.

When he'd figured it out, he'd rolled off her immediately like a good guy. Unfortunately, she'd followed him all the way across to his side of the bed. Still dead asleep, she'd wrapped herself around him, somehow slid her hand underneath his shorts and wrapped her fingers around his cock, as if he were her security blanket and she needed him for comfort.

And there she'd stayed for the last hour, her steady breathing against his neck like a hot wind of desire on his flesh. His entire body was rigid with need, and his cock was hurting from being so hard for so long. He'd sworn off women a long time ago, and it hadn't been difficult, because he'd had no interest in breaking his vow. All the shit he'd dealt with as a bull rider had been enough to cure him of the need to sink himself into a woman, unlike most of the other guys who seemed to think that the more women they could nail, the better life was.

And yet, Taylor had shredded every last resolution. He hadn't even kissed her yet, but his need for her was growing exponentially by the hour. He didn't like sleeping with women, but all day long while he'd been out on the range dealing with broken fences and learning about the horses Chase had on the ranch, he'd been thinking about the moment that he was going to crawl into bed with her tonight. While Chase had been talking horses, Zane had been fantasizing about how it would feel to have her body wrapped around his. Yeah, he'd been thinking about sex, but he knew sex was a long shot, and he'd been okay with that. He'd just wanted to be with her.

But now, with her fingers encircling his cock and her body so relaxed and soft against his, the stakes had changed.

She moved slightly, nestling deeper against him, and her fingers tightened on his cock. *Shit.* He grimaced and stared more intently at the ceiling, trying to find more knots in the wood to count. He clamped his fingers behind his head so tightly that they were beginning to ache. "Seventy-six," he muttered, trying to distract himself with his own voice. "Seventy-seven." There was another one in the corner, a small one, he hadn't seen yet. "Seventy-eight."

But it didn't help. Nothing was helping. His penis was like a steel rod, and the nerves ignited each time she adjusted her grip on him. Her tee shirt had slid upward, which meant her bare stomach was against his side. She'd thrown her thigh over his so that her knee was between his legs, and she'd slipped her foot underneath his thigh, tucking herself in. She smelled faintly of something flowery and feminine, but it was so subtle, layers deep beneath the simple scent of woman, of her, of promise and seduction.

He was half-tempted to get out of bed and head to the bathroom to give himself a little release. Normally, he'd do that in a heartbeat, but he didn't want to move. As painful as it was to lie there and not be able to do anything about the need amassing inside him, he didn't want to move. He liked having Taylor on top of him. He liked the way she trusted him enough that in her sleep, she didn't feel the need to protect herself from him. He wasn't going to lie, it was sexy as hell that when her inhibitions were erased by sleep, that her instinct was to wrap her hand around his cock. Despite her protests, there was something hot between them, and it was definitely mutual.

If he got up, she might slide back to her side of the bed for the rest of the night. Yeah, he could go after her and wrap himself around her, but having *her* being the aggressor changed everything. She wanted him. She trusted him. She needed to touch him. That shit felt really good, and he wasn't going to screw up by his need to get relief.

So, he didn't move.

She didn't either.

When dawn finally began to streak its golden rays through the small windows, Zane hadn't slept for even a minute, his cock hurt like hell from being hard for so long, and his entire body ached from holding so much tension in it.

He was pretty sure it was the best damn night of his life, and he was never going to forget it.

❧ ❧ ❧

She was in over her head. She knew it.

Taylor strode toward the ranch house, keeping her head high and refusing to look around as she walked. Refusing, specifically, to look for Zane. She'd awoken slightly several times in the night just enough to snuggle deeper into the heat of his body and bask in the feel of his body against hers. Each time, the best feeling of contentment had filled her, and she'd fallen back asleep.

But this morning? She'd woken up to an empty bed.

No note. Nothing. Just alone.

She was used to waking up alone, but this morning, she'd felt so achingly empty to find Zane gone.

That kind of reaction to his absence wasn't good. Not good at all. Of course he'd be gone already. They were on a ranch, and he'd probably been out the door before dawn to ride with

Chase. There was absolutely no reason to expect him to lounge in bed with her, or to have left her some sweet note, and yet she'd been sort of crushed anyway.

She couldn't afford to need him, or anyone. Her survival depended on her being okay with a solo life, but Zane was breaking through her resolves at warp speed, even though she hadn't even kissed him.

This had to end. No more sleeping in the bunkhouse. She'd get a hotel room, or something. But even the mere thought of moving to a hotel made her sad, not just because of Zane, but because she'd come out here to be with Mira, not to cloister herself in a hotel room, like she did almost every other night of her life.

Resolutely, she lifted her chin as she neared the house. She was not going to let Zane drive her away. She was here for Mira, and no man was going to interfere with that. She'd just drag one of those dusty mattresses out and sleep on that. Situation solved.

She smiled, feeling better as she pulled open the front door, looking forward to breakfast with Mira. Some girl time would be great. She could talk to Mira about Zane and—

Conversation stopped, and five faces turned toward her as she stepped inside. At the kitchen table, visible from the front door, were Mira, Chase, Erin, Zane, and a man who looked enough like Zane and Chase that she was willing to bet it was Steen. The table was littered with nearly-empty serving plates, and the scent of bacon and fresh bread filled the air. It looked like a genuine down-home breakfast, filled with warmth, camaraderie, and family. Longing swept over her, quickly followed by a discomfort and awkwardness. There was so much intimacy in the room, and she wasn't a part of it.

Mira waved at her, not getting up from her seat between Chase and Erin. "Hey, girl! You just made it! We saved a couple pieces of bacon for you. Pull up a chair."

"I'll get one for her." Zane stood up quickly, flashed her a smile that eased a little bit of the tension in her body, and then he disappeared around the corner.

"Um, okay." She walked into the kitchen, aware that conversation had stopped, as if her presence had derailed it.

She managed a smile at the man she didn't know. "You must be Steen."

He stood up immediately and leaned across the table to shake her hand, his face creasing into a warm smile. He was wearing jeans, cowboy boots, and a crisp plaid shirt. "Steen Stockton. It's great to meet you, Taylor. Mira has been so excited about you coming."

"Thanks." His grip was warm and strong, his hands slightly roughened from all the work he'd been doing on the house. His eyes were a brilliant blue, just like Chase's, and he had the same angular jaw as his brothers. "It's great to be here."

"I got a chair." Zane walked back into the room, carrying what looked like a hand-made wooden chair. Had one of the brothers made it?

"Put it there." Mira pointed to a spot between Chase and Steen, close to where Zane was standing.

He obediently set it down, holding it out for her. He gave her a private smile as she sat down, and her heart fluttered in response. "Thanks."

He nodded, and retreated back to his seat on the other side of the table.

Taylor helped herself to some cold eggs, a couple pieces of bacon, and half a muffin. Everything was cold, and everyone's plates were empty, making her realize that breakfast had been going on for quite a while. Why hadn't anyone come to get her? She bit her lip as she started to eat. The conversation swelled again, a rapid-fire exchange as everyone made plans for the day.

"Chase and I are headed into town to do some shopping," Mira announced. "We really need to finish furnishing the baby's room."

"Steen and I are heading into town too," Erin said. "We're picking up more stuff for the house and the clinic. You want to meet for lunch?"

"Totally." Mira grinned at her. "Maybe we could go shopping for clothes after lunch?" She patted her belly. "I need a couple more tops. I can't fit anything over my belly anymore." She beamed at Chase. "You and Steen can do some man stuff."

He smiled and put his arm around her. "You know I'm happy to shop with you. I'll go with you."

Taylor bit her lip, listening to the exchange. "Um, you need any help from me?" She wanted to be the one buying clothes with Mira, but she wasn't sure she was invited.

"Oh, no," Mira laughed. "You take the day off. We have it covered. We'll get back to work on the basement tomorrow."

"You sure? I mean, I'm here to help you—"

Mira rolled her eyes. "You've done so much, Taylor. Take a day off and relax. You never do that."

Taylor let out her breath. Yes, that was true, she never relaxed, but she had no clue what she was supposed to do for fun, especially here. She hadn't come here to relax. She'd come here to help Mira, and now it seemed like Mira didn't need her help.

Before Mira had met Chase, she and Mira had been the primary support for each other. They'd both gone through some tough times, and they'd always picked each other up. Mira had more people to count on now, which was great for her, but Taylor's life was the same as it always had been. The one place she'd fit, that she'd always belonged, no longer had as much room or need for her. "I don't mind. I can work in the basement while you're gone. Just tell me what to do."

"No." Mira leaned forward, her familiar eyes soft. "Seriously, Taylor, this is a beautiful ranch. Breathe it in. Let it fill your heart. Let yourself get off the treadmill for one day. You might find you like it."

Taylor's cheeks heated up when she realized everyone was looking at her. Suddenly, she felt like a charity project, like Mira had invited her here to save her, not because she'd needed help. "Oh, I'll be all set," she said brightly. "You go and have a good day. I have lots to do."

"No." Mira shook her head. "Don't do. Just be."

Just *be*. What did that mean? Taylor managed a smile. "Right, okay, I got it. I'll be fine."

But it was a total lie. She didn't even know what fine meant anymore...especially not with the way Zane was watching her so intently, and not saying a single word.

❀ ❀ ❀

Zane watched Taylor carefully as she discussed the day's plans with Mira. Her smile was as gorgeous as ever, but he already knew her well enough to notice it wasn't reaching her eyes. She was holding her fork a little too tightly, and her shoulders were stiff. She was clearly feeling uncomfortable and out of place, and he knew it, because he felt the same way.

Walking into that cozy little scene at the breakfast table had been his idea of hell. He'd been hungry, and he'd smelled food, but he hadn't expected Steen and Erin to be there as well. The foursome was in high gear when he'd walked in, and he'd turned to walk right back out the door, until Chase had seen him and roped him in.

The family scene wasn't his style, not in any way. It was harder than he'd thought, being back here, being a part of this group that claimed him as family, but it didn't fit him at all. But, they were all he had when it came to belonging anywhere. So, he was here, but he didn't want to have to play nice. He didn't even know how to play nice.

It was a major relief that everyone was taking off for the day. "You need me today?" Zane asked, lounging back against his chair. His arm was stretched over the back of Steen's chair, his body language lazy and relaxed, putting on the same facade of nonchalance he'd perfected as a teen when he'd learned to pretend he didn't give a shit what anyone thought of him.

"No, we already got stuff done for the morning. I'm all set today." Chase raised his brows, his brown gaze too knowing. "Take some space, bro. I know you need it."

Zane nodded. "I'll be back tomorrow, then." Taylor's gaze snapped to his, and he saw the surprise in her eyes that he was leaving for the night.

Regret thudded through his gut. Did he really want to miss a night with her? No, not really. But hell, he needed to get out of here. Tomorrow was going to be a rough day, and having tonight off from trying to play the dedicated brother was a good thing.

"Sounds good." Chase met his gaze. "Keep your phone on, though."

Mira laughed softly and whacked his arm. "Oh, come on, Chase. The baby isn't coming tonight. You need to stop worrying."

"I'm not worrying," he said, but his eyes held volumes of concern that Zane had never seen on his brother's face before. "I'm just making sure we have everything covered."

"It's all good, Chase. We've got your back." Steen stood up, gathering his plates. "Okay, so we'll see you guys in town."

Erin hopped up, grabbing more debris from the table. "Steen and I will get this cleaned up in two minutes. You guys cooked, so we'll clean."

"Oh, that's okay. We'll do it together. It'll go super-fast." Mira and Chase got up, and Zane watched as Taylor started to stand, her half-eaten plate of food in her hand.

"Oh, no, sweetie, you keep eating. We've got this one." Mira waved her off, and Taylor sank slowly back down to her seat.

Zane didn't move, watching Taylor wage some internal battle. He could tell she wanted to help, but her assistance had been summarily rejected. Plus, it was true she hadn't eaten yet. She glanced across the table at him, and vulnerability flashed across her face, so much vulnerability that his chest constricted.

She didn't belong here anymore than he did, and she knew it. "You want to go with me?" The question was out before he could stop it.

Shit. Had he really just asked that? He needed space, not a woman.

She stared at him, a sliver of hope flashing across her face. "What? Go where?"

It was that flash of hope, that momentary whisper of need for help, for someone to notice and care, that got him. He knew what that felt like, and he knew that it hurt like hell. And he wasn't going to lie. He wasn't looking forward to the next twenty-four hours, and the thought of having Taylor along felt like a breath of relief in the darkness that had been trying to suffocate him. As a rule, being around people made him feel crowded, but Taylor was an exception. She brought him peace. Maybe it was because she didn't want anything from him, at least nothing that he wasn't willing to give. She was leaving town soon, so there was no future to worry about. Just a present that made his day better.

So, yeah, he'd rather have her along than go by himself. "I have to go to a funeral." He said it quietly, for her ears only. He didn't want to get into it with his brothers. He didn't want to get into it with anyone, but somehow, it felt right to bring her along. It was going to be a dark twenty-four hours, and Taylor was the only thing that had brought him relief in a long time. He wanted her with him.

She glanced over at the others, and then back at him, clearly realizing that he didn't want anyone else to know. "Okay."

Just one word. Okay. She didn't ask questions that he didn't want to answer right now. She didn't press for details. She gave him exactly what he needed. Space. Privacy. And the answer that he'd wanted. *Yes.*

He nodded, taking a deeper breath into his lungs than he'd been able to take since the world had gone dark five days ago. "Can you be ready in a half hour?"

"Sure." Her gaze searched his, and suddenly, it felt like the two of them were the only ones in the room. The clank of dishes being loaded into the dishwasher vanished. The murmur of animated conversation faded. The presence of too many bodies faded. All that remained was his intense awareness of her, as a woman, but also, as his anchor.

He'd never had an anchor. He'd never had anything to hold onto when the shit tried to come down on him. Chase had created a solid foundation for the Stockton's, fostering a connection that Zane always came back to, but he'd returned to the ranch like a moth circling a light bulb, receiving the light but never touching.

Taylor was different. It felt like she was his, an anchor that would dig into him and lock him down when he started to slide. He knew he should be walking away, running, retreating into the solo existence that he'd carved out for himself, but he didn't want to.

He wanted her, on his bike, holding onto him, refusing to let go. "Pack light."

Her eyes widened. "You want me to ride on your bike with you?"

His gut clenched. Of course Taylor wasn't a motorcycle kind of girl. Shit. "We can take your rental."

"No," she said softly, a thoughtful gleam growing in her eyes. "I've never been on a motorcycle. Let's do that."

He grinned, satisfaction pulsing through him. "You'll have to hold onto me. Tight."

Her eyebrows went up. "Okay."

"Okay." He grinned, and she grinned back, and suddenly, the next twenty-four hours held a promise they hadn't held before.

Chapter 7

Taylor liked motorcycles.

It was a surprising discovery, especially given that she'd spent her life ridiculing those who were foolish enough to utilize such a high-risk mode of transportation, but she certainly understood the appeal now. She laughed with delight as Zane sped around a bend on the isolated stretch of highway, and she leaned with him, her knee only inches from the pavement.

She supposed she should be scared, but it was the most exhilarating experience of her life. She was pressed up against Zane's back as if she were attached to him, and her arms were locked around his waist. He was solid muscle, a sheer immovable force that anchored her to the seat. She felt completely secure holding onto him, and she loved the strength he gave her. Her inner thighs were flanking his hips and legs, and the leather seat vibrated beneath her. She couldn't believe how amazing it felt to have the wind whipping past her. She loved breathing the fresh air, basking in the sun as it beat down on her shoulders. The sensation of speed was incredible, and she felt freer than she ever had before.

They'd been on the bike for almost three hours, and she still wasn't tired of it. Breakfast had been tough for her, and she'd been so relieved when Zane had invited her to tag along. But despite the fun of the bike ride, she couldn't help thinking about the pain in his eyes when he'd told her he had to go to a funeral. Who had died? She could tell he didn't want to talk about it, so she hadn't asked, but it was on her mind. Losing someone you loved sucked, and she imagined it was even more difficult for a man like Zane who held his emotions so tightly in check.

"You hungry?" Zane asked, his voice easily audible over the built-in headset in the helmet.

She smiled. He'd asked her that every half hour for the last three hours, always checking in to make sure she was okay. "Maybe a little."

"Great. I love this place up ahead." The roar of the engine eased, and he pulled off the highway. They drove down a dirt road for about five minutes, and then he eased into the dirt parking lot of a small building that looked like it had been a railway car a hundred years ago. An old wooden sign declared it was "Casey's Place."

Behind the building stretched plains of grass that went on forever, and above her head was an endless blue sky, dotted with a few puffy white clouds. She couldn't believe how small she felt, and how huge the sky was. No conference rooms, crowded airports, computers, or rental cars. There was nothing but trees, shrubs, and untouched land extending in all directions. She couldn't see the highway anymore, and she felt like they were the only ones alive on the entire planet.

All her tension melted away, and her life seemed like a distant memory. "It's magical, being out here," she said.

"I know. I love the open road." Zane pulled off his helmet, and grinned at her as he swung his leg over the bike and stood up. His sunglasses hid his eyes, giving him a mysterious aura that merely added to his sexiness. His jeans were low on his hips, and his leather jacket made his already muscular shoulders even bigger. He was primal male, the ultimate bad boy, everything she'd never been attracted to in a man. He was nothing that she wanted, and yet she was completely drawn to him, in every way.

She'd always gravitated toward men in ties and dress shoes, the ones who kept their hair short and their faces shaved. Zane had two days of whiskers on his jaw, his hair curled over the collar of his jacket, and his entire demeanor told everyone to stay away from him, everyone except her.

There was no mistaking that the go-away vibe was not being sent in her direction at all, which she had to admit was incredibly sexy. To be the only one who was allowed in his personal space made her feel special, like some red carpet had been laid out just for her.

She unfastened her helmet and took it off. She shook out her hair and closed her eyes, letting the sun beat down on her face. It was a beautiful day, the perfect temperature with a slight breeze.

"Helmet head." Zane's voice was affectionate as he ruffled her hair, fluffing it up.

She self-consciously touched her hair, her fingers brushing against Zane's. She was the queen of always looking put together, but she hadn't bothered today. No bun, no curling iron, just a quick shower and blow dry. "I must look terrible."

"No." Zane's fingers closed around hers, stilling her attempt to smooth her hair. "You look gorgeous. I like being able to see the real you. I've seen enough women with so much makeup and hairspray they're practically made of plastic. Unlike you. You're just you. It's hot." His voice was low and throaty, and she felt heat rise in her cheeks.

"Really?"

"Yeah." He moved closer, and suddenly, the bike felt confining between her legs. She had nowhere to retreat to, unless she swung her leg over the massive machine in some awkward and obvious attempt at avoidance.

She swallowed, as his hand slid from her hair to her jaw, his fingers so light as they drifted across her skin. "Zane—"

"All the women on the tour get all fancied up, thinking that if they wear enough makeup and hairspray, that they'll get laid. It's all fake shit out there." He was so close now that his thigh bumped her knee. He didn't back up, and she didn't move away, but her heart was hammering now. "Unlike you."

"I dress up to go to work," she whispered. Was he going to kiss her? She wanted him to so much, but at the same time, she was terrified. She was starting to like him already, more than she could deal with. "I wear my hair in a bun, and I use hairspray." She was babbling now, trying desperately to make him see that she wasn't really the woman sitting on his bike. "I'm kind of a workaholic, and I don't do things like ride motorcycles—"

"Shut up," he said softly, the irresistible dimple appearing in his cheek as he smiled. "I know who you are, and I like it just fine." His mouth was a breath from hers now. "The last few hours of having you wrapped around me has been killing me. I need to kiss you, right now. It's not my style to ask first like I'm a good guy, but I made you a promise. So, say yes." His fingers slid along her jaw and down the side of her neck, sending chills ricocheting down her spine. "Ask me to kiss you," he whispered, his voice rough across her skin. "Beg me."

Heat flared in her cheeks, and her knee was burning where his thigh was pressed up against it. "Beg you?"

"I made the dumbass promise that I wouldn't touch you until you begged me. I won't make you feel unsafe, so you have to beg." His lips were almost on hers, his voice throaty and low, rippling with a carnal desire that made heat pool between her legs. "I trapped myself, darlin', and it's up to you to cut me loose."

She wanted him to kiss her desperately, but *asking* him to kiss her was such a statement. It forced her to make a choice instead of simply allowing it to happen. But, God, she wanted to feel his mouth on hers, so badly. What harm would it do? It wasn't like it could go too far, given that they were in the dirt parking lot of a diner at noon. She was leaving, too, right? So, it would just be a kiss with a man who made her feel alive for the first time in a very long time. She wanted the kiss. She wanted *his* kiss. She wanted *him*. So, she nodded once. "Okay."

He grinned, and brushed his lips past hers, not quite touching. "Okay doesn't cut it, darlin'. You need to be explicit in your instructions."

She rolled her eyes and pulled back, setting her hands on her hips. "Really?" She couldn't keep the exasperation out of her voice. "You want me to beg? Can't you just accept the unspoken body language and the implications of the word 'okay' and do your man thing and sweep me into your arms for a kiss that will rock my world? Seriously, Zane. A woman should not have to beg for her first kiss with a guy. There's just nothing remotely romantic about that—"

He locked his arm around her, yanked her up against him, and kissed her.

The kiss wasn't gentle or tentative, and there was nothing

gentlemanly or uptight about it. It was sizzling, unadulterated heat, a searing demand that ignited every part of her body. It was a kiss of relentless need, as if he were pouring every broken fragment of his soul into the kiss and into her hands.

Her heart tightened, and she dropped the helmet to wrap her arms around his neck. He dragged her off the bike so their bodies were flush against each other. Her breasts were crushed against his chest, her nipples aching with need as he palmed her hips, locking her against him. His cock was hard, pressing against her belly, and the kiss was beyond hot, beyond scorching, beyond anything she'd ever experienced, and she loved it.

She was used to polite, perfunctory sex. None of this raging inferno that seemed like it was going to melt the clothes from her body. She'd had no idea that this kind of heat even existed, but it was perfection, it was everything she needed, it was everything she wanted, even though she hadn't known it until this moment.

His hand slid through her hair, tangling in the strands as he angled her head for a deeper kiss. His tongue was demanding, finessing her with such intoxicating passion that she felt her entire body explode into uncontrollable desire. Never had she wanted anyone the way she wanted Zane. She wanted his kiss, his touch, his soul, and his body. She wanted him to make love to her until they were both so spent that they couldn't move even an inch, and then she wanted him to make love to her again.

He tasted sultry, with something faintly sweet beneath the surface. Vanilla from his morning coffee? She wasn't sure, but she knew she wanted more. He was addictive, a force larger than she could imagine, blowing into her life like a hurricane, stripping her of every careful control set around her, and her entire being burned for more.

His hand slid up beneath her jacket, and cupped her breast. She couldn't contain the gasp of pleasure as he thumbed her nipple, sending heat cascading down her trembling legs. He swallowed her gasp with his kiss, a devastating assault that made her heart tumble. How could one man affect her like this? She could barely think over the roar of need sweeping through her, and she tightened her grip on him, pressing her body against his as he deepened the kiss—

A horn honked next to her, and she jumped, letting out an involuntary yelp. Zane caught her as she stumbled over the bike, holding her upright as a pickup truck with two men in it honked again, hooting and hollering as they waved their cowboy hats at them.

Zane grinned at her, and gave the truck a wave as it pulled into a spot on the other side of the parking lot. "Well, shit," he said, turning back to her. "That was the best first kiss I've ever had."

Lightness filled her heart, and she couldn't help but grin back at him. "It wasn't bad, I'll admit—"

"Not bad?" He grabbed her wrist and yanked her against him, his eyes still hidden behind those dark sunglasses. "You better admit I'm the best damned kisser you ever had, or I'm going to maul you out here in the middle of this parking lot for all the world to see until you come clean." His hand slipped to her butt. "'Fess up, corporate girl. I'm the best you've ever had. Say it."

She grinned, letting herself melt into him. God, it felt amazing to feel the hardness of his frame against hers. "Is that like ordering me to beg you?" she teased. "Don't you know it takes all the romance out of it if you have to command a compliment? Wasn't it obvious from the way I responded?"

He studied her for a moment, and then a small smile curved the corner of his mouth. "You don't usually kiss like that?"

She gripped the front of his jacket, and tugged lightly. "Zane, I've *never* kissed like that in my life. I'm not really that passionate. I'm controlled, contained, and deeply protective of myself when it comes to men. Kissing like that...it's not me."

His hands softened on her hips, and he shoved his sunglasses on top of his head. His gaze searched hers, and she felt her heart tighten at the understanding on his face. "Does it scare you?" he asked. "The way you react to me?"

She shrugged. "It should, and it might later, but right now, it just...I just feel well...I feel alive for the first time in a really long time."

His grin widened, lighting up his eyes. "Me, too."

She smiled, then. "But I'm still not going to have sex

with you tonight. That's a different line to cross." But even as she said the words, she knew she sounded just a little too desperate. If they'd been alone, there was no way that kiss would have ended before full nakedness had occurred. "Two rooms tonight?"

He shook his head. "Sorry, darlin', but my place has only one bed. You're stuck with me."

"Your place?" She was surprised by his comment. She doubted Zane was the type of man who let anyone into his private domain. "We're going to your place?"

"Yeah." He shoved his sunglasses back down over his eyes, cutting off his emotions from her view. "It's a pit. You'll hate me after you see it." He put his arm around her. "Come on. This place has the best burgers for a hundred miles. I'm starved."

He made no more comments about his place as they walked inside, but he'd said enough. She'd heard the edge to his voice, and she knew he was dead serious when he'd said she'd hate him once she saw his place. If he was so sure of that, why was he taking her there? Another test? Or maybe, he was as afraid as she was of the direction this thing between them was going. If she hated him after she saw his place, then neither of them would have to worry about what was happening.

She kind of hoped she hated it.

And she really hoped she didn't.

Chapter 8

Zane slowed the bike as he neared the old warehouse on the outskirts of town. When he saw the familiar sight that he'd been so proud of, he felt something sink deep in his gut, and regret and failure dug into his heart.

He paused the bike in the middle of the road. For the first time in the two years since the place opened, he didn't want to go in there. How the hell could he walk in there again?

"Is everything okay?" Taylor rested her chin on his shoulder, looking past him, her arms still tight around his waist.

Her voice wrapped around him, jerking him back to the present. He looked down at her hands locked around his waist. Her fingernails were painted a pale pink, so light he could barely see it. She was wearing a ring on her right ring finger, an antique-looking design with a pale blue stone in the middle. It looked like something she'd picked up in a thrift store, not at a fancy department store counter, but he was willing to bet it was real, not some fake shit that was supposed to look like it cost thousands when it was actually worthless.

She squeezed him lightly. "Zane?"

"Anyone you know ever die?" he asked, still not driving forward.

"Yes," she answered without hesitation. "Mira's parents were very dear to me, especially her dad. My parents weren't around much, but her dad took care of me. I was devastated when he was killed in a car accident." Her voice was soft, but steady. "It's horrible when you lose someone you love."

"Yeah." He took a breath. "You ever fail anyone?"

She was silent for a moment. "Yes."

"Who?"

"My ex-husband."

She'd been married? Jealousy surged through him, a sudden, inexplicable hate toward the man who'd once been lucky enough to see his ring on her finger. "I doubt you failed him," he said, his voice harsher than he'd intended.

"I did." She shifted behind him, and he felt her lean her forehead against the middle of his back between his shoulder blades, like she was trying to hide from the memories. "It sucks."

"Yeah, it does." Suddenly, going into that building didn't feel so overwhelming. He wasn't the only who'd failed someone. Taylor understood. He was suddenly damn glad she was there with him. He revved the engine, and rode forward, turning into the parking lot behind the metal building.

He parked on the far side, not in his usual spot, then swung his leg off the bike. Taylor was still sitting on the bike, watching him. The ends of her hair were peeking out from the bottom of the helmet, and he could see a thin gold necklace resting on her collarbones, just visible under the edge of her jacket. The big helmet made her look tiny, and utterly feminine. Shit, he liked seeing her on his bike, which was weird, because he didn't let anyone near his bike. "You want to come in with me?" He hadn't intended to bring her inside, but now that he was here, he didn't want to go in alone.

She unfastened the helmet and pulled it off, glancing at the weary-looking warehouse. "What is it?"

"A place." He took the helmet from her and hung it from the handlebars. "No one will bother it here. They know my stuff."

"A place?" She swung her leg off the bike. "Did anyone ever tell you how uncommunicative you are? I mean, seriously. A place? What kind of answer is that?"

He caught her wrist and pulled her over to him, framing her face with his hands. "I need to kiss you." That was the only warning he gave her before he kissed her. He didn't ask this time, because he couldn't afford to give her the chance to say no. He did need to kiss her, more than he could ever articulate. He needed to feel her against him, and he had to taste her, to lose himself in her kiss, before he faced what was inside that building.

She responded without hesitation, her body melting against his as her arms slipped around his neck. Her lips were as silky soft as they'd been the first time he'd kissed her, and it felt like his entire soul stilled the moment he tasted her. Her body felt surreal against his, warm, pliable, and curvy in every place he could have dreamed of. He slipped one hand under her jacket, sliding up her spine to her shoulder blades. She wasn't bone-skinny, like some of the women he was used to avoiding. She had a real body, with actual curves, and her breasts were the right size for her frame, not a pair of huge knockers that would give a man a black eye if he wasn't careful.

Maybe she was used to a life on airplanes and shit like that, but she was more real than any person he'd met in a long time. Kissing her seemed to chase away the darkness that had haunted him for so long, because he knew she was kissing the man she'd just met, a man she knew only in the present. She had no idea who he'd been his whole life. She simply saw him for who she'd seen these last few days, and he liked that. He liked that a lot.

He liked the fact that she didn't date, and he liked being the one who'd broken through her walls. Shit. He liked everything about her, including having her tongue tangled up with his, and her nipples crushed against his chest.

Keeping one hand splayed over her upper back, he slipped his other hand into her hair, weaving his fingers in the soft strands, tugging lightly as he deepened the kiss. A need to claim her began to build inside him, a need to declare that she was his, to trap her against him so that he never had to worry that he'd look over and find her missing.

"Zane!" A familiar voice broke through the haze of the kiss, and he swore, jerking his hand out from under her jacket.

He kept his arm around her, however, as he turned toward the building. Approaching them was a familiar guy in faded jeans, old cowboy boots, and a cowboy hat that had seen better days. Just seeing the old man made Zane's jaw tighten. Jesus. He didn't know if he could do this. "Ross." He inclined his head.

"You heard?"

"Yeah." Of course he'd heard. That's why he hadn't been back. "Sucks."

"Yeah." Ross searched his face. "You okay? This happens sometimes. You can't blame yourself. We do everything we can."

Zane cleared his throat. "Yeah, well, I take responsibility."

Ross sighed. "Zane—"

"This is Taylor Shaw," he interrupted, not wanting to have that conversation. "Taylor, this is Ross Stevens. She's from out of town."

Ross tipped his hat to her. "Nice to meet you, Miss Shaw."

She smiled at him, warm and genuine. "Taylor," she corrected. "Just call me Taylor."

He grinned. "Then you need to call me Ross, young lady."

Taylor smiled wider, and Zane tightened his arm around her shoulders. "Ross it is, then," she said. "What is this place?"

Ross glanced at Zane. "He didn't tell you?"

"No, he's being completely uncommunicative, as usual. You know how he can be." She said it cheerfully and intimately, as if she'd known Zane forever, not just a couple days. But she was right on target, which made Zane grin.

Ross laughed. "Yeah, I do." He held out his arm. "Would you like a tour, Taylor? I'll show you everything Zane has never told you about himself, the shit he should have known I'd spill if he brought you here."

Taylor glanced at Zane, and he realized that, somehow, she understood that something was going on, something that was affecting him, and she was checking to make sure it was okay if she accepted Ross's offer. She was putting him first. Shit. He didn't even know what to say, so he just shrugged.

She smiled, then turned to Ross. "Give me a tour, then, Ross. I'm in." She took his arm, and then held out her other hand to Zane. "I want both of you to escort me. It will fulfill my childhood fantasy of feeling like a queen." There was laughter in her eyes, and Zane couldn't help but grin as he walked up and held out his arm for her.

She slipped her hand into the crook of his elbow, and let

the two men escort her toward the building. "I could so get used to this," she announced. "Two devastatingly handsome cowboys all to myself."

Ross grinned, his leathery face creasing. "If Zane ever treats you badly, you come knockin' on my door, and I'll beat the hell out of him."

She laughed, her delight making Zane grin despite the foreboding pressing down upon him. "I'm sure you could take him down, Ross," she said. "But I don't think I need to worry about that." She glanced at Zane. "Zane's a far better man than he thinks he is."

He could tell she meant it. Something shifted inside him at her words, and his smile was real as they walked into the building.

❃ ❃ ❃

Taylor wasn't sure what she'd expected to see inside the decrepit warehouse, but a gleaming new, full-sized basketball court, a computer center, extensive free weights, and a library complete with couches and a dozen bookshelves weren't top on the list. She was even more surprised to see the cavernous space being used by an assortment of boys, ranging from scrawny six-year-olds to beefy older teens who were well over six feet tall, and who looked more than a little dangerous. She saw tattoos, earrings, scraggly facial hair, and tee shirts packed with more attitude than she'd encountered her entire life. They were bold, arrogant, and absolutely lost at the same time.

For a moment, she stared in shock at the boys, then tears sprung to her eyes before she could catch herself. She jerked her eyes off the kids and looked at the ceiling, clamping down on sudden onslaught of grief, longing, and sadness. Dammit. Usually, she was okay with kids if she knew she was going to encounter them, but she hadn't prepared for children, especially not ones who were so obviously in need of someone to care. She bit her lip, fighting back emotion. God, she had to pull herself together. It was just the sight of a few kids. She was way overreacting, even for her, at least given how much time had passed since the days of her broken dreams.

"Welcome to the Garage." Ross swept his hand out. "This place used to build and service farm equipment, but now we try to keep kids out of trouble. There's not a lot to do in these parts, so we try to give them a chance."

Taylor took a deep breath and focused on Ross and Zane. This was about them, not her. "This is what you do when you're not at the ranch?" She asked Zane, and then her heart seemed to freeze when she saw the look of raw anguish on his face as he stared across the warehouse. The pain in his eyes jerked her out of her own melodrama and twisted at her heart. Instinctively, she wrapped her hand around his arm, trying to support him. "Zane? What's wrong?"

He didn't answer, and she tore her gaze off him to try to ascertain what had caught his attention so ruthlessly. On the other side of the basketball court, a boy was leaning against the wall, staring at Zane. He looked about fourteen years old, all bones and ratty, baggy clothes. His eyes were big and dark, sunken into the shadows on his face and his arms were folded across his chest. His dark hair was a little long, and even the light brown tint to his skin couldn't hide how pale he looked. He looked lost and so much younger than his years.

"Shit," Zane muttered under his breath.

"Talk to him," Ross said. "You have to do it. He needs you to do it."

The other kids saw Zane, and he got some shouts and waves that were clearly very enthusiastic, and he acknowledged them, but he never took his gaze off the boy by the wall. "I don't know what to say," he said, his voice strained.

"It doesn't matter. He just needs to hear something from you."

Zane's face was pale, but he nodded. He glanced at Taylor. "I'll be right back."

"Okay." She squeezed his hand, her fingers drifting off his as he walked away. The basketball game stopped as he neared the court. The boys swarmed him, all of them talking over each other in their attempts to get Zane's attention. He took the time to acknowledge all of them, but the boy on the other side of the court continued to stand silently, waiting. "What's going on?" she asked Ross.

Ross sighed. "One of the kids Zane had been working with died a few days ago. He got in trouble with some kids, some shit went down, and he wound up dead. Zane had been trying to get him to spend more time here, but he wasn't interested. This place wasn't his thing, but Zane thought he could help him."

"Oh, no. How awful." Now she understood Zane's earlier question about whether she had ever failed anyone, and she knew who the funeral was for. He blamed himself for the death of that boy, a devastating burden that he was carrying silently. Her throat tightened, and tears burned at the back of her eyes. Her own trip down self-pity lane seemed so pathetic now, in comparison to what Zane was going through. "And the boy over there?"

"Luke? It was his older brother, Brad, who was killed."

"Oh, God." As she watched, Zane made his way over to the boy. Luke turned his back on Zane and walked away. Zane's hands clenched, and for a moment, he hesitated, then he followed the boy, clearly talking to him. Luke stopped, his arms still folded across his chest, his back toward Zane. He cocked his head, however, clearly listening to Zane, even though he wasn't facing him.

"Zane started coming by a year ago," Ross said. "He's made a big difference for the kids. Zane's not some big star trying to throw some charity their way for PR purposes. He *was* them, when he was younger. He lived their life. They know that, so they listen. Zane paid for the basketball court to be built indoors. He wanted them to be able to play even during the winter. Before that, they just played in the dirt parking lot."

Taylor's throat tightened as she watched Zane and Luke. There was so much tension in both their bodies, so much distance between them. "Zane was homeless? Poor?" She'd seen only evidence of family and love on the Stockton ranch. What else did she not know about him?

Ross glanced over at her. "That's for Zane to tell you, not me. Ask him."

She nodded, tears burning in her eyes as Luke finally turned around to face Zane. His jaw was thrust out, and he looked hostile and angry, but his earnest gaze was riveted on Zane's face, as if he were inhaling every word Zane spoke.

It was clear there was a deep connection between the two, and this time, Taylor didn't need to turn away to protect herself from her own emotions. She watched them, her heart aching for the depth of caring so evident in the way Zane was talking to Luke. He was such a good man, so caring, so different from how he pretended to be. "It looks like they're talking. They might be a while," she said, hoping she was right. She had a feeling Luke needed Zane in a big way. "How about a tour while we wait?"

Ross smiled back, and in his eyes, she saw decades of wisdom, kindness, and understanding, the kind of patient man it would take to work with kids who carried trouble on their backs. Suddenly, all the lies she'd been telling herself about the importance of her work were shattered. Ross and Zane were the ones making a difference. They were the ones giving hope and opportunity to kids who had no one else. She did what? Sat in boardrooms talking about how a company could earn more money? God, no, she couldn't think like that. She had to live her life. She couldn't see it for what it was, or she'd never survive it.

"Sure thing, Taylor," Ross said, jerking her back to the present. "It's not much, but we do what we can." He led the way, and she hurried across the cement floor, glancing back just in time to see Zane hug Luke.

Her throat tightened, and she turned away. Zane wasn't the man she'd thought he was, an isolated loner who didn't connect with anyone. He wasn't the man he'd claimed he was, either. He was the man she'd feared he might be, the kind of man who could never accept her for who she was. He was the kind of man she could really fall for…and lose.

She had to let him go. *She had to.* She couldn't play this temporary game with him anymore, not now that she'd seen the side of him he'd kept hidden so well.

But as she followed Ross up a set of narrow, metal stairs, she realized she didn't want to let him go. It was too late. *It was too late.*

Chapter 9

Zane knew he was cranky. He knew he wasn't in the right frame of mind to have any kind of constructive discussion, but by the time he and Taylor walked into his apartment, he was too pissed to hold it in.

He shoved the door open, no longer caring about how small his place would look to Taylor. He didn't give a shit about the peeling paint on the walls or the mismatched chairs and kitchen table that had come with the place. He'd gotten the place to prove a point, even though he could have bought a damned ranch with the money from his earnings. He'd felt the need to be in this kind of place after he'd walked away from the spotlight. He'd been prepared for Taylor to hate it and walk out, and he'd been planning to let her, but now, he didn't even care what she thought of it. They were way past that.

He slammed the door shut behind her and leaned against it, folding his arms, anger building inside him as he watched her walk into the middle of the one bedroom apartment, slowly turning around as she inspected it. "It's not exactly high fashion," she said, "but I'm impressed with how clean it is. I was expecting some typical bachelor pad, but it's immaculate." She turned toward him. "What exactly was I supposed to hate about it?"

"What's going on?" He didn't mean to snap the question, but he was tired and felt like shit from going to the Garage today. "You've shut down ever since the Garage. Dinner was like trying to twist answers from you. I'm tired, and I don't want to deal with this. You don't like the kids? You think they're shit just because they don't have money? You think it's a waste of time to try to help them? That they'll all end up like Brad, dead after some bad choice, because they have no parents to guide them? A waste of the earth's resources?"

He spat the words that he'd heard so many times, unable to keep the venom out of his voice. He wasn't a kid anymore, but he'd never stop being one of *those* kids, and the words still felt like a personal insult every time he heard them, because they were. He didn't have to take that kind of shit anymore, and he didn't, but as hell was his witness, he never thought Taylor was the type who'd say them. Some people, he expected to feel that way, and he wasn't disappointed when they proved him wrong.

He realized, too late, that he'd had faith in Taylor, and he was shocked that she was like the others. It pissed him off that he was wrong about her. He felt like she'd betrayed him, and that made him even more angry. Not that she'd betrayed him, but that he'd let himself trust enough that she could make him feel like this.

Her eyes widened, and she stared at him. "What?"

"Just say it." He shoved himself off the door and tossed his bag on the ratty couch. "Just admit what you were thinking when you walked in there. The minute we got in there, you shut down." He stalked over to her. He couldn't believe how pissed he was. He hadn't expected her to be like that. He hadn't even considered it as a possibility, but he shouldn't have been surprised. He knew what to expect from people, and her nice rental and well-mannered ways should have told him what she was like. She'd just been so real. He'd believed in her, and he didn't believe in many people. "I'm surprised you didn't demand I take you to a hotel tonight, although you can probably guess there aren't a lot of luxury accommodations in this town."

"Hey." She narrowed her eyes at him. "I completely understand that you're going through something really difficult right now, but it's not fair to strike out at me—"

"Strike out?" He ran his hand through his hair. "I know what it's like when a man strikes out, and I've had the broken bones to prove it. I'm not lashing out. I'm pissed, and I'm calling it like it is. I have no time for this crap."

"What crap?" She put her hands on her hips, her eyes flashing with anger. "You think I looked down on those boys because they're poor, and come from broken homes? Is that what you really think of me?"

"Yeah, I—" He stopped mid-sentence at the expression on her face. There was something about the outrage in her eyes that made him pause. It wasn't indignant anger. There was something else there. Hurt? Vulnerability? "Isn't that what's going on?" he asked, hesitating ever so slightly. "You shut down. I know you did." He searched his mind for anything else that had happened, but he couldn't think of any other explanation. "You were fine, completely wrapped around me before we went in, and after I talked with Luke, you put up a wall so fast I couldn't have gotten through it with a jackhammer. If it's not the boys, what is it?"

"It's not—" She paused, her face stricken.

A cold chunk of ice settled in his gut at her refusal to answer. "It *was* the boys, wasn't it?" He couldn't keep the bitterness out of his voice. "You think they're dangerous and should be in juvie instead of someone giving them computers, don't you?"

Wordlessly, she shook her head, and suddenly he saw tears shimmering in her eyes. His anger stalled out instantly, and he stopped, staring at her, his heart clenching at the pain in her eyes. Shit. What was going on? "What? Tell me what it is."

She let out her breath, staring past him at a spot on the wall. "My whole life, I've loved kids," she said softly. "All I ever wanted was to be a teacher, and I wanted a dozen kids of my own. I'm an only child, and my mom died when I was little, and my dad was always working, so I grew up in a quiet house. I hated it. It felt so lonely, which is why I wound up hanging out at Mira's all the time."

Zane's fists unclenched, and he rocked back on his heels, trying to wrap his mind around the story she was telling. "You didn't have a mom?" He'd figured her for a perfect childhood, not a one-parent household like he'd had. Well, he'd had more like a sliver of one parent, and that was on his mom's good days. He'd hadn't spent much time at the Stockton hellhole once his mom had ditched the old man, but he'd been screwed no matter which parent he was with.

"No." Taylor dropped her bag on the floor. It landed with a soft thump, and she walked over to the window, staring out at the landing of his apartment. Her only view was the parking lot and another tenement apartment building across the street, but that didn't seem to bother her. "I got married a week after I graduated from college. Dan Parker. He wanted a family as much as I did. We got jobs as teachers in the same school district. It was perfect."

Dan Parker. The name of the man she'd given herself to. Zane took a deep breath, trying to let go of the sudden surge of jealousy. Taylor wasn't his, and he had no claim on her, not her present, not her future, and certainly not her past. "What happened?"

She looked back at him, and there was a single tear trickling down her cheek. "I can't have children. I had an infection when I was a little girl." She shrugged. "I didn't know. Dan was mad. He said I should have known, and that I misled him."

Zane swore softly. "Bastard."

His reply made her laugh, a teary, heart-wrenching laugh that hurt to hear. "We talked about adopting. He said he'd be okay with it." She shrugged again, a casual gesture that was a total lie. "And then he got one of the other teachers pregnant, and he left me for her. He said he could never love a woman who was broken."

"Broken?" Outrage began to pour through him. "He said you were *broken*?"

She held out her hands. "I am," she said quietly. "Everyone at the school knew what had happened. I...couldn't stay there. I left the school. I couldn't be a teacher and look at all those children I could never have. I found a corporate job, and I got away."

He stalked across the room and grasped her shoulders. "He's an idiot," he said. "And a scumbag."

She met his gaze, ignoring his comment. "Since then, I've kept it light. I didn't get serious with guys, not enough to talk about the long term. But there was one man who got under my skin. We started to get serious. I was falling in love with him, and he said he was, too. He was talking about getting married, so I had to tell him. He said it was fine, that he didn't care, that we could adopt or not have kids. I was so happy." She managed a half-smile. "Then a couple months later, one of his friends had a baby, and he said it made him realize that he wasn't willing to give up on the chance for a biological family. He was too young to settle. If he didn't find anyone in a few years, then maybe we could try again." She looked at him. "Do you know how much that hurts, Zane? To be told by the man I loved that I should try him again in a few years and if he was desperate enough, maybe he'd be willing to settle for me?" She shook her head. "I believed in him, and I was so wrong."

His fingers tightened on her arms. "You have shitty luck to find two guys who believe that. Not all men are like that—"

"In their hearts they are. It's human nature." She met his gaze. "I won't take that future away from a man, because someday he'll resent it, and he'll hate me for it." There were tears shimmering in her eyes. "I wasn't expecting to see all the kids there today. I wasn't prepared. Sometimes it hits me hard, you know? I've worked really hard to create a great career and a fulfilling life, and it's enough for me, but sometimes..." She shrugged. "I'm sorry. I just let it get to me." She met his gaze. "Those boys are beautiful," she whispered. "Every single one of them deserves the world."

He saw the honesty in her eyes, and her voice was soft with the kind of genuine passion that could never be faked, and he knew she was telling the truth. She believed in those boys as much as he did, but he'd misinterpreted her response completely. He'd judged her the way he *hated* to be judged by others. He swore at himself, disgusted by how he'd treated her. "I'm such a bastard," he said softly. "I'm so sorry for what I said to you. I had no idea—"

She shook her head, putting her finger across his lips. "No, no apologies. How would you have known?"

He wrapped his hand around hers and pressed a kiss to her fingertips. "I have a huge chip on my shoulder when it comes to being poor and from the undesirable part of society," he said. "I shouldn't have judged you like that just because I have issues. I'm sorry. Really."

She smiled, watching him trail kisses across her palm, tears still glistening on her cheeks. "You and me," she said softly. "No wonder we connect. We're both a mess."

"You're not a mess." He slipped his hands around her waist and tugged her against him. His body relaxed when he felt the heat of her body against his. "But I'm not going to deny that I'm an insensitive, judgmental bastard."

A small, tearful laugh escaped her, and she laced her fingers behind his neck, gazing up at him. "If you could have seen the way you were interacting with those boys today, you would never be able to call yourself an insensitive, judgmental bastard. It was beautiful." Her blue eyes shined with warmth that seemed to wrap around him.

No one had ever said anything like that to him. Ever. They'd praised his skill with the bulls. They'd coveted his bank account. They'd ogled his body. And before that, they'd ridiculed his old clothes and boots. They'd scorned everything about him, and the girls had wanted him only to shock their families or make their boyfriends jealous. No one had ever, *ever*, looked at him and seen anything real that was worth saving.

Until Taylor.

"Thank you." He bent his head and kissed her, brushing his lips over hers in the only way he knew how to tell her what it meant.

She sighed and leaned into him, welcoming the kiss. Her lips were responsive and warm, encircling him with a sense of belonging he wasn't accustomed to having. With a low growl, he tightened his arms around her and deepened the kiss. Her breasts were crushed against his chest, and his palms were tight on her hips. Still kissing her, he ran his hands over the curve of her ass, jamming his hands in the back pockets of her jeans and pressing her against him.

She tasted amazing. Pure, fresh, with a hint of something darker and sexier.

They were alone now.

No one was going to walk in.

No one was going to stop them.

He broke the kiss, his lips whispering against her ear. "I want to take you to bed," he whispered. "My bed. No rules.

Just us."

She didn't answer, but she pressed a kiss to his throat, and tightened her arms around his neck. He smiled to himself as he scooped her up, wrapping her legs around his hips as he carried her across the small room to the tiny bedroom off the back. "Sometime," he said between kisses, "I want you to actually tell me that you want me with your words. I can read between the lines with you now, but it's okay to admit you want this, you know?"

"No, it's not." She pulled back to look at him, her hands still loosely linked behind his neck as he carried her. "If I say I want it, then it's harder to deny that it matters to me. I need to protect myself, Zane."

His heart tightened at the pain in her voice as he lowered her to the bed. She fell back into the pillows, and he lowered himself on top of her before she could scoot away, using his weight to pin her to the bed. "You don't need to protect yourself from me, Taylor." Damn, it felt good to have her beneath him. Kissing her in a vertical position had been good, but there was nothing like the sensation of being tangled up with her along the entire length of their bodies.

She laid her hand on his cheek, her eyes searching his. It was dark out, but the streetlights gave just enough illumination for him to see her. "But I do, Zane. You affect me in a way that makes me vulnerable to you."

Satisfaction pulsed through him, and he turned his head into her hand, pressing a kiss to her palm. "I'm not going to lie to you, darlin'," he said, as he kissed the inside of her wrist. "I don't want anything from any woman, and I don't want a relationship, but I can't help it that I absolutely fucking love the fact I affect you." He caught her lips in his before she could answer.

He didn't want to say anything more. He didn't want to make promises, or ask for something which would never fit into his life. He didn't want her vulnerability to bring out some delusional knight-in-shining-armor side of him that he could never deliver on. She'd run into enough bastards, and she didn't need him adding to it by making promises he could never keep.

But he needed her. He needed her kiss, her

companionship, and her support.

She broke the kiss. "I'm not staying forever, Zane. We don't have a future." Her voice was desperate, as if she were trying to remind herself of that, not just him.

"No one really has a future," he said. "No one knows whether they have a tomorrow." He tangled his fingers in her hair. "You're the first woman who has mattered to me in a long time," he said. "Maybe ever. You're sure as hell the first one I've ever trusted, so, yeah, I don't really care what might or might not happen someday. I just don't want to miss out on this moment with you, the one we have right now."

She searched his face. "I don't know how to do that. I don't know how to let go of the forever and the future. I just worry that I'll get my heart broken, or that I'll let you down, or that it will be too hard to leave, or that—"

He kissed her, hard, deeply, cutting off her words. He had long ago given up any thoughts of a future, because every one that he could envision sucked. It was better to just be in the present and take it day by day, because then he had a chance to breathe. Anything was endurable in the present. It was when he thought of doing it for a lifetime that it became too much.

He didn't want to think about the future with Taylor, because the future was like trying to hold sand between his fingers. It just slid out of reach, every time, with steady, relentless ruthlessness. But this moment, her kiss, her body...it was real. It was something he could hold onto for the rest of his life.

With a sigh, Taylor wrapped her arms around his neck. He could tell the moment she gave up resisting. Her body softened, and her kiss became more fluid, a searing, heated interplay of lips and tongues.

"I need skin," he whispered, rolling off her long enough to jerk off his jacket and shirt. He was back on top of her before she'd even reached for the hem of her shirt. "Let me." He pulled her up to a sitting position, then slid her jacket off her shoulders, kissing her collarbone as he did so.

"That feels amazing," she whispered, leaning her head against his as he pulled her hands free.

"You ain't seen nothin' yet, darlin'." He slid his hands down her arms to her wrists, then raised her arms, clasping them together over her head. For a moment, he held her there while he kissed her, a deeper, more penetrating kiss than before, one of mounting anticipation. He'd never seen her naked, never kissed her in all the places he wanted to, but he knew it was going to happen tonight. He wanted to tear his clothes off and attack her, but at the same time, now that he knew where this was going, he felt a sense of patience utterly foreign to him. He wanted to take his time and savor every moment, to slow time to a crawl so he could make it last as long as possible.

His cock was already hard and ready, straining against the front of his jeans as he grasped the hem of her shirt and slipped it upwards, his thumbs skimming along her skin as he pulled the fabric along her body, over her arms, and off.

He leaned back, his hands sliding down her arms again as he ran his gaze over her body for the first time. Her bra was pale blue, with just the faintest bit of lace around the edges. Demure, but sinfully sexy. So much better than the black and red overstated and overfilled bras that women used to show him when they'd corner him on the way back to his hotel. "Perfect," he whispered, lowering his head to press a kiss to the swell of her left breast.

She sighed, her fingers sliding through his hair as he kissed his way across her chest to her right breast. "You know what?"

"What?" He hooked his finger over the lace of her bra and tugged it down, exposing her nipple. It was hard and erect as he took the nub into his mouth, swirling his tongue over it as he sucked on it.

She made a small noise that made him grin, as she shifted her hips. "I've been kind of neurotic about sex since Dan left me. Insecure. Uptight, you know? But—"

He bit her nipple, grinning when she yelped and grabbed his shoulders. "But what?" He blew on the taut peak, easing the burn.

"Um...yeah..." She twisted restlessly under him as he lightly tweaked her other nipple between his thumb and forefinger. "With you...I just want more. It just...it's just right, you know? I mean..."

Feeling her gaze on him, he looked up at her. She was

staring down at him, her fingers trailing through his hair.

He pressed a light kiss to her mouth. "What is it, Taylor?"

She ran her fingertips across his whiskers. "You make me want to forget all the noise in my life, and just be here. I can't even tell you how amazing it is to be in your arms. I don't want to be anywhere else, but there's so much to consider—"

"Shh." He kissed away her protest. It wasn't until she began to kiss him back that he broke the kiss, stroking her hair back from her face. "I know you want the marriage and kid thing, Taylor, and you deserve it. I'm not going to lie and mislead you. I can't do that. I don't know anything about creating a family, and I don't even know how to stay in the same place for more than a couple nights. If I wanted kids, though, I'd be perfect for you, because I don't give a shit about kids being biologically related to me. My parents were biologically mine, and they sucked beyond words. Biology doesn't create a family or love, or anything good, and I've lived that. I'm not the only man in the world who knows that, either." He cupped her breast. "You're amazing, not broken, and I want to make love to you until neither of us can move, but I have to be honest with you. I'll never be able to be that devoted husband you deserve. I can be your today, but for me, that's all there is anyway. That's what matters, that's where the living is done, so to me, that's everything. My today is my everything, and that's what I can give you."

He kissed her again, deeply, pouring every last bit of who he was into the kiss. He didn't have much to offer her. Shit, he had nothing to offer her. He was the one who was broken, lying in scattered fragments in his past, fragments that could never be rebuilt into anything whole or decent. "I'm not worthy of you," he whispered. "But I'll give you everything I have to give."

She pulled back, searching his face, and for a moment, time seemed to freeze inside his heart. He'd said too much. He never talked like that. He never said words like that. What the hell had he been thinking? He kept things clean, simple, and detached. That was how he lived. That was—

Then she smiled, wrapped her arms around his neck, and kissed him. "Make love to me, Zane," she whispered between kisses. "I'm begging you."

Chapter 10

The way Zane kissed Taylor took her breath away. His kiss seemed to sear every cell in her body, burning away all the tension and stress, leaving nothing behind but relentless, untainted need for him. She felt more alive than she had in so long, maybe ever.

His hands were like magic where they roamed her body, gliding over her skin as if she were made of the most beautiful, fragile porcelain, as if he believed he was the luckiest man on earth to be able to touch her.

The kiss was sensual and tempting, a slow, decadent seduction. It wasn't carnal heat, but something deeper and more powerful.

She'd never lived in the present. She was always trying to fix today to make tomorrow better, constantly looking ahead to where she was going, or looking behind her to make sure she didn't wind up in the same place she'd once been. But Zane's words had entranced her, making her want to crawl into his arms and never move, to simply be with him in the moment.

He slid down her body, trailing his lips along her throat, her collarbone, and to the swell of her breasts. His hands spanned her hips, his thumbs sliding below the waistband of her jeans in slow, tantalizing circles. Desire began to roll through her more intensely, and she shifted her hips restlessly. She clasped his shoulders, her fingers digging into his muscles.

She loved having his body against her. The feel of his skin sliding over hers was amazing. So much intimacy, so much sensation. She'd missed this kind of connection. She'd missed it far more than she'd realized. Or maybe, it wasn't simply that she'd missed it. Maybe it was that being touched by Zane was what she'd been waiting for all this time.

He lightly bit her nipple, and she gasped at the flood of desire…then he unfastened the button on her jeans. She tensed. Was she really going to do this? Was she really going to let him get her naked? Because she knew where it was going to lead. The need between them was too great. Nothing was going to stop them once they crossed that line. She closed her eyes, her fingers sliding through his hair as he kissed his way down her belly, pausing to lave her belly button as he unzipped her jeans.

Oh, God, really? She focused on his touch as he gripped the waistband of her jeans and began to tug them down her hips, his mouth trailing kisses lower and lower as he pulled her jeans down. Instinctively, she lifted her hips, helping him. That was all he needed, and within a second, her jeans were gone. He'd left her underwear on, but he was already raining kisses over the soft fabric that provided no useful barrier between them.

He pressed a kiss to her swollen nub, and she gasped, twisting beneath him. His fingers traced circles along the edges of her underwear, brushing over the lace, making her want to beg for him to tear it off her. But she didn't. There was something about the teasing that was amazing, making her feel he wanted to savor every last second.

She'd never been savored before. She had to admit that she really liked it.

"I want to take my jeans off," he whispered. "Is that okay with you?"

She opened her eyes to look at him. He was stretched out between her legs, an arm wrapped round each of her thighs, his gaze searing into her as he waited for her to reply. She could see the muscles rippling in his back and shoulders, along with a few faded scars she assumed were from his bull riding days. He was rugged and raw, far from perfection, and her entire body clenched with the need for him. She nodded. "Take 'em off, cowboy."

He flashed her a grin, showcasing that dimple of his that made her want to melt, and then he eased himself off her.

He stripped off his boots quickly, and she rolled onto her side, riveted as his muscles flexed while he disrobed. She couldn't help the sigh of anticipation as he stood and began to unfasten his jeans.

"You have a six pack," she said, her gaze trailing over the smattering of hair on his chest and his abs. "I didn't think real guys actually had them. I thought it was a myth created by skilled photo editing."

His fingers stilled on the bottom of his jeans, and he looked over at her. "Darlin', this here is all real, and it's all yours." He took his hands off his jeans. "You want the honors?"

She let out a choked laugh of embarrassment. "No, that's okay. I like to watch."

He sauntered over to the bed and leaned over, his palms sinking into the covers. "Go ahead," he said softly. "Indulge yourself. I want you to."

She had to admit, the idea of taking charge was a little intoxicating, especially when it came to a man who was twice her size and had enough muscle to dominate her easily if he chose to. He was so much stronger than she was, but right now, in his bedroom, she felt like she was the one with the power. She couldn't keep the grin off her face. "Okay."

"That's my girl." He stepped back and clasped his hands behind his head, his biceps flexing so ridiculously much that she felt like she had to be imagining things. Was this man really here for her, and just her? Had he really said that she was the first woman he'd ever trusted, in his entire life? Was it really possible that she was special to *him,* a man who was not only a physical specimen, but also who had a beautiful heart and so much vulnerability?

She swung her feet over the edge of the bed, and stood up. The moment she did, his eyes raked over her, burning her from head to toe. She was no svelte, gorgeous model, and couldn't even pass off her body as an athletic build. She wasn't even on the same scale as he was when it came to physical beauty, but the appreciation in his eyes made her feel like the most beautiful woman in the world.

Her nipples tightened, and she walked over to him. His eyes darkened as she neared, but he kept his hands laced behind his head. A part of her wanted to go right for his jeans like he'd invited her to do, but another part of her wanted to savor the moment, the way he'd done to her.

She splayed her hands on his chest, feeling the softness of his chest hair, and the hardness of the muscles beneath. His jaw tightened, as she slid her hands upward to his shoulders, and then across and down his arms. His skin was hot to the touch, and so incredibly sexy. Need pooled in her belly when she saw the desire darkening his eyes. "I like your body," she said.

"I'm glad. Feel free to make it yours." His voice was low and rough, curling through her like a private seduction.

"Mine? Hmm..." She smiled, and put her hands back on his chest, running them over the ridges of his torso as she moved them downward. He sucked his stomach in as she touched it, the muscles quivering beneath her fingers. Resting her fingers on his waistband, she stood on her tiptoes to kiss him.

His kiss was ravenous, immediately taking control, pouring such desire into her that her entire body began to melt into a boiling pool of need. He kept his hands clasped behind his head, though, still giving her the power, even while he stripped her soul bare with the intensity of his kiss.

She pressed her breasts against his chest, loving the feel of his skin against her nipples while he kissed her. Allowing her fingers to dance over the waistband of his jeans, she unfastened the button and then unzipped his fly. His erection was straining against the front of his jeans, and she couldn't help the shiver of anticipation. She couldn't remember the last time any man had wanted her this much, let alone the last time that she'd responded so intensely.

She hooked her thumbs over the waistband of his jeans, and tugged downward. She realized almost immediately that she'd accidentally grabbed his boxer briefs as well as his pants. She paused, hesitating. Did she really want this? This moment, this man, this magical experience?

He stopped the kiss, as if sensing her hesitation. He waited in silence, his lips resting against hers, giving her the chance to make her choice. Time seemed suspended as she waited, struggling with need and her own sense of self-preservation. A part of her wanted him to take charge, to be the one to rip off their clothes, to be the one taking ownership of what happened between them, as if that would somehow safeguard her heart, if she didn't actually admit to herself that she wanted this.

She pulled back to look at him. His dark eyes were hooded with desire, his gaze steady. Somehow, seeing his eyes made everything settle. This was Zane she was with, not some ridiculously hot stranger who meant nothing to her. Whatever happened in their future, she knew that this moment mattered deeply to both of them. Maybe it was the most either of them could give, maybe this was the pinnacle of what could ever be between them, but it didn't change that this moment was special, extraordinary even, a gift that she didn't have to fear.

She smiled, tightened her grip on his jeans and boxer briefs, and then tugged them down over his hips. His cock sprang free as his pants hit the floor, and she wrapped her hand around it as she stood up. The skin was velvet soft over the hardness, and her stomach fluttered in anticipation as Zane sucked in his breath.

"Nice," he whispered. "Did you know the second night we slept together, you were doing that to me? Holding me just like that?"

Heat flared in her cheeks. "What? I wouldn't have." She started to let go, but he grabbed her hand and held it where it was.

"You were asleep," he said, his voice rough with desire. "I thought it was awesome that you felt safe enough in your sleep to do that. A hell of a turn-on, too, I have to admit." He palmed her lower back with his free hand, lowering his head to nip at her earlobe. "I have never stayed so still for so long in my entire life, desperate not to disturb your sleep."

She let out a giggle, imagining Zane frozen for hours, afraid to dislodge her hand. "You're such a dork."

"Nah." He locked his arm around her waist and dragged her up against him, so his erection was against her belly, her hand trapped between their bodies. "I'm just a hot-blooded guy who knows when the right woman is in his bed. Speaking of which..." He scooped her up in his arms and tossed her into the middle of his mattress.

She'd just barely landed when he lunged after her.

A scream of laughter burst from her as she scrambled up the pillows away from him, but he caught her ankles and dragged her back down toward him. She had no time to escape before he was on top of her, pinning her mercilessly to the bed with the weight of his body.

"And now, you're mine, my precious," he teased, sounding like some evil wizard who'd trapped her in a dungeon. He kissed her hard, deeply, mercilessly, claiming her in a kiss so searing she was pretty sure steam would soon be rising from her body.

He broke the kiss and lightly bit her ear, and then began working his way in small nibbles and licks down the side of her neck. "You're at my mercy," he continued in his mock evil voice, "to do whatever I wish. I warn you, my darlin', the fantasies I have about your naked body will shock you."

She giggled again, sliding her fingers through his hair as he worked his way down toward her breasts. It felt totally different having them both naked, except for the wisp of her underwear. So much skin, so much heat, so much intimacy, and so much trust. "I'm too innocent for a bad boy," she teased. "I think you should let me go."

"Never." He grabbed her wrists and pinned them above her head, his hips pressing down against hers. His eyes were dark, and impenetrable. "You're mine, darlin', and I intend to keep you."

She knew he meant his words in play, and that he was referring just to this moment, but that didn't keep her heart from constricting. *I intend to keep you.* How amazing did those words sound? She wanted to be kept, to be fought for, and to be treasured beyond all words. Maybe there was no future for them, but in this moment, she felt like she had everything she wanted. "I don't think I can keep up with you." She grinned, tugging at her wrists just to see if he'd let her go.

He didn't. "I'll teach you everything you need to know." He paused at her breast, drawing her nipple into his mouth, using his tongue, his teeth, and his lips to torment her. Desire spiraled out in all directions, and she couldn't help but move her hips restlessly, needing more, already under his spell even though he'd barely begun to touch her.

"Like what?" She couldn't keep the breathlessness out of her voice.

"Like telling me what you want." He moved up again, and captured her mouth in a devastating kiss. "Take ownership of your body, Taylor," he whispered between kisses. "Claim me. Direct me. Make me your fantasy." He moved his hips, tempting her. "What do you want, darlin'? I want to give it to you."

"Kiss me," she whispered. "Kiss me."

"Like this?" He immediately captured her mouth in a kiss that plunged right to her soul. His tongue claimed hers, his mouth a sinful tool of seduction. She tried to get her hands free to wrap them around his neck, but his grip on her wrists tightened.

Excitement began to pulse through her at his refusal to free her. She liked the dichotomy of his relentless, bossy strength, combined with the fact he was demanding she take control. Power and submission combined into a heady place. "Let me go," she whispered, testing him.

"Not yet." He shifted his grip so both her wrists were in his left hand, and then slid his right hand over her breasts and down her belly. "What else do you want me to do, darlin'?" His breath was hot against her mouth, a temptation that was just out of her reach.

"Touch me."

He grinned, his dark eyes smoldering. "Here?" He put his hand on her elbow.

"You're a jerk."

He laughed. "That's not what you want? How about here?" He cupped her breasts, his finger flicking over her nipple.

She shifted under his touch. "Better."

"Where else?" he whispered, between kisses.

"Lower."

"Here?" He cupped her knee, making her laugh.

"You're such a pain," she said with a giggle.

"I just want you to feel the power of telling me what you want." He kissed her again, an intoxicating assault on all her senses, while his thumb drew circles on the inside of her knee. Okay, so she hadn't *thought* she wanted him fondling her knee, but the way his thumb was sliding over the skin on the inside of her knee was sending tendrils of desire though her body.

"A little higher," she whispered into the kiss.

He moved his hand to her thigh, his fingers tracing designs on the skin, making chills race down her leg and up her spine. "Here?"

"To the left."

His hand slid to the inside of her thigh, still tracing designs on her skin. "Here?" He kissed her again, taking her breath away before she could answer. The kiss was so amazing she could barely think, and her hips shifted even more restlessly, moving of their own accord, as if she could force his hand to go where she wanted just by sheer force of will.

"Higher," she whispered.

He moved his hand upward, until his fingers were brushing over the delicate fabric of her underwear, tantalizing her with the soft, barely-there touch as he glided across her body. "Nice," he whispered, as he ran his tongue down the side of her neck.

She shifted beneath him again. "Take it off."

"Take what off?" He pressed his palm to her folds, igniting a rush of desire, even through her underwear.

She groaned. "You're so impossible. Just take off my damned underwear and make love to me."

He laughed softly and kissed her, a kiss so penetrating that her body clenched in response. "You're so bossy." He finally released her wrists to drag her underwear over her thighs, trailing kisses down her leg as he slid the scrap of material off.

When she was finally naked, she had a brief second where she felt utterly exposed and vulnerable. There was nothing between them now. *Nothing.*

Then he kissed her toe, making her giggle. "You have such a sexy toe," he murmured as he kissed the arch of her foot. "And under here. I've been dying to kiss this very spot." His hand was warm where he'd wrapped it around her ankle, trapping her just as he'd immobilized her wrists. He kissed her anklebone, and then the front of her shin.

She swallowed, watching him as he worked his way up her leg. His eyes were on her, his dark gaze swallowing her up in its heat. He kissed her kneecap, and then the inside of her knee.

And then he began working his way up the inside of her thigh, never taking his gaze off her face.

He hooked his arm under her right thigh, moving her leg to the side as he kissed higher, and then locked his other arm across her hips, pinning her to the mattress.

She didn't think she would ever tire of his strength. "You like to do that, don't you? Trap me."

"Yeah, I do. You mind?"

She shook her head, her body taut with anticipation as he moved her legs further apart. He met her gaze, his mouth inches from her most private parts. "What do you want now, darlin'? Tell me."

"Kiss me. Touch me. Do everything you've fantasized about." Her voice was breathless, and her heart seemed to skip a beat when a slow, dangerous grin spread across his face.

"Be careful what you wish for," he said. "You have no idea what I'm capable of imagining."

"No one has ever fantasized about me before," she whispered. "Show me."

"You're in trouble now," he said. "Big trouble. Cowboy trouble." Then he swept his tongue across her folds in a single bold swipe that made her entire body clench. He gave her no respite, still pinning her to the bed with his forearm as he invaded her body with his mouth, his tongue, and even a few light nips with his teeth. Sensations cascaded through her like fireworks in her blood. Her hips bucked under his sensual assault, but each time she tried to move, he simply exerted more force with his arm, holding her in place effortlessly.

She loved how he held her down. It was incredibly sexy, especially since she knew that if she ever asked him to release her, he would in a heartbeat. It was the illusion of being trapped that was so intoxicating, plus the way his muscles flexed to resist her was completely sexy as well.

He released his tight grip on her leg, and slid his fingers inside her. She gasped at the invasion, suddenly no longer able to focus on anything but his touch, and the way it felt to have him inside her. He didn't let up on his assault with his mouth, his tongue swirling over her folds as his fingers slid deeper inside her, unfurling a cataclysm of need inside her.

She gripped his shoulders, gasping as her body burned with need. She could feel an orgasm building inside her, getting tighter and tighter until she thought she'd burst. "Stop," she gasped. "Make love to me. Now."

He responded instantly, crawling up her body to take her mouth in a devastating kiss as he kneed her thighs apart. She felt his erection pressing against her, and she wrapped her legs across his hips, trying to draw him into her. He didn't give in. Instead, he broke the kiss and framed her face with his hands. "I don't have any condoms." His voice was rough. "I haven't done this in a while, and I wasn't prepared. I was so pissed this afternoon that it didn't even occur to me this would happen."

A little part of her died at what she had to say. "It's okay. I can't get pregnant. It doesn't matter."

"I got tested a year ago," he said, not even appearing to notice her comment. "I wanted to know if I had paid the price for any of the shit I'd done. I'm clean, and I haven't been with anyone since."

She nodded, some of the tension easing from her body at his utter nonchalance about her confession. She realized that it truly didn't bother him in the least. He didn't see her as flawed or broken or anything. She smiled, her heart suddenly a thousand times lighter than it had ever felt. "My last boyfriend and I did the testing thing. He didn't want to use a condom if he didn't have to. I'm good."

His eyes darkened. "I don't like it when you talk about your last boyfriend." He moved his hips against her, his cock straining at her entrance. "I want this about us. Me. You."

Her breath caught at the sensation of his body pressing against hers, so close, so tempting. "It's only about you, Zane. I feel like..." God, could she say it? Wouldn't it make her too vulnerable? But she wanted to say it. She felt, somehow, that they both needed to hear it. "I feel like I need this with you. I need *you*. I thought I came here for Mira, but really, it was because I needed to meet you."

He didn't ridicule her or pull away. He simply nodded. "I feel the same way." His fingers tightened where he was framing her face, and he kissed her again. There was something else in the kiss this time. Something new. A tenderness. A vulnerability. She wasn't sure, but it made tears burn and her throat tighten. She felt utterly and completely cherished, treasured beyond words, despite all he was.

Zane pulled back to look at her, his eyes boring into hers. "You're mine," he said, his voice rough. "Mine."

Her throat tightened even more, and she nodded, not quite able to speak.

His eyes still boring into hers, he moved his hips, sliding his cock past her barriers and plunging deep inside her. She gasped, her heart tightening at the feel of him buried inside her. "It feels so right, doesn't it?"

"Yeah." Still not taking his gaze off her, he withdrew, and then thrust again, deeper this time, making her body ache for more. "It does. You do. We do." He braced his hands beside her head, looming over her on the bed. "I give you my everything, Taylor Shaw. It's not much, and you deserve more, but it's my all."

Tears filled her eyes, but before she could answer, he kissed her, a devastating, sensual kiss that seemed to carve a path through the aching loneliness in her heart. She wrapped her legs more securely around his hips, locking him against her as he drove deeper again and again, each thrust coiling desire more and more tightly through her, until she felt as if her entire body was going to explode.

She met his gaze, unable to drag her focus off his face. He was watching her so intently, as if he were trying to memorize her every feature so he could hold it in his memory forever. He was so present in this moment with her, making her feel like it was only about them, that this moment had meaning because it was the two of them coming together.

He cupped the back of her head and kissed her again, a feverish dominating kiss that tore through her like a fire that would never be stopped. Her entire body coiled, and she gripped his shoulders, gasping at the tension amassing inside her. This was her moment, her man, her everything.

"I'm yours, forever yours," he whispered, and then he took one final plunge that thrust her over the edge into an abyss of sensation.

"*Zane.*" She clung to him as the orgasm raked through

her. He bucked against her, and she knew the moment he surrendered. His entire body went taut, his muscles became rock hard beneath her hands, and then he shouted her name, driving deep inside her as the orgasm took him, sending him over the same precipice as she, until there was nothing left to hold onto but each other.

Chapter 11

Zane wanted to stay right where he was and never move...for at least ten minutes, until he recovered, and then he wanted to make love to Taylor again. And *then,* never move again. Until he recovered, and then—

"Wow." Her sigh of contentment interrupted his fantasies, making him smile.

He grinned as Taylor nestled against him, her hair tickling his chest. "Yeah, it was."

She splayed her hands over his stomach, tracing designs on his skin. "You're going to make it hard for me to go back to my real life," she said.

His amusement faded, and his arm tightened around her instinctively. "When are you leaving?"

She shrugged. "I promised Mira I'd stay 'til after the baby is born and help out. I have about six weeks of vacation accumulated, but I doubt I can take them all. They need me."

Six weeks. Or a week. He wasn't a long-term guy in any way, but the thought of Taylor getting on an airplane didn't sit well with him. But shit. What did he have to offer her? Nothing.

"Can I ask you something?" Her voice was slurred with contentment, making something inside him warm.

He liked that she was relaxed. He liked that he was the one she was relaxing with. "Yeah, sure. Ask away." Anything was better than dragging himself down about her leaving.

"Why did you quit bull riding?"

A cold wind swept through him, and he stiffened.

Taylor lifted her head to look at him, her brow furrowed. "What's wrong?" Her guileless gaze was fastened on him, utterly devoid of ulterior motive. He realized her question was genuine, not some tabloid wannabe trying to get the scoop on him.

Shit. He had to chill. Taylor was different. She wasn't like the others.

With a sigh, he stretched out on his back, staring at the cracked ceiling as he ran his fingers along her spine. He never talked about his past, not to anyone, but for some reason, he wanted Taylor to know. She'd trusted him with her deepest secret, and he owed her that much. "Before I was born, my mom shacked up with my father. They never got married, but he knocked her up. We lived with him for a while, and then moved out." He concentrated on the feel of her skin beneath his hand, trying to distance himself from the story he was telling. "She never held a job. She just hooked up with assorted men and slept with them in exchange for being able to live with each of them and have him support us, until she got tired of him and moved on."

Taylor frowned, and propped herself up on her elbow to look at him.

He didn't look at her. He didn't want to see what she was thinking. Instead, he kept his gaze on the ceiling. "Most of the men she was with were bastards. I learned fast to vacate when her boyfriends were around. By the time I was five, I was spending my days on the streets. I was already trouble, I'll admit that."

Taylor scooted on top of him, so she was laying on his chest, her chin resting on her palms, while she watched him.

Zane scowled at her for interfering with his attempt not to make eye contact, but she smiled gently. "It's okay, Zane. I already knew you grew up poor, and you told me you were like those boys. I knew that before I slept with you. I'm not going anywhere."

At her words, something inside him eased, a tight knot that had been there for as long as he could remember. She knew who he was, and she wasn't going to leave him. With a sigh, he lifted her hair off the back of her neck and let it slide through his fingers. "When I was six, I ran into Chase. He took one look at me, and he said I looked too much like a Stockton not to be his brother. I asked my mom, and she said yes. I was psyched, you know? I had brothers. I had family. I belonged somewhere."

She smiled. "Chase seems like a good guy."

"He's a great guy." Zane couldn't keep the faint smile off his face. "He dragged me out to the ranch, which was owned by some old guy named Skip back then. Chase and his brothers, my brothers, used to go out there all the time and take care of the horses, and I got to tag along. The ranch wound up being my salvation. I had a talent for riding, and I loved it. Dealing with those bulls gave me a place for my anger and aggression." He picked up her hand and pressed a kiss to her palm, needing to ground himself in her presence. "I was poor, my mother was a slut, and everyone thought I was worthless, until I met Chase and started riding bulls. I had a major chip on my shoulder, and if it wasn't for the bulls, I would have wound up in prison for life."

She smiled. "So, you found your place?"

"Not really." He sighed. "My brothers had mostly grown up together. They had a closeness I never quite broke into. Yeah, I was one of them, but at the end of the day, I went back to whatever shit hole we were living in at the time, and they went home together. I hated being an outsider, both with my own brothers and in society. I figured if I became a star bull rider, I'd matter. I'd belong."

She cocked her head, her eyes sharper than he'd expected. "It didn't change anything, did it? The money? The fame?"

"I tried. I filled my life with women and parties and big trucks. I thought I was the man." He twisted her hair around his index finger. "I found a woman I thought was right. We were engaged. I was on top of the world."

"And then?" Her voice was soft, non-judgmental, and he found himself looking at her, wanting to see her, needing to connect with her.

"We were leaving a bar late one night with some other riders. There were some boys hanging around outside, kids like the ones you saw today, kids like I used to be. They wanted autographs, but a couple of the guys told 'em to take a hike." He gritted his jaw, that same anger returning. "They treated

those kids like shit. My fiancée actually called them filth. *Filth.*"
He met her gaze. "I'd once been one of those kids, Taylor. The
people I called my friends treated them the same way that all
those people had treated me as a kid. I felt like I'd betrayed who
I was, and that my friends had betrayed me. How had I become
the kind of person whose friends were like all the bastards who
treated me like shit when I was poor? They liked me now, because
I was rich and famous. It was just...it was crap." The same fury
and self-loathing boiled through him. "I quit at the end of that
season. I was done. I didn't want to live that life or be with those
people."

She was still watching him. "But bull riding is all you
know," she said, far too observant. "It's your identity, isn't it?
Without it, you don't know what to do."

He shrugged. "I don't belong anywhere. I don't belong
with any people. Which is fine. I don't care. I live my life, and
I'm free to go where I want. No one counts on me, and I don't
count on anyone. It works."

She was still resting her chin in her hands, studying
him. "I count on you," she said softly.

His hands stilled in her hair, and something shifted in
his chest. "Shit, Taylor, I told you—"

She put her finger on his lips to silence him. "I didn't
mean that I'm counting on you to marry me. I just meant that I
count on you to be the man I trust, the one that makes me feel
like I matter. I don't belong anywhere either, Zane. My parents
are long gone. I travel so much that I don't even know if my
fridge actually works. Mira is my only connection, and now I've
lost her too, in a way. But when I'm with you, I feel like..." She
paused, as if she were trying to find the words. "I feel like my
soul can stop fluttering around, and it can just rest in your arms
and breathe."

He stared at her, shocked by her words, by the way
she'd articulated exactly how he felt when he was with her. He
wouldn't have been able to explain it, but the moment she'd said
it, he'd known she was right. "That's how I feel."

She smiled, a gentle, genuine smile that seemed to light
up her eyes. "I'm glad. You deserve to feel like that, but you
know, I get the feeling that Chase and Steen would be willing for

you to land there, on the ranch."

"I know." He started trailing his hands through her hair again. "But it's not my thing. I'm not that kind of guy who connects like that. Trying to put down roots is a trap. It makes you blind."

"Like when you didn't see the true nature of your friends and fiancée?"

He nodded. "Exactly like that. I won't make that mistake again. I like my brothers, and I've got their backs, but I don't fit with them, not on a permanent basis." He lifted his head to kiss her, needing to feel the softness of her lips against his.

She melted against him, returning the kiss with such warmth that his gut seemed to twist inside him. Suddenly, he didn't want to talk anymore. He just wanted to lose himself in Taylor, in her kiss, and in her body.

In a single swift move, he rolled over, flipping her beneath him without even breaking the kiss. She slipped her arms around his neck, kissing him back as he moved his knee between her thighs. He was already hard, needing to be inside her. After working so hard to create a solid, immovable foundation under him that no one could derail, he suddenly felt like he was standing on quicksand, and everything he knew was slithering out of his grasp.

He nudged his cock at her entrance, and found she was ready for him. Heat roared through him, and he sheathed himself inside her, desperate to ground himself in her, needing her to be his rock.

She whispered his name, wrapping her legs around his waist as he withdrew and then slid even deeper. As he made love to her, he pulled back, searching her face for the answers to questions he couldn't articulate.

Her fingers laced behind his neck, and she smiled at him. No words, just that private smile that seemed to unleash a thunder inside him.

Suddenly, he felt lost, so unbearably lost, like he was a four-year-old kid, standing on his front porch, trying to understand where he was supposed to go, and how he was supposed to survive. "Taylor." Her name tore from him with a rawness he hadn't intended, and he captured her mouth in a desperate kiss.

He didn't know what he wanted, all he knew was that it was Taylor he needed. Her kiss, her touch, and her voice. Somehow, she filled a void inside him that he hadn't even known was there, but at the same time, being with her created a restlessness inside him that he didn't know how to fix. He plunged deep inside her, and he felt her muscles contract as the orgasm took her. He didn't hesitate, abandoning all vestiges of control so that he tumbled into the orgasm with her, holding her more tightly than he'd ever held anything, or anyone, in his life.

And he still felt like his grip on her was slipping...

⚅ ⚅ ⚅

Taylor awoke to the shrill ring of her phone. It was the ringtone she'd assigned to Edward, back when he'd been her boyfriend as well as her boss. He'd promised to allow her an actual vacation, but apparently, he was a liar. Too asleep to open her eyes, her hand shot toward her nightstand.

When she didn't find her phone, or even a nightstand, she became aware of Zane wrapped around her, his arms tucking her securely against him. She smiled sleepily, and nestled more deeply into his embrace, as she recalled the previous night. She, the queen of being attached to her phone, had actually left it in her purse when she'd been distracted by an entire night of loving with Zane. She ran her hand over his bare shoulder, and smiled. Her body ached in a thousand places, and all of it was perfect.

Her phone rang again, jerking her back to the present. Her smile fading, she started to slide out from under the covers to retrieve her phone, but Zane's arm snaked out and locked around her waist. He dragged her mercilessly back into the bed without any apparent effort. "Don't answer it," he mumbled, sounding half-asleep.

"It's my boss. I have to." She tried to wiggle out from under his arm, but he gripped her more tightly.

"You're on vacation," he muttered. "In my bed. No phones allowed."

The phone rang again, an incessant beckoning she couldn't ignore. "Zane. It might be important. Let me go." She tried to roll away from him again, but this time, he dragged her all the way into the middle of the mattress, lifted himself up just enough to scoot her beneath him, and then lowered himself on top of her, pinning her to the mattress as he buried his face in the crook of her neck.

"Love this," he said, his voice muffled. "Waking up with you."

The sleepy honesty of his voice chased away her irritation at being banned from her phone, and she sighed, relaxing back into the sheets. It felt absolutely decadent to have him wrapped around her. She felt like she was waking up in a cocoon of love... well...not *love*, but love. "Zane." She wrapped her arms around his neck and tangled her feet over his calves, feeling her whole body shudder with relief as she allowed herself to focus on him.

He was right. This was where she wanted to be. With him.

Her phone buzzed that Edward had left a message, and she grimaced. "I should at least check the message—"

He shut her up with a kiss designed to distract her completely from anything but the feel of his body.

It worked.

Yes, real life was hovering in the background, but Zane was right. She was on vacation, in his bed, being kissed most deliciously by a naked cowboy with a heart the size of Wyoming.

Why in heaven's name would she answer her phone?

She wouldn't.

Forget the phone.

For now.

❧ ❧ ❧

The tightness of Zane's grip on her hand told Taylor all she needed to know about the emotional state of the cowboy sauntering into the funeral as if he owned the place. He was wearing dark blue jeans, a collared shirt, and he'd even shaved. She noticed that he'd selected cowboy boots, despite his avowed aversion to the cowboy identity anymore. He looked incredibly handsome, but at the same time, there was a vulnerability and pain in his eyes that he couldn't hide from her, and his grip on her hand was relentless, as if he were afraid she'd walk away and leave him to face it alone.

He'd sat on his bike for ten minutes down the street from the church, watching everyone walk in, his hands so tight around the handlebars that it was as if they'd become fused to the bike. It had taken him so long to move that she'd begun to think he wasn't going to attend when he'd finally started the bike rolling forward again, sliding it up beside the dumpster on the far side of the lot.

"Zane!" The boy he'd spoken to yesterday at the Garage ran up as they entered the church, throwing his arms around Zane.

Zane swore under his breath, but he wrapped his free arm around the youth, despite the death grip he still had on Taylor's hand. "I'm sorry, Luke." His voice was rough and harsh. "It's my fault."

Luke's brow furrowed as he pulled back to look at Zane. "How is it your fault?"

"I should have been there. I should have found a way. I—"

Taylor squeezed his hand gently, and he looked over at her, pain etched on his face. "You did more for him than anyone else ever did, I would bet," she said softly. "Didn't you?"

He stared at her for a second, then shrugged.

"Zane," Luke said, gripping Zane's arm tightly. "Will you be at the Garage today?" His young face was eager, almost desperate. "I'll shoot hoops with you."

Zane sighed and shook his head. "I told you about my brother, right? The one with the ranch?"

Luke frowned. "Yeah."

"He's about to get married and have a kid. I told him I'd help him out. I have to go to the ranch for a couple weeks. I'll be back soon, though, okay?"

Luke nodded, but there was no mistaking his crestfallen face. "Okay. Sure. Whatever."

"Hey." Zane caught his arm as the boy turned away.

Luke looked back at him. "What?"

"I *will* be back. I'm not abandoning you. You can count on me." His voice was fierce, almost angry, but Luke didn't look scared. On the contrary, he looked relieved.

Luke nodded. "Okay." This time, however, he was smiling.

"Okay." Zane held his arm for one more second, and then released the youth. Zane didn't take his eyes off Luke as he walked across the church toward the front pew, joining Ross, the manager of the Garage, two other women, and a young boy maybe four years old, who was leaning on the back of the pew, watching Zane with wide eyes.

"Is that Luke's family?"

"That's his kid brother, Toby, but they don't have any other family. They're foster kids. His mom's in prison for drugs, and his dad is some deadbeat that no one can find. Ross footed the bill for the funeral, since his brother came to our place." His gaze was moody as he watched Luke put his arm around Toby. "They have no chance," he said softly. "It's a no win for them. They have nothing."

Taylor's heart tightened. "What about aunts or uncles?"

Zane looked over at her. "You got any of those?"

She shook her head.

"Neither do they. Most of the people here didn't know Brad. They're just coming because it's at their church." The anger in his eyes burned, and her heart turned over at the depth of his emotions. But before she could say anything, another boy came up. She recognized him as Luke's little brother, Toby. He slid his hand into Zane's, and Zane immediately crouched down to eye level, engaging in a whispered conversation that she couldn't overhear.

She let out her breath and looked around. The service was sparsely attended, but there were a few adults and some kids, mostly boys. The church was simple, but well-kept, and it had the aura of a place that was pulsing with life and vitality. She was glad that Ross had arranged for the funeral to be held in the church. Maybe the people in attendance hadn't known the boy, but they were there for him.

Toby ran back to the front of the church and climbed up next to Luke in the front pew. Zane had moved away from Taylor, talking in low tones to a woman wearing a navy suit and sensible heels. She looked like she could be a social worker, or a teacher, there to take note of the proceedings. As she watched, another boy tugged on Zane's hand, and he broke off the conversation to talk to the boy, crouching down to give him his full attention.

Her heart began to tighten as she watched Zane interact with the boys. He treated every one of them as if they were the most important conversation he'd had all day, and she could see in their eyes how much his respect meant. He was a natural with them, his soft heart obvious.

He might not want children of his own, but he had enough of a heart to encompass the world.

Tears burned in her eyes, and she had to look away, taking a deep breath to combat the sudden sense of loss. Zane might think he was broken and isolated, but he lived with his full heart and soul more than anyone she'd ever met. He cared, and he used his time to matter. What did she do? All she did was run around with a smartphone and laptop, making sure the hotel had pressed her suits in time for her next meeting.

She couldn't remember ever having the kind of community that Zane was clearly surrounded by.

The music began to play, and Zane walked back over to her. "Hey." His face was taut, and the muscles in his jaw were tense. He grabbed her hand, gripping her tightly as he pulled her toward him.

She realized that despite the show of ease he was putting on, and the connection he had with so many of these kids, in truth, he was nearly undone by the situation. The loneliness she'd felt drifted away, replaced by a need to be there for him. "Let's sit." She led him to a nearby pew, one that was empty.

He sat next to her, so close that his shoulder was against hers. He leaned forward, bracing his forearms on his thighs. His shoulders were bunched, and his head was down, and he'd sandwiched her hand between his. The tension radiating from him was palpable, and she leaned forward, resting her face against his. "Do you want to leave?"

He nodded. "But I have to stay."

"Okay." She leaned against him as the minister began to talk about the value of life, and honoring those who are no longer with us.

Zane's grip tightened on her hand. "This shouldn't have happened," he whispered. "I couldn't get him to come to the Garage. He thought it was a bunch of crap. I tried. I fucking tried, but not enough. I let him go. I figured he'd find his way. *Shit.*"

Her heart twisted at the depths of his self-recrimination. "Everyone chooses their own path, Zane." She kept her voice low, quietly speaking just to him. "You couldn't force him. All these other kids respond to you. You're doing a lot right. Don't let this make you doubt yourself."

He looked over at her, the desolation stark on his face. "When I was fifteen, my best friend wanted to steal a car. I had a rodeo to go to. I went to the rodeo. He crashed the car and died. If it weren't for the bulls, I'd be dead. Chase gave that to me, but I couldn't give it to the one kid who needed it."

She had no words to ease the torment on his face. "I'm sorry, Zane."

He nodded, crushing her hand between his as he faced forward again, but he was still hunched over, his arms on his thighs, and his head bowed. He wasn't moving, and appeared to be deep in thought, but the death grip he had on her hand told her the truth that he wasn't letting anyone else see: that he was barely hanging on.

She moved closer to him, resting her shoulder against his, giving him the only comfort she could give, which was the knowledge that he wasn't alone. With her, he didn't have to pretend to be anything other than who he was.

It wasn't much, but she knew that it was all he wanted from her, and she would give it to him.

Chapter 12

Being on his bike had never felt so good.

Zane gripped the handlebars more fiercely as he sped along the winding roads. He'd skipped the highway, needing the silence and solace of nature to cleanse the funeral from his system. What the hell had he been thinking, going there? He didn't belong there. Luke's face. Hell. The kid's face had been devastated when Zane had told him he was leaving.

How had that kid come to count on him? When had that happened? He'd shown them all what happened when he got involved with those kids. They died. So why had Luke and Toby looked at him like he could fix everything for them?

Shit.

He kicked up the heat, flying through the winding roads.

"Zane?" Taylor's voice echoed in his helmet.

He swore at the sound of her voice, his gut lurching. He couldn't believe he'd lost his shit in front of her. He was embarrassed as hell at the way he'd clung to her, like some pansy. But at the same time, he wasn't going to lie that if she hadn't been there, he would have walked out. She was the only reason he'd managed to stay. "Yeah?"

"You're scaring me."

He gritted his jaw. Just because he'd been silent and uncommunicative, she was getting upset? See? That was the problem when he got close to people. They wanted more from him when he had nothing more to give.

"Can you slow down?"

"Slow down?" He glanced at the speedometer, and swore when he saw how fast he was driving. He immediately eased off the gas. "That's why you're scared? Because of my speed?" Not because he'd been moody. Because he'd been driving too fast. *Hell.* He noticed suddenly how tightly she was gripping him. Her knuckles where white from holding so hard, and her thighs were clenched around his hips.

"I'm sorry," she said. "I know you needed to go fast, but it's just too much around those curves."

Shit. He was an ass for not noticing she was worried. "Sorry." He slowed even further, and he felt her take a shuddering breath and lean her head against his back.

"Thanks. I just need a minute." Her grip on his waist hadn't lessened, even though they were at a crawl now. "I'm really sorry. I don't want to interfere."

"It's okay." His irritation at her disappeared, replaced by guilt about failing to notice what he was doing to her. He burned for the adrenaline rush of speed and danger. Since he couldn't get it from the bulls anymore, he got it from the bike. He'd been an insensitive ass not to be aware that she might not feel the same way. "Let's take a break." He pulled the bike off the road, driving a few yards off the main road into a cluster of trees. He stopped the bike and turned it off.

Taylor sagged against him, her entire upper body limp against his back. She peeled her hands off his waist. As she moved them, he saw they were trembling. Guilt hammered hard and he took her hand in his, pressing a kiss to her palm. "I'm sorry," he said. "I'm really, really sorry."

"You're upset. It's okay."

"No, it's not." He swung his leg off the bike and jerked his helmet off. Taylor already had hers off. Her face was pale, and her hair was a mess. A sexy-as-hell mess that he wanted to bury himself in and forget all the crap. Except he couldn't. He'd betrayed her by scaring her. "Listen." He ran his hand through his hair, wishing he was anywhere but where he was, and living any life except the one he was living. "It was a complete asshole move to drive that fast. I didn't even realize you were scared. *Shit.*" Unable to take the steadiness of her gaze, he moved away, his boots kicking up dust from the parched ground.

He heard Taylor sigh behind him, and his jaw tightened. Maybe this was for the best, a steady reminder for both of them that he wasn't a man she should count on. Even if he wanted to be the kind of guy people could depend on, he couldn't do it. Better that they both remembered.

He hopped up onto a six-foot boulder, sat down, and draped his arms over his knees, glaring at the foothills in the distance. How was he going to go back to the ranch right now? How was he going to keep sleeping with Taylor? This was why he never committed to a place. If no one expected anything from him, he could take off when he wanted. Right now, he just wanted to ride until he was so far away from everything that it felt like he never had to go back.

Taylor's boots scraped on the rock, and he tensed, listening to her as she climbed up beside him. His fists bunched, but he didn't look at her as she sat next to him, mimicking his pose.

He ground his jaw, waiting for the recriminations that he knew would come. Which would she start with? His antisocial behavior at the funeral? The fact he'd scared her on the bike? It didn't matter. He'd already apologized. There was nothing more he could do.

"After Dan left me for that other teacher, I left town for six weeks," she said quietly.

He didn't look at her, but his jaw tightened at the reminder of the man she'd given her heart to. He wasn't worthy of her, and he didn't want the obligations of a relationship, but the thought of her with anyone else hurt like hell.

"I just got in my car and drove over seven thousand miles."

He glanced over at her then, but she wasn't looking at him. She was staring across the parched plains, hugging her knees to her chest and resting her chin on them. She looked vulnerable and small, and he wanted to drag her into his arms and protect her. Why did he have the hero complex with her? He wasn't meant for that role.

She continued, apparently ignoring his turmoil. "I was trying to find a place to settle down. I drove through so many small towns, looking for the place that called to me, but, as you might expect, there were children and men everywhere I went."

A small laugh escaped him. "Bastards."

She managed a half-smile, but she didn't pick her chin up from her knees. "I finally realized that any kind of home would make the loss too great. So, I got a job that required me to travel almost all the time, and that was it. I basically gave up a home and connections. Mira is the only friend I still have who's not a part of my work, and my work friends are just colleagues."

He frowned, listening carefully now. "So, you're like me, only you use a plane and I use a bike."

"Yep. That's why I knew what you were doing today." She finally looked over at him. "Here's the thing, Zane. You might think you're not worthy or you don't belong, but you're wrong. The reason Luke and those boys look up to you is because they know you respect them and would do anything to help them." She smiled when he started to feel mutinous again. "Your brothers want you home, too. You have so many people who care—"

"I didn't ask them to care."

"I know, but they do." She turned to face him. "They all know the real you, and your background, and they see value in you anyway. Believe them when they say you're worthy."

He ground his jaw. "I know I'm a decent guy. I just don't want to owe anyone anything. When people count on you, you're going to fail them."

"Like how your mom failed you?"

He shrugged. "My mom sucked. She's not worth talking about." His dad was a bastard too. A perfect team. At least his mom had moved out of the Stockton house before his dad had started beating him, unlike his brothers.

"Maybe you're more worried about people failing you, than you are about failing them."

Okay, that was enough. He wasn't interested in this kind of discussion. He stood up to vault off the rock. "Let's get going—"

"I'm scared that people are going to fail me," she said softly, not moving. She was staring out across the plains again. "I didn't realize it until I met you. You made me see that I was living in a cocoon. When I got here, and I was shut out by Mira, I wanted to leave. Yesterday morning, I wanted to leave, too. When everyone was sitting around the table, I felt like I didn't belong."

He got that sentiment. He wanted to leave right now. But he was rooted to the spot, unable to drag himself away from her. He needed to hear what she was saying.

She looked up at him, her eyes shimmering with emotion. "In the last few days, you've made me laugh. You've made me feel joy, sadness, love, and connection. You've given me the best love making of my life. You brought me to life. I didn't want it. I wanted to stay in my shell, but today with you has been the best day of my life, I'm pretty sure."

He stared at her, barely able to process her words. He'd been an ass. He'd scared her. He'd come clean about what a mess he was. She'd seen the real him on every level, and that had been a *good* day for her? "I don't understand." He knew he sounded like an idiot, but he was absolutely confused about how she could say those things after how he had been.

She smiled, a tender smile full of such warmth that he slid to his knees before her, unable to keep the distance between them anymore. She touched his cheek, a gentle caress that made him want to close his eyes and lean into it. But he didn't. He just waited, not even sure what he was waiting for. He just knew that she had something he needed, something he was desperately craving, even though he had no idea what it was.

Taylor laced her fingers behind his neck, resting her wrists on his shoulders. "Just you," she said softly. "You're enough, just the way you are. If you were different, you wouldn't be what I needed so badly."

He wrapped his fingers around her wrists. "You deserve a man who will be there for you. You want the picket fence and babies. I can't do that—"

She shook her head. "The picket fence dream is long gone," she said, with a conviction that made something in his gut ache.

He didn't want her to give up on that dream. It pissed him off that she could even say it, because he knew how much she craved it in her soul. "Don't say that—"

She pressed a finger to his lips. "I wouldn't trust a picket fence even if it came knocking at my door. The reason I can relax with you is because that life is off the table. I needed you, just you, to bring me back to life. I see your greatness, Zane, and maybe it's because of your refusal to see it in yourself that I see it so clearly. Maybe it's because I need to see someone worth believing in, because I haven't had a lot of people in my life to believe in."

He swore under his breath. A part of him wanted to stand up and announce that he'd never, ever let her down, that he could be the guy that she could believe in, but there was a dead kid who would prove that was a lie. "Don't believe in me." He hated to say the words. If there was one person on the planet that he'd want to be worthy of, it was Taylor. He didn't want to drive her away, even though he knew he had to.

"You know what I think?" she asked, ignoring his orders, much to his selfish relief.

"What?"

"I think you should take your portion of the ranch, and create a place for kids to come and learn about horses, the way you did. Brad didn't want to play basketball or use computers, but maybe horses would have reached him, the way they did you."

For a split second, he stared at her, shocked by the idea. A part of him ignited with fire at the idea...and then he shook his head. "That would require me to commit to them. I can't do that. I don't know how to stay in one place."

She cocked her head. "That's a bunch of crap, Zane. You know it. You're just scared, but you know what? You're a bull rider. You, of anyone, should know how to overcome fear."

"It's not fear. It's reality. I know how much it sucks when someone lets you down, and I know myself well enough to know that I'll screw up eventually."

"Of course you will. Everyone does. That's okay."

"No, it's not. Not when people are counting on you." He sighed and ran his hand through her hair. "You're such an idealist," he said softly. "How do you see so much good in the world?"

"I don't. You made me."

He saw the truth in her eyes, and something inside him shifted. Was it really possible that he'd done something decent in his life, something that mattered? Because if he'd made a difference to Taylor, then, yeah, that was worth doing. He slipped his hand into her hair and kissed her, his lips gliding over her softer ones.

She responded instantly, telling him without words that she wasn't mad, that she didn't judge him. She truly accepted him, and wanted nothing from him except whatever it was he felt like giving her. A part of him didn't like that, because he wanted her to demand the world from him and anyone she trusted, but at the same time, it was a tremendous relief, the knowledge that he didn't have to be more than he was.

He cradled her face, kissing her more deeply, needing the connection with her. He loved the taste of her mouth, the feel of her lips, and the softness of her skin. He could lose himself forever in her and never want to go back to the world he inhabited.

She made a small sound of pleasure, and wrapped her arms around his neck. He pulled her against him, using his weight to keep their balance so they didn't tumble off the rock. They were exposed to the world in all directions, perched on their pedestal, but he didn't care. He just wanted her.

In the distance, he heard her phone ring, and she tensed slightly in his arms. "Work?" he asked between kisses.

"Yes. That's the ring I have for my boss."

"He gets his own ringtone?" Damn. He wanted her to assign a ringtone to him. The phone rang again, and he felt her attention wander toward it.

No. This was *his* moment with her. No one else got to intrude.

Zane angled his head, deepening the kiss, dragging her attention back to him. When she sighed and wrapped her arms more tightly around his neck, he felt a primal sense of satisfaction. He knew how much her work meant to her, and she'd chosen him. He didn't want her to invest in him, but at the same time, he wanted her to choose him, give him his own ringtone, and park herself in his life and never leave—

His phone rang next, echoing across the parched earth

from where he had it stashed in his bike.

"Who is it?" she asked.

"I don't know. Everyone gets the same ringtone on my phone." He caught her mouth in a kiss again, whispering against her lips. "The only person I want to talk to is right here, so I'm not answering."

She smiled. "You do realize when you say things like that, it makes me melt for you, don't you?"

He grinned and dragged her into his arms, his cock rock hard. "You're at my mercy, woman. I love that." He cupped her breast as he nipped her earlobe.

She gripped his upper arm. "We're in plain view, Zane. Don't—" He cut off her protests with a kiss. He didn't care where they were. He just wanted her now. He had so much emotion swirling inside him, and Taylor seemed to take away all the shit and leave behind relief.

She sighed and kissed him back, arching into him as he slipped his hand beneath her shirt and pinched her nipple—

Her phone rang again, and this time it was a different ringtone.

She stiffened again, breaking the kiss "That's Mira's ringtone."

"When do I get my own ringtone?" He didn't stop kissing her.

"I don't even have your phone number." She put her fingers over his mouth, seriously impeding his seduction skills. "What if the baby's coming?"

Zane shook his head. "She said it wasn't coming for a while—" Then he cut himself off, remembering the call that had just come in on his phone. He didn't get many calls. What if that had been about the baby? Sudden tension poured through him. He leapt down off the rock and sprinted over to his bike. He unearthed his phone as Taylor climbed down from the rock.

He had a missed call from Chase. Swearing, he called his brother as Taylor ran over.

Chase answered on the first ring. "The baby's coming. Something's wrong. We're at the hospital. Can you take over at the ranch?"

Taylor grabbed the phone from him. "Chase? What's

happening? I want to talk to Mira!"

"We don't know what's going on yet. Mira can't talk to you right now. I was using her phone to call you because I didn't have your number. If you guys can go back to the ranch and take care of the animals, we'll call—"

"No!" Tears glistened in Taylor's eyes. "I'm not going to the ranch. I'm coming to Mira. Where are you?"

Chase swore. "Listen, there's nothing you can do—"

"She's my best friend," Taylor interrupted fiercely. "You don't get to send me away. Where are you?"

Zane held out his hand for the phone. Wordlessly, Taylor set it in his hand. Zane held it to his ear, while Taylor pressed her head next to his to listen. "Bro, shut the hell up. I'll find someone to do evening feed at the barn. You don't get to play solo on this one, and you know Mira would want Taylor there if you'd just ask her. Their bond is like ours. We're coming. Got it?"

He felt Chase's relief over the phone. "Yeah, okay, thanks. It's rough, man. I could use you, as long as the animals are okay."

"They'll be fine. You're at the regional hospital?" He'd been there many times, after assorted bull riding accidents when he was growing up.

"Yeah." Chase lowered his voice. "I'm scared, man. Mira and this kid are my life."

"We're on our way." Zane hung up, and jammed his phone in his bag. Taylor was already reaching for her helmet, and her face was ashen. The helmet slipped out of her fingers and thudded to the ground.

Zane retrieved it for her, and set it on her head. Her hands were shaking so much she couldn't even grab the chinstrap. He folded his hands in hers, squeezing gently. "She's in a great place," he said. "It's a great hospital."

"Just go," she said, pushing him toward the bike. "We need to go—"

"Hey." He grasped her shoulders, forcing her to look at him. Her blue eyes were wide, her forehead furrowed with anguish. "Listen to me, Taylor. Mira is in good hands. They'll do everything possible for her, and Chase will make sure of it."

She gripped his wrists, her hands trembling violently. "She's all I have in my life, Zane. She's it. If I lose her—"

"You have me, too. I've got your back, for whatever you need. Understand?"

She stared at him. "But you said—"

"I'm made for crisis situations. I'm not going anywhere. Lean on me. I'll catch you. Got it?" Strength poured through him, an absolute determination to carry her through this, as well as Chase and Mira. This was why he'd hung around all these years, keeping his tenuous connection with his brothers. Because sometimes, all hell broke loose. He wasn't the nightly dinner kind of guy, but when the shit hit the fan, it was his party.

She nodded, tears filling her eyes. "Thank you."

"You got it." He caught her chin and kissed her, a kiss meant to reassure her that she could count on him. As he'd hoped, she gripped the front of his jacket fiercely, dragging him against her as she kissed him back, pouring all her fear and worry into her connection with him.

He locked his arm around her back and kissed her hard and deep, taking all her worry and accepting it as his own, offering her his strength.

After a long moment, she broke the kiss, and buried her face in his neck. He wrapped his arms around her and held her tight. He loved the feeling of her body pressed against his, of the way she was leaning on him for comfort and strength. He knew he wasn't a long-term guy, but in this moment, he could see the appeal of doing this for the rest of his life. Being the strong guy, the source of comfort, the one who could make her day better, felt damn good. He pressed a kiss to her hair. "Ready?"

She nodded and pulled back, her eyes searching his. "You think she'll be okay?"

He wasn't going to lie to her. He had no idea what was going on at the hospital. "Whatever happens, we're going to handle it. I promise you that."

She nodded once, biting her lower lip. "Okay." She didn't take her gaze off his as he finished strapping her helmet on. He brushed his finger over a tear sliding down her cheek. "You can do this, sweetheart. Mira needs you to be strong for her and believe in her, but you can be as scared as you want when you're with me. I've got you. Lean on me."

She nodded again. "Thank you," she whispered. "Thank you for being here with me."

"I wouldn't want to be anywhere else." He swung his leg over the bike as she climbed on behind him. As she wrapped her arms around his waist and pressed herself against him, he squeezed her hand. "I'll keep the speed reasonable."

"No. Don't. Please hurry."

He hit the ignition and the bike roared to life. "You got it." Yeah, he'd go fast, but he wasn't going to take the kind of chances he'd take when he was alone. He'd learned his lesson on that one. Taylor's safety mattered more than any kind of speed, no matter what the reason, including running away from the life he didn't want to live. "Hang on, sweetheart."

Her arms tightened around his waist, and he eased the bike forward, swinging it around to head back to the main road. The moment the tires hit the pavement, he opened it up. The wind hit hard, just as he loved, but for the first time in his life, his bike wasn't about an adrenaline rush or a chance to be alone. This time, his bike was about something more. It was his chance to do something for someone else, and it felt good.

Damn good.

Chapter 13

Taylor felt like her entire world was crumbling. The waiting room was tense and silent. Zane was sitting beside her on the couch, his arm around her. Steen and Erin were sitting beside each other on another vinyl couch, and Chase was pacing restlessly. The hospital smelled of antiseptic and broken dreams, and the white walls were unbearably stark. Nurses and other patients bustled past, a blur of activity that didn't matter, that barely registered.

Only Mira and the baby mattered, but there had been no news for too long.

"They should know by now," Chase said. His face was ash white, and he looked like he was on the verge of passing out. He sank down next to Zane, his face in his hands. "I can't lose them," he whispered. "They're my world."

Zane leaned forward, his head beside his brother's as they exchanged quiet words. Steen stood up and came over. He sat on the edge of the coffee table, leaning forward to join the conversation between the brothers.

The three men sat with their heads together, talking quietly. The intensity of the bond between the brothers was evident, and Taylor's throat tightened. This was Mira's world now, surrounded by people who loved each other and cared so deeply. She was so happy for her friend. After having to support others for so long, Mira had found a family who would never walk away from her. She'd found Chase, and acquired a posse.

"She's going to be okay," Erin said. "They both are."

Startled, Taylor looked over at Erin, who was also leaning forward, her hands clasped together. She was looking at Taylor, addressing her, bringing her into the circle that she didn't fit in. "You think so?"

Erin nodded. "She's an incredible woman, and she's so protective of her baby. There's no way she's going to give up."

Tears filled Taylor's eyes. "I know how strong she is, but—"

"No buts." Erin's eyes were glittering with unshed tears. "You can't think that way."

Taylor took a deep breath, and nodded. "Okay. They'll be fine, right?"

Erin nodded. "Of course they will—"

"Chase Stockton?" A nurse appeared in the doorway. "Come with me, please."

Chase leapt to his feet so fast he almost knocked over Steen, who had to scramble to get out of his way. "Are they okay?"

"Come meet your son. He's completely healthy."

"My son?" Chase's face paled. "And Mira? What about Mira?"

"She's still in surgery. Come on." She nodded at the others as Chase followed her. The two of them disappeared down the hall, leaving the others sitting there.

Taylor felt like she couldn't breathe. She looked around, and saw the others were equally grim. They should all be elated that there was a healthy baby boy, but with Mira's fate uncertain, there was no room for celebration. Zane pulled her against him. She sagged into his side, barely able to hold herself together.

Steen went to sit with Erin, and she nestled into his side exactly as Taylor was doing with Zane. She couldn't remember the last time she'd looked at a couple and not felt a deep pang of envy in her heart, but right now, when she looked at Steen and Erin, she just felt camaraderie. With Zane holding her, his warmth wrapping around her, even though she was facing the scariest moment of her life, she felt the safest she'd ever felt.

"How do you like living on the ranch?" Zane asked, his gaze steady on his brother.

It felt weird to have him ask a question like that when

Mira's life was so precarious, but she knew he was trying to distract them from the uncertain fate trying to crush them.

Steen looked at him in surprise. "I like it. I'm psyched about the house, and Erin's vet clinic is shaping up well." He shrugged. "I like being back with the horses. I didn't realize how much I missed them." He grinned. "There's nothing like connecting with a horse that no one else can reach. That moment when trust happens is amazing. There's nothing else like it." He looked steadily at Zane. "You need to get back in the game, bro. It's in your blood. You won't be complete until you're around the ranch. Stop fighting it. Get off the bike and get back on the bulls."

Zane stiffened, a move so imperceptible she knew that she was the only one who could tell, because she was leaning against him. "It's not my thing anymore."

Steen regarded him without flinching. "It *is* your thing. It's in your blood. The reason you can't stay still anywhere is because you're not where you should be. Live, bro. You only get one chance at life."

Taylor glanced at Zane. His face was stoic, not inviting further comment.

Erin didn't seem phased by Zane's body language. She just nodded her agreement. "You should see Steen with the animals. He literally comes alive."

He grinned at her. "I never would have tried it again if not for you."

She smiled at him, a private adoring smile filled with love. "And I'm so glad you did." She grinned at Zane and Taylor. "He comes on my rounds with me when I have an animal I know is going to be difficult. He can calm any animal. He's really amazing. And my clinic is going to be wonderful. We're going to have a full equine surgical center, the only one within a thousand miles." She laced her fingers with Steen's. "That's my specialty, you know. I mean, I love all animals, but equine surgery is my thing. I didn't think I'd be able to keep doing it out here, but there are so many horses. Steen and I combined our funds to make it happen." She squeezed Steen's hand. "He made my dreams come true. I couldn't have done it by myself."

He put his arm around her, and smiled at her, a smile so

tender that it seemed to light up the entire room. "You should see her operate," he said to Taylor and Zane. "She's gifted."

Erin was beaming now. "You guys really need to come see the clinic. It's just amazing."

Zane made a non-committal grunt, but Taylor couldn't resist. "I'd love to see it." How could she not? Erin's passion for her work was contagious, and she wanted to be a part of it, to see what it was like when someone lived a life that illuminated them so much. The happiness of the other couple was evident. It was clear they were very much in love, and that they were also following their dreams.

Taylor remembered being that excited the day she'd first walked into her own classroom. She'd forgotten what it was like to be so excited about life. She'd forgotten about being willing to love someone and be loved back. She'd forgotten about it all, until Zane had reminded her. She and Zane were exactly the same. Both of them walking away from what they loved because the baggage around it was too painful. She'd thought it was better to play it safe, but seeing how happy Steen and Erin were made her wonder if she'd been wrong all this time.

Chase appeared in the doorway, his face haggard and drawn. They all bolted to their feet, silence descending upon the small group.

Taylor gripped Zane's hand, her heart pounding as they all waited.

"She—" Chase's voice broke, and he cleared his throat.

Taylor felt the blood drain from her face, and she started to sway. Zane tightened his arm around her, keeping her on her feet.

"She's okay," Chase finally managed. "She's going to be okay. Everything is going to be okay." He looked at them all. "We have a son," he said, his voice raw with wonder. "A baby boy."

The waiting room erupted with congratulations, relief, and tears of joy. Taylor found herself swept into a circle of hugs, not just from Zane, but from everyone, the family that had taken in her best friend. She might have felt like an outsider at breakfast, but in this moment, she knew she belonged, and it was perfect.

ß ß ß

"He's so beautiful." Taylor held the tiny baby in her arms, terrified she would drop him. He was so small, so vulnerable, and so perfect as he slept in her arms. She couldn't believe how much love she felt for such a tiny bundle. Her heart felt like it was going to explode. "I can't believe you're a mom."

Mira smiled at her, her face pale but radiant as she lay among the pillows. "Me, either. I never would have thought I was ready, but here I am."

"You'll be a great mom." Taylor leaned forward, to press a kiss to his tiny forehead. "You listen to your Aunt Taylor," she told him. "Appreciate your mom, because she's the best."

Mira grinned. "Keep telling him that. I'm sure he'll need reminding if we're going to brainwash him sufficiently to listen to everything I tell him to do."

"I'll be happy to brainwash him." Taylor grinned at her best friend. "Can't you at least tell me what names you guys are considering?"

"Chase swore me to secrecy. He's afraid we'll be harassed by you and his brothers to pick a certain one, so I'm not allowed to tell."

Taylor wrinkled her nose. "I would never try to influence you."

"No?" Mira raised her brows. "I doubt that." She cocked her head, a new gleam in her eyes. "What's going on with you and Zane? What happened on your trip?"

Taylor glanced toward the door, but the men weren't back yet. They'd been down in the cafeteria getting food when the nurse had let Taylor in, so she'd had a chance to meet the baby first. "He's a great guy," she hedged.

Mira didn't let her off the hook. "Did you sleep with him?"

Taylor couldn't keep the goofy, deliriously happy grin off her face, and Mira clapped. "I love that smile, sweetie. You look so happy."

She shrugged, trying not to smile, but totally failing. "He's such a good man, Mira. He really is. We get each other, you know?"

Mira raised her eyebrows. "So...maybe you'll stay in town, then?"

Taylor's smile faltered. "What?"

"Listen, I didn't want to say anything or pressure you, but I miss you."

A lump formed in Taylor's throat. "You do? I miss you, too. So much it hurts," she admitted softly.

Mira nodded. "I love my new family, but you're in my heart, too. I can't imagine my child growing up and not knowing his Auntie Taylor. I know you don't love your job. Maybe it's time to quit. Start being a teacher again. Move here." Mira cocked her head thoughtfully. "Hang out with Zane. Maybe he's the guy for you."

Taylor cradled the infant against her chest, her fingers brushing lightly over the soft fuzz on his head. Tears burned in her eyes, and she fought not to cry. "I miss you so much," she whispered, "but I can't move here."

"Why not?"

"I have my job—"

"Which you don't like. Who wants to work for an ex-boyfriend? It's been a nightmare and you know it. And there's Zane—"

"Zane and I connect because I'm leaving. We have an understanding that it's a short term thing—"

"Chase said it doesn't look like that," Mira interrupted. "He said Zane couldn't keep his hands off you, out there in the waiting room." She met Taylor's gaze, deep understanding in her blue eyes. "These Stockton men have had really tough lives. They don't trust anyone. They don't believe that life can bring them good things. It takes a special woman to reach them, and you've done that with Zane. They don't love lightly, but when they love, it's forever."

Taylor stared at her in shock. "He doesn't love me." Did he? He didn't. He couldn't. He wasn't made that way. Love was just...there was no room for love.

Mira raised her brows. "Do you love him?"

"No," she said quickly, too quickly. The moment she denied it, she felt something constrict in her chest. She looked desperately at Mira, who had a sympathetic expression on her face. *Did* she love him? Was it possible? "Well, I mean, I do, as a human being. How could I not? He's such a good man. But that's different than romantic love—"

"Is it?" Mira challenged. "Can you really tell me that you haven't fallen completely in love with him, not simply as a human being, but as a man? I can see it in your eyes, Taylor. I know you do."

"I can't. I can't go there again," she whispered, staring in horror at her friend. Her stomach felt like there were a thousand butterflies spinning around in it.

"You can. You need to learn to trust just like he does." Mira smiled gently. "You're an amazing woman, Taylor. It was only a matter of time until a great guy noticed."

"But—"

A light knock sounded on the door, and Taylor snapped her mouth shut. She glanced toward the door, and heat flared in her cheeks when she saw the three Stockton brothers in the doorway, along with Erin.

Chase looked back and forth between the women. "Are we interrupting?"

"Yes," Mira said, at the same moment that Taylor said, "No." She was so grateful for the interruption. She just didn't want to go where Mira had been trying to take her.

Chase grinned, and walked into the room. "It doesn't really matter. I want to show off my son." He held out his arms for the baby, and Taylor reluctantly handed him over. The moment the baby was out of her arms, she felt a sudden sense of sadness, a gaping loneliness she hadn't felt in so long.

She sank back in her chair as she watched Chase turn toward his brothers, the baby so very tiny against his broad chest and muscular shoulders. Zane was hanging back, looking uncomfortable as Steen and Erin fawned over the newborn.

Taylor's loneliness faded as she watched Zane step awkwardly around the cooing threesome, heading across the room toward her. She might want a baby more than her heart could manage, but Zane clearly wasn't suffering from the same angst. It was apparent by his discomfort that he didn't have the baby gene. He hadn't lied to her when he said he wasn't a baby guy. Was it possible that he truly didn't have the instinct to be a father? That there was a chance that he would really be fine with who she was? So maybe, just maybe, if she did love him, it would be okay?

Her heart started to hammer in her chest, and she had to fight to breathe as he reached her. His fingers wrapped around hers as he sat down on the arm of her chair, sliding his other hand over her back. "You okay?" he asked softly, nodding toward the baby, as if he understood it might be hard for her.

She smiled at him, the emptiness fading from her heart as he settled in next to her. She nodded. "I'm good." Was Mira right? Was she falling in love with Zane? Was it really possible he was the right guy for her? What if she did give up her job? Could she be happy as a teacher if she had a man who loved her for who she was?

Chapter 14

Her phone rang, and she sighed, recognizing the ring. It was the fifth time Edward had called, and she hadn't answered once. Yes, she was on vacation, but he wouldn't be trying to reach her so much if something wasn't going on. She reached into her pocket and pulled out her phone, but Zane's hand closed over hers. "No cell phones in the hospital," he said.

She frowned up at him. "Since when do you care about the rules?"

His eyes narrowed, and for a moment, she thought he was going to say something, but he didn't. He just shrugged, and took her phone, folding his hand over it before tucking it back in her pocket.

"Zane." They both looked up as Chase walked over, holding the baby. "Here. Hold him."

"No." Zane didn't hesitate, folding his arms across the chest. "I'll take the kid on my bike when he's sixteen, but I don't want to—" He swore as Chase set the kid on his chest. He had no choice but to take the baby as Chase stepped back.

Taylor couldn't help but laugh at the horrified expression on Zane's face. "Here. You have to support his head." She helped rearrange the baby in Zane's arm, so that he was tucked up against Zane's chest, his little head leaning against him.

Zane grimaced, staring down at the child as if it might leap up and bite his head off.

The room filled with laughter, and even Taylor giggled.

Zane looked up at Chase, his face desperate. "He

blinked. I think he's waking up. You better take him."

Chase folded his arms over his chest, a broad grin making his eyes dance with happiness. "Nope. He's all yours."

Taylor leaned over Zane's shoulder, watching as the baby's eyes flickered open. His radiant blue eyes seemed to focus on Zane's face, and her breath caught as he wiggled his little hand at Zane. "Let him grab your finger, Zane."

"Seriously?" Zane looked like he was in pain as he shifted his position and poked his index finger awkwardly at the baby. The tiny fingers wrapped around Zane's finger, holding him still.

Zane frowned, staring at the baby. "Strong grip."

"Good for bull riding," Chase said.

Mira threw a pillow at him. "My son will not be a bull rider! It's too dangerous."

"Honey, he's going to be a cowboy. There's no way around it." Chase settled down on the bed, wrapping his arm around Mira and pressing a kiss to her head, leaving Zane unattended with the baby.

Taylor expected Zane to panic, but he didn't look up. He was still studying the baby.

She glanced at him, and her heart seemed to flutter when she saw the look of pure awe on his face. His head was bent over the baby, and he was whispering something to him about bull riding, his finger still trapped in the baby's tiny hand.

Taylor sat back in the chair, unable to take her gaze off Zane's face. The wonder and emotion was evident in his expression. She realized with a ripple of shock that he'd fallen in love with his nephew. She could see it on every line of his face, in the protective way he'd tucked the baby against his chest, in the softness of his expression. He no longer looked like an awkward uncle. He looked like a guy who would lay down his life for the child in his arms.

She glanced around the room to see if anyone else noticed, and she saw everyone in the room watching Zane with the same expressions of awe and delight on their faces. They all knew he'd fallen in love with the baby. It had taken less than a minute, and Zane had become a baby person.

He looked up, his gaze meeting Taylor's. His eyes were

bright, filled with more warmth than she'd ever seen. "He's perfect, isn't he?"

She nodded once, unable to speak over the lump in her throat.

"I had no idea." Zane held the baby up so he was eye level with him. "Listen, little man, I want you to know that your dad's a great guy, but I am definitely going to be your coolest uncle. Anytime your parents drive you crazy, you give your Uncle Zane a call, and I'll straighten them out. Got it?"

"You know," Chase said, his voice so deceptively casual that Taylor looked over at him. "You could move onto the ranch, and then he could just run over to your place and not waste time calling you. Steen will probably be his favorite uncle if he's the only one he sees on a regular basis."

Zane looked at Chase sharply, but instead of snapping back with his customary refusal to move to the ranch, he said nothing. Chase's eyebrows shot up in surprise at Zane's lack of resistance, and the room fell silent. Taylor's heart froze in her chest. After all his rejection of the ranch, it was the idea of being around for his nephew that made Zane pause long enough to consider breaking all his rules and moving onto the ranch.

A baby. He was willing to uproot his life for a baby, for his nephew.

At that moment, she knew the truth, the truth she couldn't deny, no matter how much she wanted to. Deep in the recesses of his scarred and broken heart was a man who would be a great dad, who had that protector, father gene deep in his soul, a man who would love his babies with every last bit of his heart. Zane was going to want children.

She let out her breath, barely able to breathe over the ache in her chest. The depth of the anguish crushing her told her all she needed to know. Too late, she realized that Mira was right. She *had* fallen in love with him. She had somehow, someway, let herself believe that this was more than a short-term fling. Her heart belonged to him, and so did her trust.

She'd been wrong to think she could keep from loving him, and wrong to believe he didn't want kids. Now her heart felt like it was shattering piece by piece as she sat there watching the man she loved falling in love with his nephew.

Not that he'd lied to her about whether he wanted to have babies, because she knew he'd spoken the truth at the time. There was no way he would have predicted his response to his nephew, but she should have known, based on how deeply he cared for the boys at the Garage.

Zane was not a man who would be content with a woman who couldn't give him children. Not anymore. No matter what he said today, eventually, there would be a time when he'd wish he'd made a different choice.

The baby started to cry, and Zane got a comically horrified expression on his face. "What do I do?"

And there it was. *What do I do?* He didn't try to hand the baby back to Chase and bolt from the scene. He asked what to do, so he could manage it himself. He wasn't even afraid of a crying baby. Just like that, his world had changed, and he was on board with it.

Chase grinned and hopped off the bed. "Unless you want to whip out a breast for him, I think this one's on Mira."

Zane laughed and handed the baby over, his fingers drifting over the baby's head as Chase took him. "Yeah, I'll pass on that one."

He sat back down beside Taylor, taking her hand in his as he grinned at her. "Did you see him? Are all babies that small?" He held up his hand. "He practically fit in my palm, but he was a real person."

She managed a smile. "Yes, they're all that small. He's beautiful." As she watched the expression of wonder on Zane's face, she felt herself falling even more in love with him. What woman wouldn't fall for a man who could love like that?

Her phone rang again, and she glanced down. It was Edward again, and for the first time since she'd arrived in Wyoming, she wanted to take the call. "I really need to get this. He's been calling for days."

Zane frowned, but she slipped out of his grasp before he could stop her. She waved her phone at the room. "I need to run outside to take this call. I'll be back in a minute." No one even really noticed as she ducked out, all of them too riveted by the miracle of life.

She let the call go into voicemail as she walked quickly

down the hall. Her heart was hammering and she wanted nothing more than to get outside and breathe fresh air. She reached the stairs and jogged down them, following the signs to the nearest exit. She didn't even care where it was. She just wanted out.

By the time she reached the steel exit door at the base of the stairs, her heart felt like it had broken into a thousand pieces. Why had Mira tried to convince her to stay? For a split second, Taylor had taken the bait and imagined that future. Living on the ranch with Zane, Mira, and the others. Being a part of a family that stood beside each other no matter what, no matter how difficult things were. It had been only a moment, but it had been enough to awaken her heart…just in time for it to be broken.

She shouldered the door open and stepped outside into the dirt parking lot behind the hospital. There were plains stretching out in front of her, and that same vast expanse of sky that looked so different over Wyoming than it did from the window of an airplane. She'd never noticed the blue before, and she'd never felt this kind of awe for the grandeur and beauty of nature.

She wanted to be here. This was the place she wanted to call home. But how could she possibly do it? She knew it would never work with Zane. So, where did that leave her? Watching him fall in love with someone else, while she played Aunt Taylor to a baby she wasn't even actually related to, trying to live vicariously through a family that wasn't really hers?

Her legs feeling like heavy weights, she walked across the dirt and sat down on a patch of grass, pulling her knees to her chest.

Her phone beeped and she looked down, surprised to see a text from Edward. As she read the words, a cold feeling seeped into her body. *Taylor. Have you even listened to my voicemails? Call me back. I've accepted a promotion. My current position is open, and it's yours. I've been trying to reach you to make an official offer. I need an answer tomorrow. Congrats on the promotion. You deserve it. Now call me!*

She stared at the phone, rereading the words over and over again. Edward was leaving. No more working for her ex-boyfriend. And he was offering her a promotion. A raise. More travel. She pressed the phone to her heart, tears falling silently down her cheeks.

Before she'd come to Wyoming, she would have been thrilled. It was everything she'd been working so hard to achieve. But now? The thought of getting on a plane and going back to that life of hotels and airports felt like it would crack her soul in half. But what was worse? Staying here and having her heart bleed every time she saw Zane or the baby?

The door to the building opened, and Zane stuck his head out the door. His brow was furrowed, and he looked so concerned that the tears started again. "Hey, babe," he said, stepping out into the parking lot. "I thought you might not be okay."

She lifted her chin and wiped the tears off her cheeks. "I'm fine. Just needed some air."

"I know." The rocks crunched under his boots as he walked across the parking lot and crouched in front of her, his forearms resting on her knees. "We need to get back to the ranch to take care of the animals."

"We? What do I know about the animals? You don't need me there." She couldn't quite keep the bitterness out of her voice.

His eyebrows shot up. "I assume you have the capability to listen to instructions, right? You seem intelligent enough to learn new skills."

She bit her lower lip and shrugged. "I guess."

He rubbed his hands over her thighs, a touch meant to comfort, not seduce, but all it did was make her tears want to fall even more. "You want to talk about it? The baby?"

"God, no." She took a deep breath. "It's fine. I'm really happy for them." How could she tell him that it wasn't the baby that had made her cry, but the fact she'd lost Zane to the baby?

He narrowed his eyes, still rubbing her thighs. "So, what's the problem then? Something wrong at work?"

"Work?" The question made her laugh, a laugh that had no joy in it. "No, that's fine." She handed him her phone with the text message on display.

Zane read the message, staring at the phone for what felt like an eternity. She frowned. How many times did he need to read it to understand what it said? "I got a promotion," she said, wondering if he'd failed to understand what Edward had written.

"I can see that." He finally looked up, an unreadable expression on his face. "Are you going to take it?"

She paused at his question. He hadn't said congratulations. He'd asked if she was going to take it. What did that mean? Was there even an option of not taking it? Was he thinking more than a few weeks with her as well? But even as she thought it, she realized it didn't matter. Falling in love with Zane would break her heart. He might not realize that he'd changed his mind about babies, but she did. "I don't know. I need to talk to Edward and get the details." She shrugged. "It's a great opportunity."

"What about teaching?" The question was blunt and without apology.

She narrowed her eyes. "I don't teach anymore."

"You could."

Frustration rolled through her. "Why are you pushing the teaching? You know I can't do it anymore. I walked away from that."

"It's your passion. Why would you reject something which makes you feel alive, and accept a safe route that drains your soul?"

His words bit deep, true words that made her angry. "Really? Isn't bull riding your passion? You rejected it because you didn't like that it put you into contact with people who don't like poor kids who tread the edges of society. Instead, you run around on that bike, not even letting yourself help the kids you want to defend."

He dropped his hand from her leg, his face going stoic. "That's my business—"

"Is it?" She stood up, suddenly so angry. "Why do you judge me, when you're just as guilty? You say you defend those kids, but even after losing one who couldn't connect to basketball in a warehouse, you still refuse to look at other options. You talk about how the horses and bull riding saved you, but you won't give those other kids the chance you had. What are you going to do with all that money you won? Let it rot in a bank account somewhere because you've convinced yourself you're worth nothing?"

He stood up slowly, his eyes narrowed. "Why are you going off on me?" His voice was even and calm, but she knew him too well not to notice how angry he was.

"Because I'm tired of being made to feel like I'm not good enough!"

He raised his eyebrows, studying her intently, as if he didn't believe her. "You are good enough. You just don't realize it."

"Really? If I'm so good, why am I not enough for a man like you? Why is it that you fall in love with a baby and not me?" Oh...crud. Had she really just said that?

Zane's eyes widened. "What?"

"Nothing." Horrified, she shoved her phone in her pocket. "I have to go." She ducked past him and raced back to the building. She grabbed the door handle and pulled...and it didn't move. She yanked again, harder, and still it didn't move.

"It's locked from the inside," he said, still standing where she'd left him.

"I can see that!" She whirled around and started stalking around the building, in what she hoped was the general direction of the front door. "You go back to the ranch. I'll catch a ride with Steen and Erin later." She pointed in the other direction. "I think you left the bike that way," she lied.

He ignored her, broke into a jog, and settled in beside her. "Taylor—"

"I don't want to talk about it. I didn't mean to say that, and I meant nothing by it, so let it go." She knew she sounded snappy, but she was just so embarrassed by what she'd blurted out. Between the baby and her job, she felt so overwhelmed right now she couldn't even think straight.

"I was just going to say that I need your help at the ranch. You promised Mira you'd help her, and this is what she needs. Erin has some critical cases she needs to attend, and one is a dangerous bull that she needs Steen's help with. They'll help out when they get back, but we're the ones that aren't needed anywhere else."

Taylor bit her lip. She *had* promised Mira. That was

why she'd come to Wyoming in the first place. So what if she'd managed to fall in love and get her heart broken? That didn't change that she owed her friend. "Fine. But you can sleep on your bike tonight."

He lightly wrapped his fingers around her elbow and leaned in, his breath warm against her ear. "Darlin', I don't know what's gotten into you, but there is no chance in hell I'm sleeping on my bike. I'll give you space for the moment, but we're talking this out tonight, whether you like it or not. Got it?"

"Fine. I'll sleep on your bike." She felt like her soul had fragmented into a thousand pieces, and she'd forgotten how to breathe. She needed space to regroup, to think, to recalibrate. She needed to find the place of equilibrium that had served her so well for so long.

"No chance of that," Zane said.

The certainty in his voice made chills run down her spine. A part of her didn't want him to give up on her. A part of her wanted him to fight for her, to prove that she was wrong for thinking that he didn't love her. But another part of her, the part that had been broken too many times, wanted him to just let her go while she could still get away.

Because right now, all she wanted to do was run.

Chapter 15

Zane leaned against the stall door, watching Taylor as she swept the aisle. They were both sweaty and exhausted, having worked for almost four hours straight to take care of all the animals. The help Zane had called in had fed and watered everyone, but the stalls had needed to be cleaned, horses turned out, and then evening rounds had been done.

Taylor had been tireless, almost relentless in her work, never slowing down long enough to talk, which was fine with him.

He hadn't figured out what to say.

Unaware that he was watching her, Taylor paused and leaned on her broom, resting her head against the handle. Her shoulders were slumped, and she looked exhausted. Her hair was a mess, she was covered in dust and shavings, and she had a smudge of dirt on her right cheek.

She was so beautiful that she made his heart stop in his chest, so vulnerable that he wanted to scoop her up in his arms and protect her forever, and so strong that he wanted to get down on one knee and bow to her. Working with her for the last four hours had reminded him of what it had been like to work on the ranch with his brothers when he was a kid. The ranch was the only time that he'd felt accepted, like he belonged. The animals never judged him, and he was so good at riding that he'd earned the instant respect of his brothers. Plus, his brothers were just as much of a stain on society as he had been, so he'd felt like their equal, not some insult to their existence.

He'd missed the ranch, he realized. He'd missed the animals, the hard work, and the smell of fresh hay and shavings. And, he'd missed the camaraderie that he'd found with Taylor, especially when she'd become too tired to remember she was mad at him.

She was tired now, and the evening had to change direction. "You ready?" he asked.

She startled, looking up at him as she pulled her shoulders back, hiding her exhaustion. "Ready for what?"

"To be finished. We're all set." He levered himself off the stall door and walked over to her, sliding his hands over hers as he took the broom. "You did great."

She didn't protest, instead sinking down on a nearby hay bale. "I'm so beat."

"I know. It was a lot of work tonight." He put the broom away. "I never could have done it without you. Between Chase, Steen, and Erin, there are a lot of animals on this ranch."

"You need help here," she said. "Especially now that Chase and Mira are going to be spending time with the baby."

"Maybe. Help costs money."

She met his gaze. "Not if they're poor kids who need a reason to believe in themselves."

And there it was, that same idea she'd been pushing at him. He sighed and sat down beside her, his shoulder leaning against hers.

She didn't move away, so he rested his forearm on his thigh and held out his hand.

After a moment, she put her hand in his. The moment his fingers wrapped around hers, he felt himself relax. He realized he'd been worried that he'd never get a chance to hold her hand again, after she'd been so mad at him earlier. Stupid thing to worry about, but he had.

"You want to tell me what's going on?" he said. The job. Her job offer. It had been gnawing at him all evening. He couldn't understand why it was bothering him so much. No, he knew why. It was because she should be a teacher, not some corporate exec living in hotels and airplanes. She was more than that. She had the biggest heart he'd ever seen, and he didn't want it killed by a sterile life.

She looked over at him, said nothing, and then shrugged. "I'm tired. I'm going to bed." Then she stood up and started to walk down the aisle.

Zane frowned, jumped up and sprinted after her, grabbing her arm just before she made it to the main doors. "What the hell is going on?"

She glared at him. "Can't you tell I don't want to talk about it? Leave me alone."

"Wow." He stiffened at her rejection, sliding back into the defensive mode he'd lived with for so long. He would not put himself out there for someone who didn't want him. Ever. "Fine." He let go of her arm, and walked away, heading back toward the shed.

Thoughts hammered through him, but he shut them out. He would not let her get to him. She didn't matter. It didn't matter what anyone thought. He reached the door, and kept walking toward his bike. He'd have to take care of the horses in the morning, but tonight was his.

He swung his leg over the bike and fired up the engine. It roared to life, filling him with the same thundering storm it always did...only it didn't work this time. It wasn't enough. He didn't want to get on that bike. He wanted to be in Taylor's arms in that bunkhouse.

Shit.

The tires began to roll, and he swung around toward the driveway, only to swear and slam on the brakes. Taylor was standing in front of him, blocking his path.

"Move," he yelled over the engine.

"No!"

He swore under his breath, backed up, and began to drive around her. She immediately ran in front of the bike again, forcing him to stop. Swearing, he stopped the bike. "Taylor—"

"Turn it off!" she yelled.

He swore and killed the engine, folding his arms over his chest as he glared at her. "What?"

"I'm sorry."

He frowned. "What?"

"I'm sorry." She sighed. "I'm sorry I took my bad mood out on you. It's not fair."

He narrowed his eyes, unwilling to trust the apology. "Doesn't matter. Is that it?"

"No!" She walked up and grabbed the handlebars. "When you turned away from me in the barn, I saw the look on your face. I knew that you thought I'd rejected you, that I'd somehow decided that you weren't good enough."

He ground his jaw. "You're wrong."

"I'm not." She sighed, suddenly looking so tired that his anger dissipated. "Listen, Zane, I'm going to say this once, not because I want anything from you, but because you need to hear it. The reason I was upset in the hospital wasn't because Mira and Chase have a baby and I don't. I was upset because you fell in love with him."

That hadn't been what he'd been expected to hear. "What are you talking about?"

"The baby. I saw the look on your face. Everyone did. You love him."

He shrugged, uncomfortable with the discussion. "He's my nephew. I'm not going to reject the kid."

She shook her head. "It was more than that. You should have seen the expression on your face. I've never seen that kind of love on a man's face. It was beautiful." She held up her hand before he could interrupt. "You've got the dad gene, Zane. You might not know it yet, but you do. Which means..." She took a deep breath.

He waited, every muscle taut in anticipation of what blow she was about to deliver.

She met his gaze. "I've fallen in love with you. So deeply that I feel like I came alive for the very first time."

His heart froze in his chest, and suddenly he couldn't breathe. He'd had countless women scream their love at him during his bull riding tenure, but never had he believed it or cared. Until now. Taylor meant it. She loved him. *She loved him.* How was that possible? She was the most giving, caring person he'd ever met. She knew all his ugly secrets, and somehow, she'd decided he was worth loving? What the hell? He could never live up to that. He could never repay her for that. What was she doing, cheating herself out of life by loving *him*? "I don't want—"

"Stop." She sighed and released the handlebars. "I think I let myself fall in love with you because you were safe. I was leaving, and you definitely wanted nothing to do with kids, so either way, I was protected. But then..." She paused.

He leaned forward, curious despite his instinct to fight back against her declaration. "Then what?" He didn't know what he wanted her to say. All he knew was that he felt his entire being was on the edge of a precipice, waiting for words he couldn't articulate.

"Then I wanted to stay."

"Stay? Where? On the ranch?" *With me?* He didn't ask the last question, because he didn't want to hear her say no. And he didn't want to hear her say yes.

"With you. On the ranch. I wanted to become a part of your amazing family."

Hell. He leaned back, his mind going a thousand miles an hour. He knew he should be telling her to find a new life, a new dream, to walk away, but the words wouldn't come. He couldn't make himself send her away, no matter how much he wanted to. He wanted to hear more.

"But then I saw you with the baby." She sighed, and he saw in her eyes a grim resignation that was heartbreaking. "You would be a great dad. You'll be a great uncle. I couldn't live with myself if I took that chance away from you. Someday, you would resent me. And I know you want your freedom anyway, so..." She shrugged. "I'll take the promotion, then—"

"No." He swung his leg off the bike and grabbed her arm just as she was turning away.

She looked at him, hope and fear gleaming in her beautiful eyes. "No, what?"

"No—" He didn't even know what he wanted to say, what he needed to say. "Just, no."

She laughed softly, that same beautiful laugh that had lifted his heart so many times. "I can't stay, Zane. I can't stay and watch you live a life with someone else—"

"There's no one else. There will never be anyone else." That much he knew was the truth. "I don't like women. I don't want one."

She laughed aloud then. "You will. You'll find someone,

and I can't watch it."

"Fuck that." He grabbed her wrist and hauled her against him. He locked his arm around her lower back, keeping her pinned against him. "Do you know what my life plan was after I walked away from bull riding?"

She raised her eyebrow and shook her head.

"I vowed to never trust anyone ever again. My plan was to count on no one, and let no one count on me. I was done with the crap of society. I just wanted to be left alone to hate the world on my own."

Her fingers wrapped around his upper arms. "That's kind of antisocial," she said. "You're worse than I am."

"But that's the thing," he said, searching her face, as if he could find in her eyes the words he couldn't come up with on his own. "That was my plan, and I was cool with it. And then I met you. And you fit me." He didn't know how to explain it any better. "I like us together."

A slow smile formed on her face. "I like us together, too," she said. "But we fit right now. We don't fit forever."

"Why not?" Shit. Had he really just said that? Was he really arguing for a forever with her?

"Because, Zane, I want to get married and be treasured for who I am. You're not ready to go there, but someday, you will realize you want kids, and I won't have you looking back and realizing that you're trapped."

His grip tightened on her arms. "What the hell are you talking about? We're wrong because you want to get married, and I don't, and also because someday, not only will I want to get married, but I will also want kids? Those two excuses are completely contradictory. You're making shit up as an excuse to walk away."

She stiffened. "I'm not making—"

"You're making shit up because you're afraid of being hurt again."

She stared at him, then a single tear spilled down her cheek. "You have the power to shatter my heart," she said softly. "I can't live through that again."

His grip on her arms softened. With a sigh, he enfolded her into his arms. She melted into him, burying her face in his chest as he held her. "I'm sorry, babe," he whispered, as he pressed a kiss to her hair.

"I'm sorry, too," she said, her face still hidden against his chest.

He pressed another kiss to her hair. He didn't even know what to say to her. He didn't know what he wanted to say. He just knew that he didn't want her to walk away from him tonight. "I don't want to hurt you," he said. "Ever."

"I know you don't." She lifted her head to look at him, her eyelashes frosted with tears. "That's why I opened my heart to you, and that's why you could break it."

He wiped his thumb over her eyelashes, brushing away the tears. "Stay with me tonight."

"Tonight?" She nodded at the bike. "I thought you were leaving."

"I don't want to leave." He slipped his fingers through her hair and bent his head, pressing a soft kiss against her mouth. "I need you." He knew he should have bailed when she'd told him she loved him, and he'd been unable to say it back. A responsible guy would step back when she'd confessed that he could hurt her. But he didn't want to let her go. He wanted to hold her in his arms and make love to her until the sun broke across the sky in one of those Wyoming dawns that he never got tired of.

She gripped the waistband of his jeans, closing her eyes as he sprinkled kisses over her cheeks, her nose, her chin, and her lips. "I don't want you to leave, either," she whispered.

Relief rushed through him, and he angled his head, taking her mouth in a real kiss, the kind of kiss that could carry a man through the very darkest of times.

He scooped her up in his arms and carried her back to their bunkhouse. She opened the door, and then he kicked it shut as soon as they were through. He didn't waste time with a shower, even though they were both grimy from working on the ranch. He needed her now, and he needed her in every way.

By the time they reached the bed, their kisses were pure wildfire. He groaned as he lowered her to her feet, sliding her down his body. Her skin was soft as he framed her waist, kissing her hard and deep, pouring everything into the kiss that he could never say. Her arms were wrapped tightly around his neck, kissing him back just as fiercely, as if she were afraid it was the last time they'd ever be together.

It wasn't.

It couldn't be.

He'd never survive without her.

Somehow, they managed to get their clothes off without breaking physical contact. The moment nakedness reigned, he picked her up again. She locked her legs around his waist as he gripped her hips, his fingers digging into her bare flesh as he relocated them onto the bed.

He was inside her before they'd even hit the mattress. He wanted to honor her with a long seduction, with kisses meant to show how incredible she was, but he couldn't do it. There was something inside him that was so desperate to connect with her that he couldn't hold back. He just buried himself inside her, needing that connection, needing to claim her, and make her his.

His kisses were desperate, his hands all over her body, his entire being shouting for her. Taylor didn't let him down. She met every kiss with equal passion, her hips moving in an invitation that ignited his need for her even more. He could feel the orgasm building, tightening around them both. It was too fast, too soon. He wanted more for her but—

The orgasm hit them both at the same time. *"Taylor."* Her name tore from him as he drove inside her, giving her all that he was, while she bucked beneath him, mercilessly caught in the same climax gripping him so hard.

It seemed to last forever, the moment of ecstasy that brought them together as one. He tried to hold onto it. He tried to make the moment last forever...but eventually, it faded, releasing them from its grasp.

Completely drained, he collapsed beside her, dragging her tightly into his arms. He locked his leg over her hips, his arms around her upper body, and buried his face in her hair, needing to get as close to her as possible.

"Zane?" She nestled into his body, tucking herself against him exactly how he wanted.

"Yeah." He pulled her even tighter.

"I love you."

He closed his eyes and pressed a kiss to her hair, his chest tightening at her words. He didn't know what to say to her. Nothing was worthy of what she gave him. "Stay," he finally said. "Don't take the job. Be a teacher."

She didn't answer for a long moment. "And what about us? What happens to us if I stay?"

He wanted to give her the response she craved. He wanted to be that guy for her, the one that would declare his love and honor her. But how could he say that? He knew he could never deliver, and he couldn't make her promises that he would later break, no matter how right it felt at the moment. "I haven't slept in the same bed for more than four nights in a row since I was fifteen," he said. "And those longer stretches were for competitions. If I can't sleep in the same bed, how could I possibly offer you a forever? Or anyone? Including a kid?" She was wrong. He didn't want kids. A nephew was different than having that kid count on you every second of every day for its entire life.

She trailed her fingers over his chest, drawing designs that felt amazing. "I think," she said softly, "that if I were to accept that answer from you and let you trap yourself with me in some sort of off-again on-again relationship with no family in the future, I would be doing you a great disservice, by allowing you to hide from who you truly are."

"Oh, come on." Frustrated now, he rolled her onto her back, pinning her to the bed. "I make my choices, Taylor, and right now, my choice is you. With me. In my bed. Wherever that is." He stopped when he realized what he'd said. Had he just invited her to be a part of his vagrant life? Shit. She deserved more. Scowling, he rolled off her, resting on his back and staring at the ceiling, chastising himself for being so weak that he actually offered her a life that she didn't deserve, just because he couldn't stand the thought of being without her.

She didn't come after him, and the two-inch gulf between them felt like a crevasse that could never be crossed.

"You know," she said, her voice drifting through the darkness. "On some levels, that sounds like the best way ever to spend my life, living on your bike with you, seeing new places every day. These last few days with you have been the best days of my life."

He stiffened, hope suddenly springing through his body. He turned his head to look at her. She was lying on her side, her hands tucked under her chin, and her knees curled up, watching him. She looked vulnerable and beautiful, and his heart softened as he rolled onto his side to face her. "Mine, too," he said.

She smiled, and held out her hand to him. He wrapped his fingers around hers. "What do you really want, Taylor? From life? If you could really have it."

"I don't think like that, Zane. We have to tailor our dreams to fit our reality, or our heart breaks a little bit with every single heartbeat."

Listening to her made his heart break a little bit. She was so brave and courageous, and he wanted her to fight for what she wanted. He wanted her to get married and have those kids and teach until her smile reached her eyes every second of every day.

But at the same time, he wanted her for himself, and those two pictures weren't compatible. Which did he want more? To make himself happy by keeping her and giving her the half-life he could offer her? Or by letting her go so she had the chance of finding that guy who could give her everything?

"What about you?" She asked. "If you could have anything you really wanted, what would it be?"

He didn't hesitate. "You."

Tears filled her eyes. "Zane—"

Before she could finish, her phone rang. Her boss's ringtone. Sudden fear rippled through him. "Don't get it."

"I have to. He needs an answer." She scooted off the bed and ran to her purse. He leapt up after her and grabbed her wrist just as she pulled the phone out.

"Don't. Let's talk—"

She looked at him. "Why, Zane? Why shouldn't I answer it? *Why?*"

He hesitated. Why? What good reason did he have? Just because he didn't want her to go off on the grand adventure of her life, accepting a great job that would propel her to the kind of stardom she deserved, so he could keep her on the back of his bike, living in shit hotels, making her live life as a teacher, just because *he* thought that was a better choice for her? The truth was, *she* was the one with the parent dream. She might not be able to have biological kids, but there were a lot of ways to be a parent. She didn't need a man who didn't want kids. What she needed was a man who wanted kids as much as she did, who didn't give a shit about where they came from.

He didn't give a shit about where kids came from, but being a dad...he couldn't do it. She could find her way back to teaching in a year or two, but if he kept her, she'd never find the man who could heal her heart.

Slowly, he dropped his hand from hers. "Never mind." He turned away and walked back to the bed, leaving her with the chance of her lifetime.

Chapter 16

Taylor's heart seemed to crumble into a thousand pieces as she watched Zane walk away from her. Yes, she hadn't truly expected him to declare his love for her when she'd told him she loved him, but when he'd said all those words, something inside her had come to life, hoping so desperately that there was a way to make it work. She didn't want to let him go, and she didn't want him to let her go...

He disappeared into the bathroom. He left the door open, but turned on the shower and got inside, giving her privacy.

The phone rang again. Edward's name flashed across her screen. For a brief second, she remembered how she used to feel when she saw his name, back when they were first dating. Her heart would leap and a huge smile would spring onto her face. But he'd never made her feel the way Zane made her feel. She didn't want his job. She didn't want that life. She didn't want to talk to him.

But at the same time...Zane had made the choice they both knew was right. Maybe that was his role in her life. Maybe his job had been to make her love again, and to teach her to have faith in the goodness of other people. Maybe his role had simply been to heal her, so she could go forward with the life that she was meant to live.

Maybe he was destined to simply be a memory.

Maybe it was time for her to stop running away from what she wanted and start fighting for herself...but what did she want?

A text message flashed across the screen from Edward. *This is the last time I'm going to call, Taylor. Answer the damn phone or the job goes to someone else.* The phone rang again, his name flashing across the screen,.

This time, she answered it. Slowly, her hand shaking, she lifted it to her ear. "Hi, Edward."

☙ ☙ ☙

Zane stayed in the shower until the hot water ran out. And then he stayed in the cold water for as long as he could take it. It wasn't until he was chilled to the bone that he finally turned off the water. Once silence reigned, he waited, listening for the sound of Taylor talking to her boss.

There was no conversation coming from the main room.

Was she asleep? Had she packed her bags and bailed on him? Sudden panic rushed through him, and he jerked the bathroom door open. When he saw her curled up in the bed, her hair spread over the pillow and her hands tucked under her chin, he was so relieved he had to grab the sink to keep from going down to his knees.

Jesus.

How could he let her go? But how could he be the selfish bastard who kept her from what she wanted?

He took a breath and grabbed a towel, carelessly wiping the droplets off his skin, never taking his eyes off her. She was asleep, her chest moving in a slow rhythm, her eyelashes soft against her cheek.

He tossed the towel on the sink, then walked across the room. He knelt beside the bed and bent toward her. "Taylor," he whispered.

She didn't stir.

He brushed her hair back from her face, his fingers drifting over the incredibly soft strands. She was so beautiful and courageous, full of love, warmth, and vulnerability. He kissed her, a soft kiss, the kind of tender, gentle kiss he'd never have the courage to give her if she were awake. "Hey, babe," he whispered, keeping his voice low so as not to wake her, so she wouldn't hear the words that he had to say. "I want you to stay, but I can't take away your dream of being a mom. You'll find the guy who will give you that. I'm the one who can't handle watching you with someone else, because there will never be anyone else for me. You're it. You're my one and only. You're my forever."

He waited for a moment, almost hoping that she'd heard him in her sleep, hoping a foolish hope that she'd wake up and somehow show him a way that it could all work.

But she didn't stir, and her breathing stayed in the deep, even rhythm of sleep.

Which was for the best.

He let out his breath in a deep sigh, then eased the covers back and climbed in beside her. He wrapped her up in his arms and tucked her against him, her back tight against his chest, her hips nestled tightly against his. She felt so good and so right in his arms. He'd never wanted anyone to have a claim on him, but he knew that if he could wake up every single day with her in his arms, he'd have found the life he didn't deserve. But not at the cost of her dreams. He wouldn't do that to her. He pulled her even more tightly against him, knowing without asking that she'd accepted the promotion. Would she leave tomorrow? If not, then would it be the day after, as soon as Mira was settled? Maybe the day after that, but it would come.

The thought that this might be the last night he would ever hold her made something inside him tighten, a raging anger fueled by gaping loneliness he hadn't felt since the night he'd sat alone on his eighth birthday, watching the shadows on his bedroom wall while he listened to his mother screw her new boyfriend, completely forgetting that it had been her son's birthday that day.

She'd never remembered a birthday after that, and he'd learned not to care. He'd learned not to feel. He'd learned to accept what he could from his brothers, and to appreciate his talent as a bull rider. And most importantly, he'd made sure to never let anyone matter to him.

But Taylor mattered. She mattered on a thousand different levels. She mattered so much that he was willing to rip his heart out of his chest and let her get on that airplane and walk out of his life.

An image of an airplane cutting across the Wyoming sky flashed through his mind, and the greatest sense of desolation rolled through him. She would be on that plane soon.

But tonight, he had her.

Tonight wouldn't last forever, but he wasn't going to waste it.

"Taylor." He pressed a kiss to the nape of her neck. "Darlin', wake up."

She mumbled something and snuggled more tightly against him. For a moment, he considered being a good guy and letting her sleep. Then he decided to fuck it. He was being the hero by letting her go. Tonight, he was going to be the selfish jerk, and he was going to use every last second he had with her to fill his soul with enough of her love to sustain him the rest of his miserable, vagrant life. He palmed her belly, and began to nibble on her neck. "Taylor," he whispered. "Wake up."

Again, she mumbled something incoherent, but, even in her sleep, she pushed her hips back into him as he moved his hand lower on her belly. This woman, who trusted no one, had learned to trust him even in her most vulnerable moments.

That was worth everything to him.

Grinning, he rolled her onto her back and moved over her. He kissed her, a slow, tantalizing seduction of lips and tongues while he slid his knee between her thighs and wedged himself where he wanted to be.

He knew the moment she woke up. Her breath changed, and her muscles tightened, but he didn't stop kissing her. There was no way he wanted to give her the chance to talk about the job offer, no way he wanted to give her the chance to steal this last time together that they had.

She didn't try to stop him. Instead, she slipped her arms around his neck and kissed him back, even as she wrapped her legs around his hips, locking her feet together behind his back. "My sweet angel," he whispered, just before he slid inside her.

Neither of them was getting any sleep tonight, no matter what.

❦ ❦ ❦

When Taylor finally woke up, the sun was low in the sky, and Zane was still wrapped around her. He was holding her tightly, tangled around her from head to toe, his face buried in the curve of her neck. He was breathing deeply, finally asleep, after making love to her all night, all morning and most of the day. He'd let her sleep twice, while he'd run out to take care of the animals, but when he'd come back at noon, he'd told her Steen was back and he was taking the rest of the day off. He hadn't left the bed since then, and neither had she.

And now, it had to be close to dinnertime, and she'd spent the whole day in bed with him. She'd thought the other day had been the best day of her life, but it had been topped. If she stayed with Zane, would every day with him keep getting better? What a life that would be to look forward to.

She sighed, trailing her fingers over the dark hairs on his arm where it was locked across her chest, his forearm angled between her breasts as if he was claiming her even in his sleep.

They hadn't talked once about the future. They'd talked about his childhood with his mother, the first time he'd met Chase, and the glories of bull riding. She'd talked about being so sick as a child, and her father's sadness when she'd had the surgery that had taken away her childbearing capability, a sadness she hadn't understood for a long time...until she finally had.

They talked about the boys at the Garage, and the one who had died. Zane had cried for the boy who'd died, for his inability to save him. He'd let Taylor comfort him and take away his grief and guilt, which had been one of the most beautiful moments of her life. She'd never felt so close to anyone, even Mira.

She knew she mattered to him. Zane was a loner, and he'd somehow, someway, found a place with her. Was that enough? Could she take that and hope it would make his life enough? "Zane?"

He grunted and tightened his arms around her.

"Zane." She lightly hit his arm.

"Yeah." His voice was groggy with sleep.

"Do you think..." God, could she really say it? "Do you think..."

His body stiffened almost imperceptibly. "Do I think

what?"

"We could...make this work?" She held her breath, her heart pounding. She couldn't believe she'd said it. God, how could she say it? That was so selfish of her. "Never mind. Forget I said it—"

She started to pull away from him, and suddenly she found herself on her back, pinned to the bed by a man who looked surprisingly irritated given that he'd been dead asleep only moments before. "You need to understand something, Taylor." His voice was rough and steady, his gaze burning through her with intensity.

She swallowed. "What?"

"I'm not letting you go because you're right that someday I'll want biological kids and you'll destroy me by taking away that dream."

Tears threatened. "Zane—"

"No." He cut her off. "Listen to me. You know how you said the fact I love my nephew means I'm going to want biological kids someday?"

"Yes." She'd never forget the look on his face.

"In case you forgot, that kid's not my biological nephew. Chase isn't his biological dad."

She stared at him, his words sinking in. She'd totally forgotten. How could she have forgotten? Chase was so in love with Mira and the baby that she hadn't even thought about the bloodlines of the baby.

"I have no blood ties to that baby, and I'd slay a demon for him. Do you understand?"

Slowly, she nodded, her heart starting to pound.

"Here's the thing, sweetheart. My mother was total shit. And so was my dad. They both sucked as parents. Biology doesn't mean anything when it comes to family and love. If I decided I wanted to be a dad, there's a thousand ways to become a dad other than knocking up a woman with my sperm. In the end, all that matters is that you've got a kid who needs a parent who will stand behind them and fight the entire damn world on their behalf. I'd be that dad, and it wouldn't matter one bit if my blood ran in their veins or not. You need to understand that." His voice was fierce and angry, so full of emotion that she could almost feel it.

She realized he was telling the truth, the absolute truth. He didn't care about biology when it came to children. He truly didn't. For the first time in her life, hope flared in her belly, a terrified, faint hope that she'd never dared have in her whole life. "Zane—"

"I'm not the only guy like that. So don't sit there in your prison cell and hide from men. Find the one who won't care."

His words made her heart freeze. "What?" Find the one? Hadn't he just said that he was the one? "But you just said—"

"Taylor." His voice softened as he framed her face. "I can't be a father. I can't do it. I don't want that responsibility, and I can't be the world to some innocent child. It's so far from the realm of who I am, and what I'm capable of. If you were to stay with me, it's *you* who would be giving up on your dreams, not me. I want to keep you, more than you could ever, *ever* know, but if you stay with me, there will be no children, and that's a violation of your soul. I won't do that to you." He put his hand over her heart. "You've spent your life trying to convince yourself you don't want kids. You do. You can have them. You can have a dozen of them. If you give yourself to me, you will lose that dream, and it's not right."

"But—"

"Look into your heart, Taylor. Do you want kids? Do you want to be a mom? Do you want a real family, all sitting around the breakfast table, arguing over who gets the last piece of bacon?"

Tears filled her eyes at the image he presented, and she nodded silently, tears streaming down her cheeks. "I do," she whispered. "I really do." As she said the words, she felt the thick walls around her heart start to shatter, tumbling down as she acknowledged what she really wanted, that she'd been trying to hide from for so long. "I want to be a mom, more than anything. I just thought—"

"You thought that if you crushed your own dreams with enough force that you could destroy them."

She nodded, silently, starting to cry hard. It was terrifying to give up the pretense that she didn't care, but at the same time, she felt like a tremendous weight had been lifted from her shoulders. She could breathe again, truly breathe again. "I didn't believe there would be men who didn't care that I—"

"That you're the most incredible woman ever?" He brushed her hair back from her face, his dark eyes searching hers. "Don't ever sell yourself short again, darlin'. You're so incredible that when you meet the right guy, he'll turn heaven and earth to have you for his own, exactly the way you are. He won't want to change anything about you."

"Like you? Do you want to change anything about me?" She hadn't meant to say it, but the words had tumbled out.

His hand stilled in her hair, and he met her gaze. "No, I don't. I wouldn't change a single thing about you, on any level."

More tears fell, but this time, they were different tears. They were the tears of being loved for who she was. Maybe he hadn't said the words, but she knew that was how he felt.

He wasn't finished, however. "I wish I could change myself, though, and be able to be a dad for you. I wish that there was something inside me that wanted to take on that responsibility, but all I see when I look inside are the losers who spawned me. That part of me broke a long time ago, and it's never going to heal."

She saw the honesty in his eyes, and she heard the truth in his voice. Maybe he wanted kids deep in his soul, on a deeper level than he was aware, but he would never, *ever*, let himself go there. He was too scarred from his own life to ever be willing to take on the responsibility of another human being, one who was innocent and dependent. He was too certain that he would eventually fail a child, and nothing was going to change that conviction, because he didn't want to change. His instinct as a protector was what drove him to protect others from the worst enemy...which was himself.

A great sadness spilled through her, as she realized the truth, that no matter how much she loved him, there was a chasm that could not be crossed. He was right. If she went through life and never had children, a part of her heart would shrivel up and die. But wouldn't a part of her heart always stay behind with him? How could she split her heart like that? "Maybe—"

"There's no maybe." He kissed her, softly, a kiss that felt terrifyingly like good-bye. "I can't be the man I wish I could be, the one you deserve. I just can't. But I can honor who you are by letting you go. I'm not the only man you're capable of loving, Taylor. There's a guy out there who will give you everything you want, and not the incomplete half-life I could give you."

She knew then, that it was over.

There wasn't going to be a tomorrow, or even a tonight.

This was the last moment of their story.

Chapter 17

Zane bent his head, pressing his forehead against the soft fur of the gray mare that had arrived only two days ago. The animal nudged Zane's chest as he ran his hand along the animal's neck. "You feeling better now?" he asked her. "Erin's pretty impressive. I've never seen anyone operate on horses the way she does. You're in good hands."

The mare had been on three legs when she'd been unloaded from the trailer, and thirty-six hours out of surgery, she was already bearing weight on her gimpy leg.

"You really going to let Taylor go?" Chase appeared in the door of the stall, holding his son in his arms.

Zane stiffened, and turned away from the animal to face his brother. "Yeah." He glanced at his nephew, who had officially been named, Joseph John Stockton. The John was for Mira's dad, and Joseph had been the middle name of the kid's biological dad. Everyone was already calling him J.J., which worked just fine. Not a bad name for the kid. Nothing that would get him bullied.

"Why?" Chase tucked the baby more securely against his chest.

"Because she deserves more."

Chase scowled at him. "That's a bunch of crap, bro. She's in my house with Mira and Erin, crying her eyes out because she's leaving here in two hours."

The ache in Zane's chest intensified even more than it already had been. For two weeks, he'd slept in an empty stall while Taylor had occupied the bunkhouse. For two weeks, he'd watched her over dinner in the main house, becoming friends with Erin and his brothers, beginning to fit into ranch life. For two weeks, he'd burned to walk into that bunkhouse and climb into bed with her. He'd wanted to talk to her, to hold her, and to make love to her again and again.

But he hadn't.

He'd kept his distance, because he knew that if he stayed with her, neither of them would do what was right for her. "She'll be fine."

"No, she won't."

Zane looked sharply at his brother. "You don't know what you're talking about."

Chase leaned against the doorjamb. His cowboy hat was tipped back on his head, his jeans were dusty, and his boots were well-worn. Except for the baby in his arms, he looked every bit the cowboy that Zane did, but Zane knew that his cowboy persona would go back in its box when he left here. "I never would have put myself into the role of a parent, Zane. I don't know anything about being a good dad. None of us do. There was no chance I was going there...until I had to. I had nothing to offer Mira, but we made it work." He grinned, the happiest damned grin Zane had ever seen, as he held up the baby. "You see this little person? He's my son. He's counting on me to be there for him, and to get it right."

Zane's gut turned over. "What if you screw up? What if you become like our dad?"

Chase's eyes narrowed. "I'm not going to become like him. I realized that there's no chance of that happening. Yeah, I don't know anything about being a good dad or husband, but Mira's dad was awesome. She said she'd help me, but she also said that she'd never have married me if she didn't think I could do it on my own."

Zane's eyebrows went up. "You haven't married her yet."

Chase grinned. "Actually, I did. I wanted my baby to be born to my wife, not my fiancée, so we got hitched in the hospital. I'm not allowed to tell because Mira still wants her big, fairytale wedding, but yeah, she's mine, and I won't have it any other way."

Zane studied his brother, surprised by how damn happy he was. He'd wanted to get married so badly he'd done it over a hospital bed, and then was going to do it again with the fancy party? "You're whipped, man."

"Finding the right woman is the best thing that could ever happen to a guy. You found yours. Keep her."

Zane jutted his jaw out. "She wants kids. I'm not going there. There's no commonality."

Chase turned John around so that Zane could see the kid's face. His eyes were closed, and he was sleeping peacefully. A deep protectiveness surged through Zane, a need to protect that kid from anything that might ever try to harm him. "You can do the dad thing, Zane. Try it."

"Try it? And if I fail, then what? Leave a string of fucked up kids behind? No way. That's not something you try. You go all in, or you don't. I'm not taking the chance of being the one to screw it up."

Chase sighed. "You won't screw it up."

"How do you know?" Zane challenged. "The three weeks I've been here are the longest I've been in the same place since I was fifteen. How do you start building a family on that? You have to give a kid a forever, not a few weeks here and there."

His brother tucked the sleeping baby against his chest again. "Let me ask you something."

"What?"

"How has it been? Staying here? Have you lost your mind? Gone insane? Developed hives or a weird rash that no one wants to touch?"

Despite his irritation, Zane couldn't help but laugh. "No rashes. It's been okay." He glanced at the horse snoozing behind him. "It's been good to be around the animals again," he admitted.

"So, there you go." John suddenly awoke with a loud wail, and Chase grinned. "He needs his mama. You going to come out to say good-bye to Taylor, or are you going to make the woman you love walk away alone?"

Zane wanted to hide in that stall. He didn't want to face that moment of watching Taylor walk away from him. He wanted to get on his damned bike and take off in the other direction, riding so hard and fast that he could feel nothing but the wind sliding into his flesh.

But this was Taylor. She deserved more. "I'll come."

❦ ❦ ❦

Taylor hugged Mira fiercely, unable to stop the tears from streaming down her cheeks, even as she forced a smile to her face. "I'll miss you so much," she admitted. "I hate leaving you."

"I'll miss you, too." Mira pulled back, her own eyes rimmed with tears. After a couple weeks of staying low key after her surgery, she was starting to get mobile, which Taylor knew was her signal that it was time to leave. "I don't understand why you're taking this job. You don't want to do it. I can tell. You're even missing my wedding for it."

"I know, but it's not your real wedding." When Mira's eyes widened, Taylor rolled her eyes. "Of course I know you secretly got married in the hospital. Why else would you be willing to move your wedding out for a couple months until you're fully recovered and all Chase's brothers can come? I know you too well, my friend, so don't even bother denying it."

Mira gave her a sheepish smile. "You're not mad I didn't tell you? I was worried that you'd feel I didn't love you if you knew I'd gotten married without you. I know that it's been hard for you, adjusting to sharing me."

"I'm fine with it." Taylor smiled through her tears. "I've finally learned that life and friendship are so much more complicated than things like that. I know you wanted to be married before John was born, and I get it. It's okay." She took a deep breath. "But, despite the fact that I would love to hang around and see you in your lacy white dress, I need to take this job, at least for a little while."

Mira bit her lip. "You're sure?"

"Yes." She was proud of how certain she sounded. She'd thought so much over the last two weeks about staying in Wyoming and trying to find a teaching job. She'd dreamed about it. She'd fantasized about it. She'd even driven by a few schools just to see how she felt, but she'd felt like she was just trying to use teaching to fill the gap left by Zane. She had to heal herself first, and then see where she wanted to be. Staying around for another few weeks with Zane and the baby was just too hard. In addition, with all the Stockton brothers descending upon the ranch for the upcoming wedding, it just wasn't where she could be right now. "I'm not ready to make a career change. I want to see this job through."

Mira wrinkled her nose. "Okay, but you have to stop by here regularly, okay? Sell your house and buy one here, so at least this becomes your home base."

Taylor smiled through her tears. "Maybe."

Erin walked up and wrapped her arms around both of them. The genuineness of her hug made Taylor feel even more desolate. She'd gotten close with Erin quickly, and she felt the real loss of leaving town just as the friendship had begun to solidify.

"I feel like I just got a new friend," Erin said, "And I have to lose you before we've even had a chance to cause enough trouble together."

Taylor laughed and hugged Erin. "I was so scared of you when I first got here. I thought there was no room for me with you and Mira."

Erin's eyebrows went up. "And now?"

"And now I know you're cool. The second sister I never had."

"Because I'm the first sister," Mira declared, tucking her arm through Taylor's. "You know, Erin, if we delay Taylor for another ten minutes, she might miss her flight. Should we do it?"

"Don't," Taylor laughed as she pulled her arm free from Mira's. "I have to go. I get to fly first class now. I'm really looking forward to those hot towels."

"I can make hot towels," Mira said, frowning. "Seriously."

"Stop." Tears threatened again as Taylor picked up her purse. Her bags were already on the front porch. "You guys stay here. I'll cry if I have to say good-bye again." Her heart felt like it was breaking, but it was a good break. She had found a home here, and she would be back. She'd arrived without roots, and she had some now. "Love you both."

The three women hugged again, a fierce, desperate hug that promised a friendship that would last forever. Tears were streaming down her cheeks again as she stepped back. "Okay, no more of that. I'll call you guys." She then turned and hurried out the door, not looking back.

When she got to the porch, her bags were gone. She looked up, and saw Zane loading them into the trunk of her rental car for her. Her heart seemed to freeze when she saw him. He'd come to say good-bye? God, how could she do this? Why hadn't he just let her go?

Chase walked up. "Good luck with your job, Taylor. You know you're welcome here anytime."

"Thanks." She hugged him, and then gave a bit of extra love to little John, snuggled in his daddy's arms. "Don't forget your Auntie Taylor while I'm gone," she told him. "I'm the best, and you need to always remember that."

John, however, seemed unimpressed. Instead of cooing, he wailed at her, his face red and contorted. Chase grinned. "He needs Mira. Travel safe, Taylor."

"I will."

She watched as Chase carried the baby into the house, calling for Mira. Her friend and Chase had come together in the most extraordinary of circumstances, but they'd turned it into something so beautiful. That was what she wanted: a relationship so full of love that the world became a more beautiful place simply by its existence.

"You ready?"

Her heart leapt at the sound of Zane's voice, and she turned toward him. He was standing by her car, his hands on his hips, watching her. His cowboy hat was tipped back, his jeans and cowboy boots were well-worn and sexy, and his shoulders were broad beneath his cotton shirt. He looked every bit the cowboy, and none of the biker, and he was gorgeous.

God, she'd missed him.

Tears tried to come again, but this time, she refused to let them. Instead, she put her sunglasses on, lifted her chin, and marched down the stairs toward her car. He didn't move out of the way, and she finally stopped right in front of him, craning her head back to meet his gaze.

For a long moment, neither of them moved. She felt like her world had come to a standstill, hovering in suspended animation, waiting for him to ask her to stay. She would. In a heartbeat. Just one word. That was all he had to say. One word. She knew he'd be okay with what she had to offer, and in this moment, she felt like foregoing her own dream of being a mother was worth it to never have to say good-bye to him. *Just ask me to stay, Zane. Just ask.*

He raised his hand and brushed his fingers over her jaw. His eyes were dark and inscrutable, a mask she couldn't penetrate. Two weeks ago, he'd cried in her arms over a boy who'd died, and now he had so many walls up, she couldn't see a single whisper of his humanity...but she knew it was there. "I love you, Zane."

Crud. She hadn't meant to say that. She'd promised herself she wouldn't beg for his attention. She was more than that. She deserved someone who would chase her down and offer everything he had to keep her.

"I know you do."

She blinked. "I know? That's how you respond? *I know you do?*" Sudden anger rushed through her, anger that she'd wasted so much emotion on him over the last two weeks, wondering if there was a way to make it work. "Forget it, Zane. I have to leave."

He dropped his hand and stepped back from her without argument. "Be safe."

"Of course." She climbed into the driver's seat and tossed her purse down. Her hands were shaking, and she wasn't sure if it was from anger or the fact her heart was shattering into a thousand pieces. "You, too." She gripped the steering wheel as he shut her door. It closed with a soft thud, and then he stepped back.

She glanced out the window at him. He met her gaze, and in that moment, she saw the depth of his pain, the agony of what he was enduring. Her heart seemed to stop, and she flung the door open. "Zane!" She threw herself into his arms, and he caught her, holding her tight against him.

He kissed her, hard and fierce, his fingers tangling in her hair as if to trap her. She melted into the heat of his body, into the fire of his kiss, losing herself to him on every level. She'd missed him so much, and being in his arms was the only place in the world she wanted to be. "Make love to me, Zane. Take me to the bunkhouse and make love to me."

His arms tightened around her, but he broke the kiss, resting his forehead against hers. "I can't break your soul, Taylor. I love you too much to do that to you."

Her heart seemed to stop. "What?"

He pulled back, his gaze searching hers. "If I didn't love you so much, I would keep you. I'd be willing to take your dreams away so I could have you for myself. But I can't do that, because hurting you would destroy me."

He loved her. She'd known he did, but hearing him say it was different. It was beautiful. Perfect. The most amazing words she'd ever heard in her life. "Maybe being an aunt would be enough—"

"No." He kissed the argument away. "You know it wouldn't. I know it wouldn't."

"Zane!" Chase walked out on the porch, and Zane grimaced at the interruption.

"Later," he said, not taking his gaze off Taylor, and not loosening his grip on her.

"Some guy is on my landline from a garage. He said that Luke and his little brother ran away. He thinks they're headed toward the ranch. Wants to know if they're here. You know what he's talking about?"

Zane's face paled and he spun away from Taylor. He raced over to the house and grabbed the phone from Chase. Taylor hurried after him, but by the time she reached him, he'd already hung up. He turned toward her, his face stricken with fear. "Luke took off in the middle of the night, apparently taking Toby with him. According to one of the other boys at their foster home, Luke's planning to hitchhike all the way here. Do you know what can happen to kids who hitchhike? We have to find them."

"I'll help." She didn't hesitate. She knew she'd miss her flight, but she didn't care. She'd seen him cry over the guilt of Brad's death. There was no way she was leaving him to face this on his own. "We can take my car."

"Okay." He shoved the phone at Chase. "I need to get

my cell. Get the car started," he ordered Taylor. He vaulted down the steps and sprinted toward the barn, while she ran for her car. He was back within a minute and a half, and dove into the passenger side of the car as she peeled out.

As she sped down the driveway, he leaned forward, searching through the windshield, scanning the road and the fields. "They could be anywhere along the route," he said, his voice rough and stark. "They'd had enough time to make it here if they got a ride immediately, but they could be two miles from their home if they didn't. Hundreds of miles that could swallow them up. Oh, God." He groaned and dragged his forearm across his brow. "They're just kids."

"Luke's a tough kid," she said. "I'm sure they're okay."

"Don't lie," Zane snapped. "We have no idea if they're safe. Toby is four. Four! Luke took his four-year-old brother!" He was gripping the dashboard, his knuckles white as he searched the road ahead. "They've been in foster care for the last year. I knew their situation was bad, but hell. It can't be bad enough to risk this. The ranch is more than two hundred miles away from the Garage. Why would he come after me?"

"Because you're all he has," she said softly, scanning the fields for two boys as she drove. "He's picked you, Zane. He's picked you to save him."

Zane glanced at her, his eyes panicked. "He's made the wrong choice. His brother's already dead. I can't save anyone."

"No, you're wrong." She shook her head. "You couldn't save Brad, but Luke and Toby are still alive. Kids are smart, Zane. They know how to survive, and it looks like Luke has realized you're his best bet."

"Jesus." Zane bowed his head, and his shoulders shuddered. "What if something happens to them? What if they die coming after me?" He sat back and ran his hands through his hair, his fingers shaking. "I should have realized this was going to happen. I should have seen it. A couple months ago, Luke asked me where the ranch was. He made me show him on a map, and asked me to point out what roads I took when I came here. I should have realized. I should have talked him out of it before I left—"

"Stop it!" She slammed on the brakes, and the car

skidded to a stop.

Zane gripped the dashboard, glaring at her. "What are you doing? Drive!"

"I am so damned tired of you blaming yourself for things that aren't your fault! People are responsible for their own choices. You did your best to help Brad, and he still went with his friends to rob that store. His choice, not yours. You're a great man, and a born protector, and Luke knows that. He's willing to do anything to save his little brother, and you're their only chance. Brad's death probably made Luke realize exactly how dire their situation is if he doesn't change it. Their life is probably like yours was, or your brothers. When you were fourteen, if you'd had someone counting on you, you would have done whatever it took to protect them, right? Even if it meant hitchhiking two hundred miles to find the one person in the world you trusted?"

"Of course. I would have travelled a thousand miles if that would have helped." He stared at her, his face ashen. "You think it's as bad as it was with my dad?"

"If it wasn't, would he be dragging his brother down two hundred miles of highway searching for you?"

Zane seemed to pale even more. "I can't—"

"Yes, you can! God, Zane, stop being an idiot! Those boys need you, and you better pull yourself together by the time we find them!" She smacked his shoulder. "They need you, Zane Stockton, and no one else. Just you!"

He bowed his head, and laced his fingers behind his head, his elbows resting on his knees. His shoulders were shaking, and she could hear his ragged breathing.

Her anger dissipated, and she leaned over, putting her hand on his back. "Zane," she said softly, leaning her head against his.

"What?" He didn't look up, his voice hoarse.

"You can do this. You can be what they need. I know you can."

He looked over at her, and she saw that his eyes were bloodshot. "Brad died," he whispered. "*He died.*"

"I know he did. It was tragic and terrible. You can let that destroy you, or you can learn from it. He died because he had no one to hold his hand and guide him. These boys are coming to you, Zane. There's no one else in their lives who can help. Without you, they have nothing. Aren't you better than nothing?"

He stared at her for what seemed like an eternity, then he nodded once. "I'm better than nothing," he admitted in a barely audible whisper, his voice raw and agonized.

"There you go." She knew he was far better than that, but at least it was progress. "Let's go find them, okay?"

He nodded. "Okay. Drive fast."

"Don't worry. I will."

Chapter 18

The miles crawled by with agonizing slowness as Taylor raced down the winding, two-lane back road. Zane told Luke he took this road because he liked the curves, but it wasn't the fastest way. Which way would Luke select? Was he wrong that Luke would go as Zane went? What if the kid decided the highway was faster? What if he and Taylor were searching on the wrong road?

No, he was sure Luke would follow his path, both to stay off the main road where the cops might pick him up, and because he'd want to be like Zane.

Shit. *Luke would want to be like him.* How the hell had this happened?

No. It didn't matter how it happened.

All that mattered was that they found them.

They'd been driving for two hours already. Two hours. Still more to go. What if they didn't find them on the road? What if they made it all the way to his foster home and the Garage and didn't find them?

Then they'd go back over it again. And again. Until they found them. He thought of the funeral, and he felt sick. "What if they're dead? What if—"

"Stay focused, Zane. Keep looking." Taylor was steady and calm, as she had been since they'd left the ranch. Without her, he knew he'd have lost his shit by now.

He let out his breath and nodded, his gaze relentlessly sweeping the roadside as they hurtled past the endless fields—

He suddenly saw a dark shadow in the field to his left. He whipped around in his seat, searching the fields, but he didn't see anything.

"What is it?" Taylor eased off the gas.

"Nothing. I don't see anything. Mind tricks."

She looked over at him. "Zane. Do you think you saw something?"

Her unwillingness to dismiss his initial reaction made him think again. Had it been mind tricks, or had he seen something real? He looked at her, then looked back at the field. His gut said it had been them. "Turn around."

She immediately slowed down, then hung a U-turn across the road. He leaned forward in his seat, scanning the grasses. He saw something dark again, and his heart started to speed up. Something was running through the grasses. "Do you see that?"

"Yes. I can't tell what it is." She sped up the car, flying down the highway, closer and closer until—

"It's them!" He could see the two boys racing through the grasses, rushing away from the highway as fast as they could. He shoved open his door, leaping out of the car before Taylor had come to a complete stop. "Luke! Toby! It's me! It's Zane!"

They kept running, frantic and terrified, running away just like he'd done so many times.

"Luke!" He bellowed his name, and broke into a sprint, racing across the field, his heart hammering. "Luke! It's me! It's Zane!"

Suddenly, the taller boy stopped. He whirled around, looking back at Zane, then he screamed Zane's name, picked up his brother, and started running toward Zane, stumbling on the uneven field.

Zane ran faster, his heart pounding when he saw Luke stumble and fall, Toby tumbling out of his skinny arms onto the dirt. "I'm coming! Just wait!"

Luke tried to pick up his brother, dragging himself to his feet as he tried to run toward Zane again. He was so exhausted, he fell again, but again, he grabbed his brother and surged to his feet, refusing to give up.

"Luke!" Zane lunged the last few feet as Luke started to

fall a third time, catching both boys in his arms. They fell into him, two skinny kids shivering from cold, even though it wasn't even that cold out.

Zane went to his knees, hauling the boys against him, shaking as hard as the kids were. They were okay. *They were okay.*

Luke flung his arms around Zane's neck, clinging so tightly that Zane couldn't breathe, not that he cared. He pulled the kids tighter against him, holding on as tight as he'd ever held onto anything in his life.

It felt like forever before Luke finally loosened his grip on Zane, who immediately softened his own hold on them, giving them space. Toby kept leaning against Zane's side, staring up at him with big, brown eyes. Zane grinned down at him. "Hey, Toby. You've been on an adventure, huh?"

Toby nodded once, still staring at Zane. "Luke says you'll take care of us. He says we can live with you."

"He did?" A cold fist jammed itself into Zane's stomach, and he looked at Luke, who was staring warily at Zane. "What's going on, Luke?"

Luke still looked scared. "You're not mad? You're not going to yell at us?"

Zane wrapped his arm around Toby and hoisted him up so the kid was on his hip. He didn't answer Luke's question. Instead he asked one of his own. "How bad is it?" He knew Luke would know what he was asking.

The teenager met his gaze. "Bad. It's real bad, Zane."

Zane took a deep breath and nodded. He knew what 'real bad' was to a kid like Luke, who had learned to cope with a lot of bad shit in life. For Luke to say it was real bad...he knew what that meant. "Okay."

"You going to send us back?" Luke looked scared, like a little boy who was terrified of what lay before him, not like a fourteen-year-old who should be thinking he ruled the world.

Suddenly, as Zane stared into Luke's face, he felt his own heart break. Little pieces that he'd kept glued together for so long began to shatter. He couldn't stop the tears, and he didn't bother to try. He just held out his arm to Luke.

For a long moment, Luke didn't move, then the fear left

his face and he walked into Zane's embrace. This time, the hug was different. It wasn't relief that the two kids weren't dead. It was a promise, the kind of promise no one had ever made to him when he was a kid, the kind of promise that he'd never thought he'd make...until now.

❦ ❦ ❦

Taylor knocked lightly on the front door of the bunkhouse and poked her head in. Zane was just closing the door to the back room, where he and Taylor had managed to right two cots and make them up with fresh linens when they'd finally gotten back to the ranch. "Are they asleep?"

Zane shook his head. "Toby's waiting for you."

Taylor's heart softened, and she hurried past Zane into the back room. The lights were still blazing, and the boys had crawled into the same tiny bed, with Luke's arm around his little brother. The bed they'd set up for Toby sat empty, abandoned in favor of the security of each other in a world where they'd learned to be afraid.

"Hey," she whispered, walking over to the bed.

Toby rolled over to face her, and he smiled, that adorable smile that she hadn't seen until an hour into their stop at a roadside tavern for dinner and ice cream on the way home. Zane had placed a few calls that had given them permission to take the boys back to the ranch for the night, leveraging his superstar reputation and his hundreds of hours of volunteer work at the Garage to get what he wanted. "How's it going?" she asked.

Toby nodded. "It's good." He held out his hand, and she took it, wrapping it up tightly in hers. Her heart seemed to melt for him, and she had to blink back tears. So much love and innocence still alive in him. He still had a chance.

She looked at Luke, who was watching her silently. "How are you doing?"

He shrugged, warily. "Okay."

"Is there anything I can get you?"

He shook his head.

Toby's fingers relaxed in hers, and she saw that he'd already fallen asleep. Quietly, she tucked his hand against his chest, and brushed her fingers over his tousled hair. When she looked back at Luke, she saw he was still watching her.

"You're nice," he said quietly. "You're not like the others."

She didn't know exactly what others he was referring to, but she could guess. "Yes," she said. "I'm not like the others. I'm like Zane."

His shoulders relaxed, and he took a deep breath. "Okay."

She smiled. "Okay, then." She lightly kissed Toby's forehead, and then looked at Luke, who hadn't taken his gaze off her. "Can I give you one?"

He shrugged again, but not before she saw a flash of yearning in his eyes. She quickly pressed a quick kiss to his head as well, then pulled the covers up around them. "Good night. See you in the morning."

Luke said nothing as he closed his eyes, pulling Toby more tightly against him.

She leaned over the boys, putting her hand on Luke's shoulder. She bent over, lowering her voice for his ears only. "You're safe here," she whispered. "It's okay now."

Luke didn't answer, but she saw the corner of his mouth turn up ever so slightly. She was smiling to herself as she ducked out of the room and pulled the door shut behind her, leaving the lights on for them. She had a feeling it would be a long time until they would be ready to sleep in the dark.

Zane was leaning against the kitchen counter, his arms folded over his chest. His cowboy hat was on the hook by the door, but his boots were still on. He looked exhausted, but there was a fire in his eyes that she hadn't seen before. "I need to talk to you." His voice was tense and clipped.

"Okay." The bed was still the only place to sit, so she walked over and sat on it. She tried not to think of all the times she'd been wrapped up in Zane's arms in that bed, and of all the nights since, when she'd lay there in silence, listening and hoping for his footsteps outside, footsteps that had never come. "What's up?"

Zane didn't join her. Instead, he gripped the counter, his muscles tense. "So, I made some more calls while you were at the main house updating Mira and Chase."

"You did? What kind of calls?" She'd made some calls, too.

"I'm making them mine."

Her heart leapt at his words, but she didn't move. "What do you mean?" she asked carefully, not wanting to jump to conclusions.

"Foster to adopt. They have no one else. I have to do it." His voice broke and he walked across the room, going down to his knees in front of her. He gripped her hips, staring up at her. "They don't have a single living relative," he said. "Do you realize that? I thought their mom was in prison, but apparently she died of a drug overdose not long ago. They're totally and completely alone. No parents, and not a single relative will claim them. Now that Brad's dead, they have *no one*."

Her heart ached at the pain in his voice, and she nodded. "I figured they had no one else once I heard that they were coming here for you." She touched his jaw, thick with the whiskers of a man who never bothered with society's conscripts to make himself presentable, unless he felt like it. "You're adopting them? Really?"

He nodded. "They've got nothing, Taylor. I'm better than nothing."

She smiled. "You're a lot better than nothing, Zane."

"I'm not." He leaned his head against her stomach, and she wrapped her arms around him, holding him tight. "I don't know what the hell to do with them. I don't know what kids need. I don't have a place for them to live. I—"

"Stop it. You're everything they need. It's not going to be easy. Kids can be challenging, but love is all that they really need. You might not want to admit it, but you love them, and that will be enough. You'll figure the rest out." Her heart ached for his pain, for his inability to see how amazing he was. "You do realize that I would never have fallen in love with you if you weren't the most extraordinary human being I've ever met, right?"

He looked up at her, searching her face. "You believe in me," he whispered.

"Of course I do."

"You're the only reason I told them I'd take them. Because you make me see things in myself I can't see alone."

She smiled. "I'm glad—"

"Adoption is forever," he said. "It's a forever promise. I can't ever take it back."

She cocked her head, studying him. "You don't sound scared," she said.

He shook his head. "I should be, but I'm not. It feels right. Like it's what I'm supposed to do, you know?"

She nodded, her heart swelling for him. "You'll be a great dad, Zane. I know you will, because—"

"Taylor?" He cut her off.

"What?"

He took her hand, sandwiching it between his palms. "I know you want babies. I know that's your dream. I don't want babies. I really don't. But...I've got these boys now. They're not little. They've got scars we'll never be able to see. They're not easy. I don't even know basic stuff about them, like if they eat bacon at breakfast. But, it's a family, kind of, you know? I mean... maybe..."

Her heart started to pound, a frenzied rhythm of hope that she hadn't felt in so long. "What are you trying to say?"

"Would it be enough for you? The boys? Me? I'm thinking I'll set up shop on the ranch. I think the animals would be good for Luke. My brothers would accept them, and the boys would always have a place, so that even if something happened to me, they'd be a part of the place. They'd always have a home, right? So, here is good for them. So, you know, I don't know, what do you think? I mean, you have a great job, and stuff, but—"

Tears filled her eyes. "I quit my job tonight."

He stared at her in disbelief. "What?"

"I called and quit. When I saw the way Luke screamed your name and started running for you, I realized I couldn't do one more day in hotels and airplanes. I believe in children, and I want to help them. But not just being a teacher. I want to help kids like Luke and Toby. I can make a difference. I know I can. I've been caught in this societal tractor beam of biological children, and I realized that it's all just stupidity that has been dragging me away from who I am."

He grinned, a slowly widening grin. "So, you're not

afraid of kids like Luke and Toby? They're from the wrong side of the tracks, you know."

She whacked him lightly on the side of the head. "Let go of that wrong side of the tracks thing, Zane. That chip needs to get off your shoulder."

"I'll never get it off my shoulder," he said, his smile fading. "I can try, but it'll never go away. I'm just me."

She sighed. "I know who you are. That's who I love. I didn't mean you have to change for me. I just meant that I want you to realize how amazing you are."

He said nothing, studying her intensely. "Tell me it's okay to ask," he finally said, his voice hoarse. "Tell me it's not selfish. Tell me that I won't ruin your life if I ask."

She went still, her breath suddenly frozen in her chest. "Ask," she whispered. "Ask me."

Silence again, then he cleared his throat. "I know that I'm not what you might have dreamed of. I know I'm not going to bring you babies, but I have a couple kids, you know? And they're going to need help. More than I can give them. And—"

She put her finger over his lips. "Just ask."

"I love you, Taylor. More than you could ever understand." He grasped her wrist, and then kissed the palm of her hand, never taking his gaze off hers. "I want so desperately, with every fiber of my soul, to wake up with you every morning for the rest of my life. I want to hold you all night, every night. I want to learn how to be a parent with you. I want to watch the boys at their first rodeo together. I want to make love to you every night, a dozen times a night, and I want to hold your hand every day until we die."

Tears filled her eyes. "Zane—"

"I need you in my life, Taylor. I can't do it without you. And by 'it', I mean survive, thrive, breathe, or even smile. I need a forever promise from you. I'll give you mine." He took her hands and sandwiched them between his. "I promise I will love, cherish, and protect you forever, if you will please, please, please, agree to marry me." He cut himself off, vulnerability etched on his handsome face as he searched hers. "Be my wife, Taylor. My forever. Our forever. Me and the boys. All of us."

A tear trickled down her cheeks, and she smiled through

her tears. "I would have married you without the boys," she said. "I would have kept the boys without you, if I could have. Together? It's everything I could ever dream of. Of course, of course, *of course*, I will marry you, and the boys."

A huge grin spread over his face, and he let out a whoop worthy of the most die-hard cowboy. Then he dragged her into his arms, and he kissed her, the kind of forever kiss that she'd long ago given up hope of ever having.

Until she'd met Zane.

Chapter 19

"Luke?" Zane finally found him in the last aisle in the barn, leaning over the door, watching the horse inside. "I've been looking for you."

Luke looked at him with sudden fear. "Am I in trouble? Did I forget to do something? I thought I fed everyone. Did I miss a horse?"

"Nah. You're doing great." Zane's heart sank at Luke's instinctive reaction. The boy had been on the ranch for almost two months now, and he was still skittish. Toby had fallen in love with riding almost instantly, but Luke had been unwilling to have anything to do with the horses, aside from doing chores around the barn. He worked hard, too hard, as if he were afraid he'd lose his new home if he wasn't valuable. Zane didn't know how to help him, and it was killing him.

"I wanted to check in with you and make sure you were doing okay." He walked over and leaned on the door beside Luke, studying the animal within.

The bay mare was in bad shape. She was all bones and had a long scar across her hip. Erin had found her on one of her outings, abandoned in a back field. She'd bought the animal on sight and brought her home. The mare had arrived yesterday, but she hadn't eaten a bite yet. She was too skinny to go much longer without getting some nourishment, but she'd refused even the hot bran mash.

"She's not eating," Luke said.

"Nope, she's not," Zane agreed, surprised that Luke had

noticed.

"Why not?"

"She's scared. She's had a rough time of it. If an animal is in a constant state of fear, sometimes they can't relax enough to eat."

"She'll die if she doesn't eat. Look how skinny she is." Luke's voice was worried, and he didn't take his gaze off the animal.

Zane thought for a moment, then an idea formed. "You know what she needs?"

Luke shook his head. "What?"

"To feel safe. To feel like someone is going to protect her. She needs to bond with someone. Horses are herd animals, and they're not used to living alone. She doesn't know how to connect with other horses because she's lived alone for so long. She needs someone to be her champion."

Luke said nothing, his arms hooked over the door as he watched her.

"I don't have time," Zane said, choosing his words carefully. "Taylor and I are working on plans to get the cabins built for the summer camp for the kids. Steen's working with the horses that come to the ranch for rehab or training, but this one's not ready for that. Chase and Mira are swamped too." He paused for an extra moment. "We'll have to sell her, and find her a new home. One where someone has time for her."

Luke said nothing, and Zane waited.

Finally, the boy said, "What if they don't take good care of her? What if it's not as nice a place as this one?"

"We'll do our best. We won't let her go somewhere that's not safe."

Luke looked at him. "But how do you know? You never know what's going on inside another place, unless you're living in it."

Zane's heart broke for the lessons that had prompted that observation. "This is true," he said evenly, "but we'll make sure—"

"No." Luke shook his head. "No. I'll take her. I'll take care of her. She needs me."

Zane couldn't stop the grin from spreading over his face,

but he quickly wiped it away when Luke looked over at him. "You think you're up for that?" he asked, keeping his expression solemn. "You'll have to gain her trust and get her to eat. When she's ready to be ridden, you'll be the only one she'll want on her back. So, you'll have to be ready for that. You'll have to learn to ride so that you'll be skilled by the time she's ready."

Luke nodded seriously. "I can do that. I'll start right away. Can we do a lesson today?"

Zane couldn't stop the grin this time. "You bet we can." He nodded at the mare. "She needs a name. What are you going to call her?"

"I get to name her?" Luke looked back at the mare, studying her. "Harley," he said decisively. "Her name is Harley. Like your bike. She'll be as fast as your bike when she's better."

Zane grinned. "Harley it is." He put his hand on Luke's shoulder as they both looked in at the mare, who was dozing in the back of the stall. "You'll have to talk to Chase and figure out what to feed her, and how to get her started eating again."

Luke nodded. "I can do that. Chase is a good guy."

"That he is." He pulled open the door. "Go on. Say hi. Introduce yourself."

"Really? Can I?" Luke couldn't keep the eagerness out of his voice, ducking inside the stall even as he asked the question. He walked right up to the mare, who raised her head nervously and backed into the corner at his approach.

Zane watched as the boy instinctively slowed down, and began talking in low undertones to the mare. Harley's ear flicked forward to listen, and slowly, ever so slowly, she lowered her head, still listening.

"Zane—" Taylor appeared beside him, and then fell silent when she saw Luke with the mare. She moved up beside Zane, her hand sliding into his as they watched Luke talk to the mare. Slowly, inch by inch, he moved closer. Harley kept lowering her head more and more as she relaxed, and her ears kept flicking forward, until he was standing right next to her. He leaned in, whispering into her ear, not attempting to touch her. Harley was absolutely still, listening.

Taylor pulled her hand out of Zane's and slipped into the stall. Neither Harley nor Luke noticed her approach, and she slid a carrot into Luke's hand before ducking back out. Zane grinned and put his arm around her as they watched Luke glance down at the carrot. He looked back at Zane, who gave him a nod, and then he held the carrot in front of Harley's nose.

She sniffed it, then turned her head away.

Luke resumed whispering in her ear, still holding the carrot out. Harley cautiously sniffed the carrot again, and then she carefully took it from Luke's hand and crunched it. Luke looked back at Zane and Taylor, a huge smile etched on his face, his light brown eyes dancing with delight.

Zane's heart tightened, and he pulled Taylor closer against him as they both gave him a thumbs up. This was it. This was what being a parent was. This was what being a family was. Sharing moments like this, with the people he loved.

He looked down at Taylor, and he saw her eyes glistening with happiness. "I love you, darlin'," he whispered.

She smiled. "I love you, too."

He kissed her, and then laughed when he heard Luke's groan. "You guys are kissing again? That's so gross."

But when Zane looked over at him, the kid was grinning, watching them as if seeing them together was the best thing he'd ever seen. "If you're done with Harley," Zane said, "the house is here."

Luke's face lit up. "The house? Our house? Really?"

"It's coming up the driveway right now," Taylor said. "I saw it myself."

"I can't believe they moved that old farmhouse," Luke said. "Is it on rollers? A truck? How are they doing it?"

"You'll have to see." Zane had decided the boys couldn't wait a year for a house to be built. Plus, who needed a brand new house, anyway? Together, they'd found a fantastic old farmhouse in the next town, and he'd bought it and paid to have it moved. The foundation was already laid, and it would take only a few days to get the house settled sufficiently for them to move into it. Four bedrooms, three bathrooms, and he was planning to build a serious game room on the back, the kind of game room that would keep the boys at home and not out on the town where they could get into trouble.

He knew what boys did, he knew what it took to keep

them out of trouble, and he was going to give them everything he had to keep them safe. He was already figuring out the dad thing, learning how to balance love with rules. Who knew he had it in him? He smiled. Taylor had known. Without her, he'd never be where he was, living the life that he was meant to lead.

"Awesome!" Luke hurried out of the stall, taking time to make sure Harley's door was locked, before taking off in a sprint down the aisle.

Taylor started to go after him, but Zane grabbed her wrist and pulled her back, pinning her against the stall door. "I need one second with you," he whispered, tunneling his hands through her hair. "Sharing that bunkhouse with the boys has seriously cramped my naked time with you."

She melted against him, their bodies fitting together perfectly, as they always did. She wrapped her hands around his neck. "It's been perfect," she said.

He grinned, thinking of how they'd woken up this morning with Toby in bed with them, snuggled up beside Taylor. "Yeah, it has." They'd had to start sleeping with clothes on, but he learned that it was so worth it. "My wife," he said softly. "I'll never get tired of saying that. *Ever.*"

She beamed at him. "Good," she said. "I'm glad to hear it." She grinned. "I'm glad we didn't wait for Mira and Erin's double wedding. Our ceremony was perfect with just us and the boys."

"I couldn't wait, and I didn't want to share." He kissed her forehead, then her cheek. "If you'd said you wanted to wait for the big wedding, I think I would have had to kidnap you."

Her smile faded. "I had the big wedding, Zane. I didn't want another one. I just wanted you and the boys."

"I love you." He kissed her again, a kiss that seemed to melt away every last bit of tension in his body. Holding her in his arms was a gift he'd never dreamed of...until he'd met her. "I love everything about you, just the way you are."

She smiled. "I know you do, and I feel the same—"

He cut her off with a kiss, the kind of kiss that still shook them both to their cores, a kiss of forever, of commitment, and of a passion that would never die. With a deep sigh, she wrapped her arms around him, kissing him back just as fiercely.

His cock growing hard, he grabbed her legs and lifted them around his hips. There had to be an empty stall around—

"Mommy! Daddy!"

He swore and set Taylor down as Toby came hurtling around the corner, his little legs pumping as fast as he could go. "You have to come see the house! It's even bigger than I remember! Come see! Come see!" He grabbed Taylor's hand and started dragging her toward the door.

Taylor laughed, tossing a smile back at Zane as she let Toby lead her out. He grinned, laughter bubbling up deep in his chest as he followed them.

Yeah, this was good. Really, really good.

Sneak Peek: No Knight Needed

An *Ever After* Novel

Ducking her head against the raging storm, Clare hugged herself while she watched the huge black pickup truck turn its headlights onto the steep hillside. She was freezing, and her muscles wouldn't stop shaking. She was so worried about Katie, she could barely think, and she had no idea what this stranger was going to do. Something. Anything. *Please.*

The truck lurched toward the hill, and she realized suddenly that he was going to drive straight up the embankment in an attempt to go above the roots and around the fallen tree that was blocking the road. But that was crazy! The mountain was way too steep. He was going to flip his truck!

Memories assaulted her, visions of when her husband had died, and she screamed, racing toward him and waving her arms. "No, don't! Stop!"

But the truck plowed up the side of the hill, its wheels spewing mud as it fought for traction in the rain-soaked earth. She stopped, horror recoiling through her as the truck turned and skidded parallel across the hill, the left side of his truck reaching far too high up the slippery slope. Her stomach retched as she saw the truck tip further and further.

The truck was at such an extreme angle, she could see the roof now. A feathered angel was painted beneath the flood lights. An angel? What was a man like him doing with an angel on his truck?

The truck was almost vertical now. There was no way it could stay upright. It was going to flip. Crash into the tree. Careen across the road. Catapult off the cliff. He would die right in front of her. Oh, God, *he would die.*

But somehow, by a miracle that she couldn't comprehend, the truck kept struggling forward, all four wheels still gripping the earth.

The truck was above the roots now. Was he going to make it? *Please let him make it—*

The wheels slipped, and the truck dropped several yards

down toward the roots. "No!" She took a useless, powerless step as the tires caught on the roots. The tires spun out in the mud, and the roots ripped across the side of the vehicle with a furious scream.

"Go," she shouted, clenching her firsts. "Go!"

He gunned the engine, and suddenly the tires caught. The truck leapt forward, careening sideways across the hill, skidding back and forth as the mud spewed. He made it past the tree, and then the truck plowed back down toward the road, sliding and rolling as he fought for control.

Clare held her hand over her mouth, terrified that at any moment one of his tires would catch on a root and he'd flip. "Please make it, please make it, please make it," she whispered over and over again.

The truck bounced high over a gully, and she gasped when it flew up so high she could see the undercarriage. Then somehow, someway, he wrested the truck back to four wheels, spun out into the road and stopped, its wipers pounding furiously against the rain as the floodlights poured hope into the night.

Oh, dear God. He'd made it. He hadn't died.

Clare gripped her chest against the tightness in her lungs. Her hands were shaking, her legs were weak. She needed to sit down. To recover.

But there was no time. The driver's door opened and out he stepped. Standing behind the range of his floodlights, he was silhouetted against the darkness, his shoulders so wide and dominating he looked like the dark earth itself had brought him to life.

Something inside her leapt with hope at the sight of him, at the sheer, raw strength of his body as he came toward her. This man, this stranger, he was enough. He could help her. Sudden tears burned in her eyes as she finally realized she didn't have to fight this battle by herself.

He held up his hand to tell her to stay, then he slogged over to the front of his truck. He hooked something to the winch, then headed over to the tree. The trunk came almost to his chest, but he locked his grip around a wet branch for leverage, and then vaulted over with effortless grace, landing in the mud with a splash. "Come here," he shouted over the wind.

Clare ran across the muck toward him, stumbling in the slippery footing. "You're crazy!" she shouted, shielding her eyes against the bright floodlights from his truck. But God, she'd never been so happy to see crazy in her life.

"Probably," he yelled back, flashing her a cheeky grin. His perfect white teeth seemed to light up his face, a cheerful confident smile that felt so incongruous in the raging storm and daunting circumstances.

But his cockiness eased her panic, and that was such a gift. It made her able to at least think rationally. She would take all the positive vibes she could get right now.

He held up a nylon harness that was hooked to the steel cord attached to his truck. "If the tree goes over, this will keep you from going over."

She wiped the rain out of her eyes. "What are you talking about?"

"We still have to get you over the tree, and I don't want you climbing it unprotected. Never thought I'd actually be using this stuff. I had it just out of habit." He dropped the harness over her head and began strapping her in with efficient, confident movements. His hands brushed her breasts as he buckled her in, but he didn't seem to notice.

She sure did.

It was the first time a man's hands had touched her breasts in about fifteen years, and it was an unexpected jolt. Something tightened in her belly. Desire? Attraction? An awareness of the fact she was a woman? Dear God, what was wrong with her? She didn't have time for that. Not tonight, and not in her life. But she couldn't take her gaze off his strong jaw and dark eyes as he focused intently on the harness he was strapping around her.

"I'm taking you across to my truck," he said, "and then we're going to get your daughter and the others."

"We are?" She couldn't stop the sudden flood of tears. "You're going to help me get them?"

He nodded as he snapped the final buckle. "Yeah. I gotta get into heaven somehow, and this might do it."

"Thank you!" She threw herself at him and wrapped her arms around him, clinging to her savior. She had no idea who he was, but he'd just successfully navigated a sheer mud cliff for her and her daughter, and she would so take that gift right now.

For an instant, he froze, and she felt his hard body start to pull away. Then suddenly, in a shift so subtle she didn't even see it happen, his body relaxed and his arms went around her, locking her down in an embrace so powerful she felt like the world had just stopped. She felt like the rain had ceased and the wind had quieted, buffeted aside by the strength and power of his body.

"It's going to be okay." His voice was low and reassuring in her ear, his lips brushing against her as he spoke. "She's going to be fine."

Crushed against this stranger's body, protected by his arms, soothed by the utter confidence in his voice, the terror that had been stalking her finally eased away. "Thank you," she whispered.

"You're welcome."

There was a hint of emotion in his voice, and she pulled back far enough to look at him. His eyes were dark, so dark she couldn't tell if they were brown or black, but she could see the torment in his expression. His jaw was angular, and his face was shadowed by the floodlights. He was a man with weight in his heart. She felt it right away. Instinctively, she laid a hand on his cheek. "You're a gift."

He flashed another smile, and for a split second, he put his hand over hers, holding it to his whiskered cheek as if she were some angel of mercy come to give him relief. Her throat thickened, and for a moment, everything else vanished. It was just them, drenched and cold on a windy mountain road, the only warmth was their hands, clasped together against his cheek.

His eyes darkened, then he cleared his throat suddenly and released her hand, jerking her back to the present. "Wait until you see whether I can pull it off," he said, his voice low and rough, sending chills of awareness rippling down her spine. "Then you can reevaluate that compliment." He tugged on the harness. "Ready?"

She gripped the cold nylon, suddenly nervous. Was she edgy because she was about to climb over a tree that could careen into the gully while she was on it, or was it due to intensity of the sudden heat between them? God, she hoped it was the first one. Being a wimp was so much less dangerous than noticing a man like him. "Aren't you wearing one?"

He quirked a smile at her, a jaunty grin that melted one more piece of her thundering heart. "I only have one, and ladies always get first dibs. Besides, I'm a good climber. If the tree takes me over, I'll find my way back up. Always do." He set his foot on a lower branch and patted his knee. "A one-of-a-kind step ladder. Hop up, Ms.—?" He paused, leaving the question hovering in the storm.

"Clare." She set her muddy boot on his knee, and she grimaced apologetically when the mud glopped all over his jeans. "Clare Gray." She grabbed a branch and looked at him. "And you are?"

"Griffin Friesé." He set his hand on her hip to steady her, his grip strong and solid. "Let's go save some kids, shall we?"

Sneak Peek: Shadows of Darkness

An Order of the Blade Novel

Levi Hart froze, his senses shocked into hyper-awareness when he caught the unmistakable scent of a *woman*. It plunged past his shields, invading his being with a force so strong he had no chance to protect himself from the sheer intensity of her presence. He swore and went utterly still. His mind went into hyper-focus as he fought to regain control, his body barely swaying on the ancient meat hook he'd been chained to for over a century.

But with each breath he took, the fragile, delicate scent of pure femininity wrapped itself tighter around him. Hot. Sensual. Tempting. And utterly dangerous to a Calydon warrior who was driven by a dark, powerful need for a woman.

His ancient instincts rose fast and hard, a driving lust that he hadn't succumbed to in centuries. Swearing under his breath, he closed his eyes, summoning what was left of his once formidable discipline to regain control of his body and his senses. It took precious seconds to shut down the lust burning through him. He had to engage strength he couldn't afford to waste in order to crush the almost insurmountable need to find her *right then*, but he did it.

The relief was instant, but a residue of emptiness resonated through him, as if his very being was stumbling in the absence of that sexual hunger. Without the distraction, however, a sharp-edged focus settled over him. He narrowed his eyes and called upon his preternatural senses, sending waves of psychic energy out into the surrounding tunnels, searching for the physical presence of the woman he had scented.

He found nothing.

A dark fury raged through him, anger that he couldn't find her. Urgency mounted, and he sent out another wave of energy, but this time, he opened his mind, sending the tentacles of his consciousness out into the air, searching with ruthless speed. Within seconds, he picked up her feminine energy again. This time, he kept his physical response contained, and he allowed his mind to hurtle toward her at a mind-numbing pace, racing through tunnels and around corners, faster and faster, gaining speed with each millisecond, her scent becoming stronger and stronger until—

He found her.

The moment his mind touched hers, she sucked in her breath, and her mind snapped to his, injecting warmth and passion into his cold, isolated being. His entire body clenched in response, and tension radiated through his muscles as he fought to concentrate. She smelled of spring and outdoors, of grass, of nature, and of a lazy sensuality, things he hadn't experienced in over a hundred years. But since he'd opened his mind to her, it wasn't simply her physical being he accessed. Her emotions assaulted him, a dizzying onslaught of fear, courage, and desperation, all of it ruthlessly contained by her single-minded focus and determination. His name reverberated through her mind, and it was layered through her entire being.

All her attention was centered on *him.*

His body responded to the knowledge, a tightening of his cock that he couldn't control no matter how hard he fought it. To have his name and his existence so intricately woven into the fabric of her being was so visceral that he could almost feel her presence, as if she was right in front of him. He couldn't keep his physical response contained, and his lust spilled over their connection into her. Instantly, desire flooded her, and he felt her body respond to his.

The connection between them was electric and intense, igniting his cells like fire licking its way through his body. He was a cold-blooded assassin who'd spent a lifetime honing his utter lack of emotion and eradicating his need for physical connection with a woman, and yet, in mere seconds, she'd stripped away every last defense and created a need in him so powerful he knew he'd be sprinting through the tunnels in search of her if he weren't locked down.

Who the hell was she? And why was she there? No one had set foot in any of the caverns surrounding his prison since he'd been chained up, and he didn't believe it was a coincidence that she was so close, thousands of feet below the surface of the earth in tunnels that no human being would ever stumble across, thinking about him. *Who are you?* He pressed the question at her, instinctively erecting a telepathic bridge between their minds.

She froze in response, and for a split second, he felt her confusion that he was speaking in her mind. Then fear rippled through her, and she slammed up her mental shields, severing their link. Emptiness assaulted him at the lack of connection, and he swore, struggling to regain his equilibrium. She'd cut him off, but he knew she'd heard him.

She'd heard him. After more than a century of complete isolation, *she'd heard him.* The sudden shock of having his existence recognized by another living creature hit him with an almost violent crash of emotion. His entire being suddenly burned with a need to be acknowledged, to be recognized, to be *seen*.

He shoved aside the emotions before they had a chance to claim him. He'd lived his whole life alone. He'd been a shadow in the night, a phantom who was everyone's worst nightmare. His solitary existence had never bothered him, not even for an instant, and he wasn't going to let it start grating on him now just because he'd been strung up like a carcass for a century and had scented a woman so enticing it could drive him mad if he let it consume him.

Her essence became stronger, and he realized she was headed right for him, on a direct path through the tunnels. *She was seeking him out.* Anticipation burned through him, an escalating need to see her, to hear her voice, to drag her against him and taste her mouth against his.

He swore and closed his eyes, raising his own shields to block her scent so he could recalibrate. What the hell? Why was he reacting like that to her? Was it just because he'd been isolated for so long? Or maybe she was some sort of seductress? Not that it mattered. He didn't want to make out with her. He wanted to *escape*.

This might be his chance.

He took a deep breath, summoning the combat-focus that had once been as instinctual as breathing and staying alive. Decades of no food, no water, and no external stimulation had weakened him, and his mind fought against his commands to concentrate so intently.

With a snarl of fury, he forced his mind to respond, channeling what was left of his strength into his mind until it coalesced into the razor-sharp clarity that had once defined him.

Straining to see in the darkness, he scanned the cave that had been his prison for so long. It had taken years for his eyes to adjust to the rampant darkness enough for him to be able to see anything, and even now, he could make out only the faintest dark shapes that indicated tunnel openings, escape routes that were only yards away, and yet completely out of reach.

She was in one of those tunnels, getting closer with each step.

Manipulating his body weight with the effortless grace of a man who'd spent countless hours figuring out how to stay fit and strong even while he was suspended by his wrists in a frigid, underground cave, Levi spun in a circle. He systematically inspected every inch of his cave, searching for indications that would tell him which direction she was approaching from.

Unable to resist the temptation, he inhaled again, and her scent wrapped around him, diffusing through his cells like a tendril of sunshine in a body that had long been dead. Energy pulsed through him, a sense of vitality he hadn't felt in decades. He reached out to her again, this time searching the space around her for more information on who she was. With his attention no longer only on her, he noticed the presence of two powerful males flanking her.

His hands clenched, and his muscles went taut. *She was with two Calydon warriors.* Possessiveness surged through him, a sudden fear for her safety. Was she their prisoner? Were they going to lock her up the way he'd been strung up? Suddenly, it was no longer about sex. It was no longer about his need to be acknowledged. It became only about protecting her. *Are you in danger?* He pressed the question ruthlessly at her mind, shattering her mental shields.

Again, she flinched, clearly hearing him, but once again, she didn't answer. Instead, she thrust him out of her mind as efficiently as he'd penetrated it.

He had to admit, he was impressed with her defenses, but at the same time, it was annoying as hell. He had no idea what the situation was. Did he need to protect her? Was she in danger?

No. No. *No.*

His job wasn't to protect *anyone.* He had one last mission to accomplish, and he couldn't afford to get distracted by a woman. He had to escape, hunt down the man who had nearly destroyed Levi's soul…and then kill him. He could allow the approaching threesome to mean only one thing to him: a chance to gain his freedom.

Sneak Peek: A Real Cowboy Never Says No

A *Wyoming Rebels* Novel

Chase Stockton knew he'd found the woman he'd come to meet.

There was no mistaking the depth of loathing in the gaze of AJ's dad when he'd glared at the woman in the pale blue sundress. There was only one woman Alan could despise that much, and it was Mira Cabot, AJ's best friend from childhood.

Chase grinned. After more than a decade, he was about to meet Mira Cabot in person. *Hot damn.*

Anticipation humming through him, Chase watched with appreciation as she ducked into the last row of pews, her pale shoulders erect and strong as she moved down the row. She was a little too thin, yeah, but there was a strength to her body that he liked. Her dark blond hair was curly, bouncing over her shoulders in stark contrast to the tight updos of the other women in the church. He'd noticed her flip-flops and hot pink toenails, a little bit of color in the chapel full of black and gloom.

Chase had hopped a plane to attend the funeral, but it hadn't been just to honor AJ. He could have done that from his ranch in Wyoming. Nope, he'd come here to meet Mira, because he'd had a feeling this was going to be his only chance.

He ignored the line of churchgoers waiting to be seated. Instead, he strode around the back of the last pew to the far side, where his quarry was tucked away in the shadows. As he approached, someone turned up the lights in the church, and the shadows slid away, casting her face in a warm glow, giving him his first view of the woman he'd been thinking about for so long.

Chase was shocked by the raw need that flooded him. Her eyes were the azure blue as in her photos. Her nose had that slight bump from when she and AJ had failed to successfully install a tire swing in her front yard, resulting in her crashing to the ground and breaking her nose. Her lips were pale pink, swept with the faintest hint of gloss, and her eyelashes were as long and thick as he'd imagined. Her shoulders were bare and delicate in her sundress, and her ankles were crossed demurely, as if she were playing the role that was expected of her. Yet, around that same ankle was a chain of glittering gold with several blue stones. He knew that anklet. He'd helped AJ pick it out for her twenty-first birthday.

She was everything he'd imagined, and so much more. She was no longer an inanimate, two-dimensional image who lived only in his mind. She had become a real, live woman.

Mira was eyeing the crowd with the faintest scowl puckering her lips and lining her forehead, just as he would have expected. She didn't like this crowd any more than AJ had.

Chase grinned, relaxing. She was exactly what he'd imagined. "You don't approve?" he said as he approached her.

She let out a yelp of surprise and jumped, bolting sideways like a skittish foal. "What?"

Chase froze, startled by the sound of her voice. It was softer than he'd expected, reminding him of the rolling sound of sunshine across his back on a warm day. Damn, he liked her voice. Why hadn't AJ ever mentioned it? That wasn't the kind of thing a guy could overlook.

She was sitting sideways, her hand gripping the back of the pew, looking at him like he was about to pull out his rifle and aim it at her head.

He instinctively held up his hand, trying to soothe her. "Sorry. I didn't mean to startle you." He swept the hat off his head and bowed slightly. "Chase Stockton. You must be Mira Cabot."

"Chase Stockton?" Her frown deepened slightly, and then recognition dawned on her face. "AJ's best friend from college! Of course." She stood up immediately, a smile lighting up her features. "I can't believe I finally get to meet you."

He had only a split second to register how pretty her smile was before she threw her arms around him and hugged him.

For the second time in less than a minute, Chase was startled into immobility. Her body was so warm and soft against him that he forgot to breathe. He had not been expecting her to hug him, and he hadn't had time to steel himself. He flexed his hands by his sides, not sure how to react. It had been so long since anyone had hugged him, and it was an utterly foreign experience. It was weird as hell, but at the same time, there was something about it that felt incredible, as if the whole world had stopped spinning and settled into this moment.

When Mira didn't let go, he tentatively slipped his arms around her, still unsure of proper protocol when being embraced by a woman he'd never met before. As his arms encircled her, however, a deep sense of rightness settled over him. He could feel her ribs protruding from her back, and he instinctively tightened his grip on her, pulling her into the shield of his embrace. In photographs, she'd always been athletic and solid, but now she was thin, thinner than he liked, thinner than he felt she should be.

She tucked her face in his neck and took a deep breath, and he became aware of the most tempting scent of flowers. It reminded him of a trail ride in the spring, when the wildflowers were beating back the last remnants of a stubborn winter.

The turbulence that constantly roiled through his body seemed to quiet as he focused on her. He became aware of the desperate nature of her embrace, reminding him that she was attending the funeral of her best friend, and she was no doubt being assaulted by the accompanying grief and loss.

He bent his head, his cheek brushing against her hair. "You okay?" he asked softly.

She took another deep breath, and then pulled back. Her blue eyes were full of turbulent emotion. "It's just that seeing you makes me feel like AJ's here again." She brushed an imaginary speck of dust off his shoulder. "You were his best friend, you know. You changed his life forever."

He wasn't used to anyone touching him with that kind of intimacy, especially not a woman. Women never got familiar with him. *Ever.* He simply didn't allow it. But with her, it felt okay. Good even. He shrugged, feeling completely out of his depth with her. "He changed mine," he said. "He did a hell of a lot more for me than I ever did for him." AJ had been a lifeline in an ugly existence that had been spiraling straight into hell. He knew exactly where he'd have been without AJ: dead, or in prison. It was a debt he could never repay.

She nodded, still not stepping away from his embrace.

She lightly clasped his forearms, still holding onto him. "He was like that, wasn't he?"

"Yeah, he was." Unable to make himself release her, Chase studied her face, memorizing the curve of her nose, the flush of her cheeks, and the slope of her jaw. "You were his rock, you know. The only person in this world he truly trusted."

And that was it, the reason why he'd wanted to meet her. He was bitter, tired, and cynical, and he'd needed to see if the Mira Cabot his friend had always talked about actually existed. He needed to know whether there was someone in this world, anyone besides his brothers, who a man could actually believe in. Hearing that AJ had died had derailed Chase more than he'd expected, and he'd needed something to hold onto, something that connected him back to AJ and to some dammed goodness in his life.

Her cheeks flushed, and she smiled. "Thanks for telling me that. We didn't keep in touch much over the last few years, but he's always been in my heart."

He stared at her, uncertain how to respond. Who talked about things in their heart? And with strangers? But he knew the answer to that. Mira did, and that's why he'd wanted to meet her.

She finally pulled back, and he reluctantly released her, his hands sliding over her hips. She moved further into the pew and eased onto the bench. "Sit with me," she said, patting the seat beside her.

"Yeah, okay." Instead of taking the aisle seat, he moved past her and sat on the other side of her, inserting himself between Mira and AJ's dad. The old man was across the church, but he hadn't stopped shooting lethal stares in her direction. AJ wasn't there to protect her, so it was now Chase's job.

He draped his arms across the back of the pew, aware that his position put one arm behind Mira's shoulders. Not touching, but present. A statement.

He looked across the church at AJ's dad, and this time, when the man looked over, he noticed Chase sitting beside her. The two men stared at each other for a brief moment, and then Alan looked away.

Satisfied, Chase shifted his position so he could stretch his legs out, trying to work out the cramps from the long flight.

He was glad he'd come. It felt right to be there, and he'd sent the message to AJ's dad that Mira was under his protection.

He glanced sideways at her as she fiddled with her small purse. Her hair was tumbling around her face, obscuring his view of her eyes. Frustrated that he couldn't see her face, he started to move his hand to adjust her hair, and then froze. What the hell was he doing, thinking he could just reach out and touch her like that?

Swearing, he jerked his gaze away from her, a bead of sweat trickling down his brow as he realized the enormity of what was happening. *He was attracted to her.* For the last decade, Mira had simply been AJ's best friend, an angel of sorts that Chase had idealized from a distance, never thinking of Mira as anything more personal than simply a bright light in a shitty world.

But now?

He wanted her.

He wanted to brush her hair back from her face. He wanted to run his fingers over her collarbone. He wanted to feel her body crushed against his again. He wanted to sink his mouth onto hers, and taste her—

Hell. That spelled trouble, in a major way.

Suddenly, he couldn't wait to get on the plane and get out of there, and back to his carefully constructed world.

He hadn't come here for a woman. He'd come here for salvation, not to be sucked into the hell that had almost destroyed him once before. Mira Cabot might be the only woman on the planet worth trusting, but that wasn't reason enough for him to risk all that he'd managed to rebuild.

Nothing was worth that risk. *Nothing.*

Sneak Peek: Ghost

An *Alaska Heat* Novel

"What are you running from?"

Ben Forsett froze at the unexpected question, his hand clenching around the amber beer bottle. For a long second, he didn't move. Instead, his gaze shot stealthily to the three exits he'd already located before he'd even walked into this local pub known as O'Dell's in Where-the-Hell-Are-We, Alaska. He rapidly calculated which exit had the clearest path. A couple of bush pilots were by the kitchen door. They were large, rough men who would shove themselves directly into the path of someone they thought should be stopped. His access to the front door was obstructed by two jean-clad young women walking into the foyer, shaking snowflakes out of their perfectly coiffed hair. The emergency exit was alarmed, but no one was in front of it. That was his best choice—

"Chill, kid," the man continued. "I'm not hunting you. I've been where you are. So have most of the men in this place."

Slowly, Ben pulled his gaze off his escape route and looked at the grizzled Alaskan old-timer sitting next to him. Lines of outdoor hardship creased his face, and wisps of straggly white hair hung below his faded, black baseball hat. His skin hung loose, too tired to hold on anymore, but in the old man's pale blue eyes burned a sharp, gritty intelligence born of a tough life. His shoulders were encased in a heavy, dark green jacket that was so bulky it almost hid the hunch to his back and the thinness of his shoulders.

The man nodded once. "Name's Haas. Haas Carter." He extended a gnarled hand toward Ben.

Ben didn't respond, but Haas didn't retract his hand.

For a long moment, neither man moved, then, finally, Ben peeled his fingers off his beer and shook Haas's hand. "John Sullivan," he said, the fake name sliding off his tongue far more easily than it had three months ago, the first time he'd used it.

"John Sullivan?" Haas laughed softly. "You picked the most common name you could think of, eh? Lots of John

Sullivans in just about every town you've been to, I should imagine. It'd be hard for people to keep track of one more."

Ben stiffened. "My father was John Sullivan, Sr.," he lied. "I honor the name."

Haas's bushy gray brows went up. "Do you now?"

The truth was, Ben's father was a lying bastard who had left when he was two years old. Or he'd been shot. Or he'd been put in prison. No one knew what had happened to him, and no one really cared, including Ben. "I'm not here to make friends," Ben said quietly.

"No, I can see that." Haas regarded him for a moment, his silver-blue eyes surveying Ben's heavy whiskers and the shaggy hair that had once been perfectly groomed. Ben shook his head so his hair hung down over his forehead, shielding his eyes as he watched the older man, waiting for a sign that this situation was going south.

He would be pissed if Haas turned on him. He needed to be here. He was so sure this was finally the break he'd been waiting for. He let his gaze slither off Haas to the back wall of the bar where an enormous stuffed moose head was displayed. Its rack had to be at least six feet wide, its glazed dead eyes a bitter reminder of what happened to life when you stopped paying attention for a split second.

Beside the moose rack was the battered wooden clock he'd been watching all evening. Adrenaline raced through Ben as he watched the minute hand clunk to the twelve. *It was seven o'clock.*

"What happens at seven?"

Ben jerked his gaze back to Haas, startled to realize the older man had been watching him closely enough to notice his focus on the clock. "I turn into a fairy princess."

Haas guffawed and slammed his hand down on Ben's shoulder. "You're all right, John Sullivan. Mind if I call you Sully? Most Sullivans go by Sully. It'll make it seem more like it's your real name."

Ben's fingers tightened around the frosty bottle at Haas's persistence. "It is my real name."

Haas dropped the smile and leaned forward, lowering his voice as his gaze locked onto Ben's. "I'll tell you this, young man, I've seen a lot of shit in my life. I've seen men who look like princes, but turn out to be scum you wouldn't even want to waste a bullet on. I've seen pieces of shit who would actually give their life for you. You look like shit, but whatever the hell you're running from, you got my vote. Don't let the bastards catch you until you can serve it up right in their damn faces. Got it?"

Ben stared at Haas, too stunned by the words to respond. No one believed in him, no one except for the man who had helped him escape. He'd known Mack Connor since he was a kid, and Mack understood what loyalty meant. But even Mack knew damn well who Ben really was and what he was truly capable of. Mack's allegiance was unwavering, but he did it with his eyes open and ready to react if Ben went over the line.

He had a sudden urge to tell Haas exactly what shit was going down for him, and see if the old man still wanted to stand by him.

But he wasn't that stupid. He couldn't afford for anyone to know why he was here. "I don't know what you're talking about," he finally said.

Haas raised his beer in a toast. "Yeah, me neither, Sully. Me neither." As Haas took a drink, another weather-beaten Alaskan sat down on Haas's other side. This guy's face was so creased it looked like his razor would get lost if he tried to shave, and the size of his beard said the guy hadn't been willing to take the risk. Haas nodded at him. "Donnie, this here boy is Sully. New in town. Needs a job. His wife left him six months ago, and the poor bastard lost everything. He's been wandering aimless for too damn long."

Ben almost choked on his beer at Haas's story, but Donnie just nodded. "Women can sure break a man." He leveled his dark brown gaze at Ben. "She ain't worth it, young man. There are lots of doe around for a guy to pick up with."

Ben managed a nod. "Yeah, well, I'm not ready yet."

"We gotta get him back on the horse," Haas said. "Got any ideas?" With a wink at Ben, he and Donnie launched into a discussion about the assorted available women in town and which ones might be worthy of Ben.

As the two old-timers talked, Ben felt some of the tension ease from his shoulders. In this small town in the middle of Alaska, he had an ally, at least until Haas found out the truth. Shit, it felt good to have someone at his back. It had been too damn long—

The door to the kitchen swung open, and a cheerful female voice echoed through the swinging door. Her voice was like a soft caress of something...damn. He realized he didn't even know what to compare it to. His mind was too tired to conjure up words that would do justice to the sudden heat sliding over his skin. But a seductive, tempting warmth washed over him, through him, like someone had just slipped hot whisky into his veins, burning and cleansing as it went.

Ben went rigid, adrenaline flooding his body. It was seven o'clock. Based on what he'd pieced together about her schedule and her life, she would be coming on duty now, walking out of the kitchen *now*. Was it her? *Was it her?* Her hand was on the kitchen door, holding it open as she finished her muffled conversation. She was wearing a black leather cord with a silver disk around her wrist. On her index finger was a silver ring with a rough-cut turquoise stone and a wide band with carvings on it. Her fingernails were bare and natural, a woman who didn't bother with enamel and lacquer to go to work. Her arm was exposed, the smooth expanse of flesh sliding up to a capped black sleeve that just covered the curve of her shoulder. She wasn't tall, maybe a little over five feet.

Son of a bitch. It might actually be her. *Come into the bar,* he urged silently. *Let me see your face.* He'd never heard her talk before. He'd never seen her in person. All he had was that one newspaper picture of her, and the headshot he'd snagged from her family's store website before it had been taken down. But her trail had led to O'Dell's, and he was hoping he was right. He *had* to be right.

The door opened wider, and Ben ducked his head, letting his hair shield his eyes again, but he didn't take his gaze off her, watching intently as the woman moved into the restaurant. Her back was toward him as she continued her conversation, and he could see her hair. Thick, luscious waves of dark brown.

Brown. *Brown.* The woman he'd been searching for was *blond.*

The disappointment and frustration that knifed through

his gut was like the sharp stab of death itself. He bowed his head, resting his forehead in his palms as the image flooded his mind again, the same memory that had haunted him for so long. His sister, her clothes stained with that vibrant red of fresh blood, sprawled across her living room, her hand stretching toward Ben in the final entreaty of death. *Son of a bitch.* He couldn't let Holly down. He couldn't let her down *again.*

"Are you okay?"

He went still at the question, at the sound of the woman's voice so close. She still had the same effect on him, a flood of heat that seemed to touch every part of his body. He schooled his features into the same uninviting expression he'd perfected, and he looked up to find himself staring into the face he'd been hunting for the last three months.

He'd never mistake those eyes. The dark rich brown framed by eyelashes so thick he'd thought they had to be fake, until now. Until he could see her for real. Until he could feel the weight of her sorrow so thickly that it seemed to wrap around him and steal the oxygen from his lungs. Until he looked into that face, that face that had once been so innocent, and now carried burdens too heavy for her small frame.

Until he'd found her.

Because he had.

It was her. Yeah, maybe she'd ditched the blond and let herself go back to her natural color, which looked good as hell on her, but there was no doubt in his mind.

He'd found her.

Son of a bitch.

He'd found her.

Select List of Other Books by Stephanie Rowe

(For a complete book list, please visit www.stephanierowe.com)

CONTEMPORARY ROMANCE

The *Wyoming Rebels* Series

A Real Cowboy Never Says No
A Real Cowboy Knows How to Kiss
A Real Cowboy Rides a Motorcycle

The *Ever After* Series

No Knight Needed
Fairy Tale Not Required
Prince Charming Can Wait

Stand Alone Novels

Jingle This!

PARANORMAL ROMANCE

The *NightHunter* Series

Not Quite Dead

The *Order of the Blade* Series

Darkness Awakened
Darkness Seduced
Darkness Surrendered
Forever in Darkness
Darkness Reborn
Darkness Arisen
Darkness Unleashed
Inferno of Darkness
Darkness Possessed
Shadows of Darkness
Hunt the Darkness
Release Date TBD

The *Soulfire* Series

Kiss at Your Own Risk

Touch if You Dare
Hold Me if You Can

The *Immortally Sexy* Series

Date Me Baby, One More Time
Must Love Dragons
He Loves Me, He Loves Me Hot
Sex & the Immortal Bad Boy

ROMANTIC SUSPENSE

The *Alaska Heat* Series

Ice
Chill
Ghost

NONFICTION

Essays

The Feel Good Life

FOR TEENS

A Girlfriend's Guide to Boys Series

Putting Boys on the Ledge
Studying Boys
Who Needs Boys?
Smart Boys & Fast Girls

Stand Alone Novels

The Fake Boyfriend Experiment

FOR PRE-TEENS

The *Forgotten* Series

Penelope Moonswoggle, The Girl Who Could Not Ride a Dragon
Penelope Moonswoggle & the Accidental Doppelganger
Release Date TBD

Collections

Box Sets

Alpha Immortals
Romancing the Paranormal
Last Hero Standing

Stephanie Rowe Bio

New York Times and *USA Today* bestselling author Stephanie Rowe is the author of more than 40 novels, including her popular Order of the Blade and NightHunter paranormal romance series. Stephanie is a four-time nominee of the RITA® Award, the highest award in romance fiction. She has won many awards for her novels, including the prestigious Golden Heart® Award. She has received coveted starred reviews from Booklist, and Publishers Weekly has called her work "[a] genre-twister that will make readers...rabid for more." Stephanie also writes a thrilling romantic suspense series set in Alaska. Publisher's Weekly praised the series debut, ICE, as a "thrilling entry into romantic suspense," and Fresh Fiction called ICE an "edgy, sexy and gripping thriller." Equally as intense and sexy are Stephanie's contemporary romance novels, set in the fictional town of Birch Crossing, Maine. All of Stephanie's books, regardless of the genre, deliver the same intense, passionate, and emotional experience that has delighted so many readers.

www.stephanierowe.com

http://twitter.com/stephanierowe2

http://www.pinterest.com/StephanieRowe2/

https://www.facebook.com/StephanieRoweAuthor

Made in the USA
Las Vegas, NV
31 March 2022